FOREWORD

The events described here took place ov
the best part of a century, they ended neaɪɪy ᴜne
hundred years ago.

Your narrator's knowledge and understanding began with
the end of this intricate story. Born in 1960 in Cambridge
to parents who were WWII refugees, and having spent his
earliest years mainly in Africa (The Gambia and
Ethiopia), thence to boarding school aged seven,
spending holidays in Addis Ababa, in Afghanistan
(Baghlan), then Yemen (Taiz), leaving school at 14 to
live in Lesotho (Leribe). It was in Taiz and on that
winding road, through often beautiful mountain scenery,
between Leribe and Maseru that this boy was told the
story of a famous early 20th Century poet, a friend of
artists, such as Picasso, Rousseau and Derain. That poet,
Apollinaire, was a member of his mother's family, a
Kostrowicki (pronounced *Kostrovitski or Kastravicki*, of
which there are various spellings*)*.

Over the years that followed, while your narrator grew up
and as a man, car journeys and other times spent with his
mother would provide the occasion for further discussion,
further stories, or speculation. In time the man would
take a harder look at the story of this relative. In doing
so, in pulling on these tangled threads, he pieced together
more and more. In effect he started at the end - his
family knew their story, the facts within their and their
forebears' experience. An unhappy story in many

respects, but nevertheless one that family members before him (including his grandfather) decided should be told, as they first did publicly in the 1950's, resulting in the publication in Polish by the Surrealist poet and author Anatol Stern of a book entitled "Dom Apollinaire'a" (House of Apollinaire). This book written in Polish and reaching only a limited audience, however, told only part of a larger, even more complex tale, as became clearer to your narrator as he was told more and himself later explored further and deeper.

The life of Napoleon's only legitimate son and heir, Franz, Duke of Reichstadt (*Ryhstadt*), overlapped the complex story of three colourful and intertwined families whose roots lay in Lithuania, in White Ruthenia, or Belarus, in Veliky Novgorod (the Novgorod Republic, that operated in Northern Russia, along the lines of the Venetian and Ragusan Republics (modern day Dubrovnik), before Muscovy (Red Ruthenia, or Russia) overran its neighbours), in Russia and in the upheavals that took place there. A story that itself had its necessary secrets, including hidden identities, until after the fall of empires, their autocratic dynastic rulers vanquished and gone.

Thousands of books and articles have been written about persons appearing in these pages. Many by learned rigorous scholars, academic historians and others with impressive credentials. Nevertheless, please read on and judge for yourself what is fact and what is fiction. Both are interwoven here, because that is the reality, a reality purposely engineered by those whose interests led them so to do and who had the power and means to achieve this, when it mattered most.

Why write this now? Because although many of the threads of this tapestry are in the public domain, the tapestry itself has not been seen as a whole and perhaps it is now time for those characters whose stories were hidden, suppressed or subverted for whatever reasons, to have their story told, when little harm can result and through its telling they may gain a kind of peaceful emancipation denied to them in life.

Apollinaire died on 9 November 1918, one hundred years ago. In the same year WWI ended, as did the Austro-Hungarian Empire and Habsburg rule there. Imperial Germany (the Hohenzollerns) and Tsarist Russia (the Romanovs) also fell. Europe was changed fundamentally. By the 1950s, if not earlier, these were old, tired secrets, ones whose telling could have no meaningful political consequences. If not told, our poet and his forefathers would have truly been captive, both in life and beyond.

No one who wrote of these matters, especially those contemporaries on whom we must rely in large part for our sources, was able to see the entire picture or to interpret and record it without the lens of perception or bias, or without motives of a personal nature, influenced by politics, in the main. In history, the victor typically held the pen.

Women are at the core of these events, daughters, lovers, wives, mothers, grandmothers and others - some of them extraordinary persons. If we look carefully, we will find that it was the women who were the strongest and who consistently picked up the pieces and saved the day.

I have been more than blessed with loving wonderful parents and my fabulous wife, Sarah and daughters Natassja, Stephanie and Olivia. This is for you and those mentioned here to whom you are related, more or less distantly.

Jeremy Moczarski

October 2018 (revised, June 2021)

Postscript:

On 10 September 2020 the State Museum of the History of Belarusian Literature (Государственный музей истории белорусской литературы), in Minsk opened the Kostrovitsky literary and documentary exposition, timed to coincide with the 140th anniversary of the birth of Guillaume Apollinaire. The National Historical Archives of Belarus, the Belarusian State Archives-Museum of Literature and Art, the National Library of Belarus, the Republican Centre of National Culture and the Predmestie Gallery took part in the creation of the exposition. This book, together with the titles "Poetry in the blood" and "A Man of Power and a Goblin on a Fork" by this author were featured in this exposition and copies were donated to the institutions that took part.

PART I – THE EMPEROR

The Aftermath

July 1815

It was over and the taste of defeat was bitter, foul, sickening – unacceptable! Days later it still alternately enraged and depressed him. The return from Russia had been intensely awful, leaving a deep scar, but this was worse. He had been on the verge of turning it all around, winning through. After Elba the margin between success and failure had been so small. The highly improbable had again seemed possible, victory within his reach. He had very nearly won the greatest reversal of ill fortune in history - the consequential differences monumental.

How the Hell did it happen? His men had come back to him and fought like lions. That farmhouse? It was an insubstantial obstacle, thinly defended. It should have broken. They should have broken it. His plans were sound. He could not be everywhere. That was no consolation now. There was none to be had, he knew. Just outcomes. Defeat. Losses. Intolerable!

He had raced back to Paris, to control the news and, he hoped, resolved and intended, the aftermath. Soon it became apparent this was not possible. He was a fugitive, in flight once again. His supporters peeling away, fair weather friends and the faint hearted in the vanguard, others standing back on the sidelines, watching, waiting, even loyalists on whom he needed to rely if he were to regroup, or even survive. The Allies were searching for him, rumours had reached him that Blucher and his Prussians were even determined to exact a final retribution and ending. He felt it. It all moved too quickly, the sand running out. Not fear, just a precipitous downward slide. A horrible sick, hollow feeling; God I am so, so tired, he thought.

Having found no advantage in Paris, no lifelines offered, no suggestions accepted, and with the Allies closing in, meeting no substantial resistance, he had given in to the pleadings of his thinned entourage and made his way towards the Atlantic Coast and, as he now contemplated, exit. He had been confronted with an ultimatum – abdicate or be deposed. It was over. A return to relatively comfortable, familiar and nearby Elba would not be offered, he knew. The provisional Government was pressing him to leave France without delay or face the consequences. He had only a short time in which to try to determine his own destiny. On his own terms? But where could he go? Where could he go and hope for a life as a free man? Certainly not in Europe. They would search everywhere, he would be recognised, and he could not, would not, skulk and hide.

The obvious solution that had presented itself to him and his reduced remaining circle of advisers was America. A new country, with whose emerging political ideology he felt much sympathy. Its appeal was now growing on him. If, as was becoming agonizingly apparent, France had lost the will to fight, had lost faith in his capacity to win, if he could not garner enough support in the Paris Legislature to pull together and lead again the armies of France against the Allies, to chase them out of France, to rebuild, then why not go to America and live as a private citizen, in a land which had only recently shared a common enemy – Britain? After all, he had doubled the size of that new country by selling to it Louisiana! Joseph, his elder brother, had useful connections and friends among the Americans, going back many years to the Treaty of friendship and commerce signed at Morfortaine in 1800, when he was Minister Plenipotentiary.

Perhaps they might have need of his exceptional administrative skills? He might establish and lead a new state. Not perhaps the New World empire that he had once envisaged, but nevertheless something worthwhile, a working retirement during which he could establish a settled legacy of his ideas. A more hopeful thought than much else on his mind.

While at Malmaison Marie Walewska (*Valevska*), his pretty Polish former mistress, had visited him with their young son[i], who looked so much like his younger half-brother, the King of Rome. Marie had offered, begged, to let them join him in exile, for their boy to be with his father. Attractive though it would be to have female companionship, and sweet and devoted though she was, he had long ago tired of her, moved on and their presence could only complicate matters, politically and personally. The presence of a famous mistress and their illegitimate child, so obviously his (his features distinct), would not serve his cause.

What, however, of Marie Louise, his wife and their little son, his heir? Was it possible her father, long his enemy, could somehow be persuaded to allow them to join him in America? Could they be brought to him? He remained deep in thought.

A few leagues away, in another world, the disciplined, drilled environment of a Royal Navy ship-of-the-line, HMS Bellerophon, its commander, Captain Frederick Maitland mused alone in his cabin.

The rich, active and varied experience he had gained as boy and man in the Royal Navy at a time when Britannia truly ruled the seas had prepared him for just about anything. His capacity for surprise was, he thought, limited.

He had returned to England in October, after a year in command of HMS Goliath (a cut-down 74) on the Halifax and West India stations. At the end of her usefulness, she had been paid off at Chatham on their return. In quick succession he had first been appointed to command the Boyne, fitting out at Portsmouth as the flagship of the Commander-in-Chief on the American Coast, Sir Alexander Cochrane. Having sailed the Boyne to Cork, where in January a fleet of transports and merchant ships congregated, they were bound for America. There the extraordinary news of Boney's escape from Elba had reached them.

Fresh orders had translated him to the venerable Bellerophon, famous veteran of the First of June, the Nile and Trafalgar. On 24 May they had departed Plymouth with the squadron of Sir Henry Hotham, Maitland issued with sealed instructions.

Subsequently events had moved quickly. After investigating L'Ile Dieu, Bellerophon arrived off Rochefort, where they observed the French war ships anchored there. They were joined by the Cephalus, an 18-gun brig-sloop, swifter and more manoeuvrable than Bellerophon, with a usefully shallower draught, more suited to close blockading river mouth ports.

Soon after the momentous and happy news had reached him of a decisive victory at Waterloo – the fate of Europe had been resolved and Boney was again on the run - thoughts of years more of war with France could again be discarded – he had received a secret message from an agent in Bordeaux, hidden within a quill. Boney was likely to try to escape France by sea, probably to America, quite possibly via Rochefort. It was clear that the Atlantic Coast was the most obvious direction of flight and that his own patrol zone fitted the case squarely.

The threat represented by the two French frigates and lesser ships at Rochefort had taken on a different dimension. England and France were no longer at war, but if these ships were under the direction of Bonaparte, they could not on any account be allowed to slip away, even if they had to be engaged and stopped by force. Once on the open sea it would be a race with unquantifiable and increasing odds!

Confirmation that Boney and his entourage were indeed in the vicinity of Rochefort had made it all very real and immediate. It was now his responsibility to prevent escape or face the inevitable music!

On 10 July the French schooner La Mouche approached Bellerophon under a flag of truce. Maitland politely and formally ushered Comte Emmanuel de Las Cases and General Savary, Duke of Rovigo to his cabin. They handed over a letter from Count Bertrand. This requested that their master be allowed safe passage to exile in the United States. Maitland replied to Las Cases and Savary that his orders were to prevent this from happening.

Instead, unable to obtain further instructions in the time available, on his own initiative Maitland offered passage aboard the Bellerophon to Britain. Discussions continued over the following days, La Mouche bearing variously Las Cases, General Francois Lallemand and General Gourgaud.

In the meantime, although he was being informed by Napoleon's ambassadors that he was at Rochefort, Maitland had discovered that Boney was in fact at L'Ile d'Aix. Rochefort was rife with rumours of escape plans. One of the more amusing and unlikely examples was the suggestion that Bonaparte would be smuggled out in a special purpose cask consigned aboard a neutral Danish merchantman. A cartoonist's delight!

As a precaution and early warning system, Maitland gave instructions for guard boats to keep a close watchful eye around the clock on the Frigates Meduse and Saale (both appeared ready for sea) and to report any comings and goings and, especially, signal a warning of preparations for sail. If they were coming out, the British war ships must be ready to intercept, to fight if need be.

Napoleon's reverie broke when there was a gentle knock on the door to his chamber. Beckoned, five men walked in and stood respectfully, the newcomer clearly freshly arrived. The first, third, fourth and last (Charles Tristan de Montholon, Henri Gatien Gourgaud, Charles Lallemand and Anne-Jean-Marie Savary), used to being in his company, still in their uniforms, were prominent members of his entourage. de Montholon introduced their companion, a strongly built and tall stranger, about forty years of age, wearing well-made travelling clothes, a self-confident man clearly used to an outdoor life. "Sire, this is Captain Henry Graham of the American merchant vessel "Pride of Charleston", presently at Rochefort. He was found there by our good friends. He has informed us that he is in Rochefort to take on fresh provisions and other supplies and embarkation of passengers and cargoes bound for America. For a fee, he might be willing and able to help us. He says he is no friend to the English".

Napoleon Bonaparte, self-made Emperor of France, man of history, remained seated for half a minute or so as he examined the face of this seafarer from the New World who looked him in the eye and returned the compliment, as he was pleased to see. He had long ago acquired the ability to assess the qualities of men - men of all ranks and walks of life. After a short interval, in the circumstances not long enough to be rude, he stood and, with the beginnings of a smile, offered his hand, which was respectfully and firmly received by the approaching stranger. "We are pleased to meet you Captain, please be seated and tell us of your ship". Turning to General Lallemand he gestured to him to pour wine for those present. Napoleon had always had the knack and winning capacity of putting others swiftly at their ease and gaining them with his warmth, charm, humour when necessary, his personal touch. He knew he was likely to have need of Captain Graham.

Graham knew he was in the presence of the greatest man he had come across in his much travelled and seasoned life. A man whose fame, or infamy, transcended all others, a living legend. Himself accustomed to judging men, his ship and the lives of those on board depending upon it, he warmed to his host. He really had not known what to expect when he was brought here. A great man, an egomaniac, a monster, disappointment? Each a fascinating possibility.

He had been approached that morning near the dockside in Rochefort by a nondescript older man dressed like any other merchant, making enquiries about his ship, his next passage, its whereabouts, speed, cargo and capacity and his willingness to take on important well-paying passengers, discreetly. It had to be interesting, and it was not unusual for him to be approached by careful voyagers, in these recent years of turmoil. Sensing an opportunity, he had allowed himself to be brought to this place with only little explanation. An important man wanted to meet him and could pay him well. It was common rumour in Rochefort that the fallen Emperor of France and other senior Bonapartists were somewhere nearby, seeking escape from their swiftly closing pursuers, blockaded by the British. A great quarry, valuable prizes, all seeking refuge.

He now found himself in the presence of a smiling man, compelling respect, an intelligent force. "Sir, I am honoured to meet you. I was told we can do business together."

When he left the Ile d'Aix, over three hours later, under cover of darkness, to return to his ship, a large deposit in gold coins reassuringly tucked away in an inner pocket of his cloak, Henry Graham had much on his mind, arrangements to make, partners to placate, his ship's freedom and safety to protect. He had agreed to provide swift direct passage to Boston for Europe's most wanted fugitive and his companions, a fair-sized mixed party of men and their wives and a few children, who would be crowded aboard. In exchange for the deposit, he had agreed to remain at Rochefort for up to 5 days, awaiting an opportunity to board his precious human cargo, with as much discretion as could be arranged (a night-time embarkation off the Ile de Lie by boat in smaller groups, luggage also - the details of which he and his new passengers had thrashed out, each finally satisfied with the others' thoroughness). After five days he must leave with or without them. As they had all understood, by then matters would be decided, their pursuers upon them. In any event no merchant ship could stay still for long, for its owners' and his employers' and their insurers', and clients' time was money and cargoes had to be moved and delivered, delays explained or paid for.

No easy task to remove and board quickly and quietly a large party, unaccustomed to the sea, with baggage, under the vigilant eyes of the patrolling Royal Navy, whose HMS Bellerophon, a 74-gun two decker ship of the line, and two consorts were off the approaches to Rochefort, ominously and aggressively blockading the entrances to the harbour, intercepting shipping, keeping a watchful eye on the two French frigates, a brig and a corvette lying at harbour there. Since the news of Boney's arrival in the vicinity of Rochefort had reached the British, Bellerophon's presence had been reinforced with two smaller and swifter 20-gun ships, HMS Myrmidon and HMS Slaney. Onshore there were also plenty of spies, turncoats, royalists or proto-royalists and others who would be quick to take advantage of an opportunity for a swift and substantial reward. The presence of an American vessel and the rumours in circulation that Napoleon would try to escape to America drawing particularly close attention on the Pride and the comings and goings of those aboard her.

The thought of running the gauntlet to beat the blockade of the Royal Navy did not daunt Graham. It stirred his blood. There was nothing new in this contest. Until three years ago the United States and Britain had been at war, the Royal Navy pursuing American ships at sea, with boardings, press ganging of sailors (deemed renegades, owing allegiance to their King) and seizure of cargoes and vessels as prizes. Clippers like the Pride were built for speed, able to outpace all but the fastest British Man o' War. If he could get them aboard and get past Bellerophon and its escorts, once out to sea he was confident he could deliver his passengers to his home port with only little danger of intervention to his vessel. He would enjoy the chase. He was being offered enough in gold and diamonds to satisfy even his partners – they could buy more ships, add to their small fleet, he mused. A steady man, nevertheless, the adventure of it stirred him.

Time passed while he was lost in thought. He and his travelling companion barely spoke. It was evening, dark save for the lights of the townsfolk and still open hostelries, when they got back to the outskirts of Rochefort, where he stepped down from the two seater buggy that, driven by his taciturn chaperone, the so-called 'friend' (an agent of Bonaparte's spymaster, Karl Schulmeister) whose name he knew as "M. Bochet", had been his means of transport to and from the quiet spot on the river where they had landed from the small boat that had ferried them at dusk to and from L'Ile d'Aix. He deliberately took a circuitous route on foot back to his ship. Used to taking precautions, usually against pickpockets, thieves or other malcontents that lurk in the shadows of any port town, he concluded he was not followed, that he could detect.

Once back in his cabin Graham washed his face and hands, changed his shirt and secured the deposit. Having caught up with the ship's news, he sat alone in reverie, barely noticing the simple cold supper brought to him, the red wine that he washed it down with, or the familiar muffled sounds of a moored ship that carried on around him. He later slept soundly, as only a man who has much to organise and who enjoys events, and their profits can do at the end of such a day.

After Graham had left the room, the four generals remained behind with the Emperor (for such they would still call him). They were joined by Emmanuel de Las Cases, who had assumed the role of the Emperor's Secretary. Savary recharged their glasses and they waited expectantly for their leader to speak, to reveal the direction of his thinking.

Minutes passed. They were used to this; knew to wait.

"So, Gentlemen, America. Our friends in Paris [was there a trace of irony?] have put at our disposal the Meduse and the Saale, both frigates, a corvette and a brig to take us to America, as we asked. The Americans have been friendly to us before. They have reason to be grateful. They have no love for the British. Now we find that the Royal Navy, which seems destined ever to flout us, has blocked our passage. The new masters of France will not permit a fight. These ships are nearly useless to us, but not entirely. We can use their presence to create a diversion, while the good Captain Graham spirits us away on his ship, which is faster."

"We have asked for passports for ourselves and for you and your families to accompany me. These we are still waiting for. As we heard, Graham can take us provided we have these passports and permission from the United States Minister, William Crawford to land in America. Again, the request has been made. We cannot simply voyage to America and present ourselves as fugitives seeking sanctuary."

Las Cases was the first to speak. "Sire, and how will we proceed if the passports are not given or the Americans say no, or more likely, do not reply in good time? Surely Paris will not risk angering Louis or the Allies, nor will Crawford risk the new peace between the United States and Britain. They will not help."

Napoleon looked at him, "nevertheless we will ask". Las Cases replied "Sire, you must consider surrendering your person to the British before you are captured. There is very little time. If you are captured anything can happen."

After a minute's thoughtful heavy silence, Napoleon nodded, saying "thank you, Gentlemen, it is time for dinner".

When soon after they were all congregated, with the ladies, the atmosphere was jolly, feverish, almost surreal. The jokes seemed funnier than usual, the laughter louder, nervous. The Emperor was at his most gracious and warm. Danger was galloping towards them and their future was opaque. They could all feel it. For themselves and this man in their midst to whom they owed so much and to whose destiny they felt bound, by individual degrees. A common factor for uneasy companions.

The Emperor clearly enjoyed the meal and then reading to the party afterwards, holding court, as was his custom, in good times and bad, until even he was ready to say good night. They had been grateful to be together, to enjoy this taste of normality and companionship. This was now the best time of the day. No more serious matters were discussed, but afterwards, when they had withdrawn to their sleeping quarters, those whose wives were present discussed their situation after their own fashion, in lowered voices and whispers.

13 July 1815

The day started well enough. The mood among the Emperor's party was even superficially gay at times, though fragile. Madame de Montholon suggested a morning walk, with which the Emperor, and so her husband and Las Cases readily agreed. Others followed some paces behind the main party, led by the Emperor who had graciously offered Mme La Comtesse de Montholon his arm. The others, attuned, had noticed her effect of lightening his mood and were grateful for it.

After an hour, during which the Emperor inspected the fortifications of Fort Liédot and teased and probed gently those of the pretty Mme de Montholon, they returned to find a worried looking visitor pacing, in dusty travelling clothes, anxious to speak with the Emperor, with whom he withdrew behind a closed door. The others making themselves apparently busy within reach, waiting for news. The new arrival did not augur well, they feared.

Only ten minutes or so later the door opened, and their visitor emerged, stony-faced, nodded to those present and took his leave. Bertrand, Gourgaud, de Montholon, Savary and Las Cases were summoned by the voice from within. Once more the door was closed firmly and quietly.

The Emperor stood before the window at the far end of the room, looking to the sea, his hands held behind his back characteristically. He turned. His visage was ominously dark and stern.

"The news from Mr Crawford is that we will not be welcome in America. Crawford says he cannot grant us entry to the United States without the approval of President Madison and there is of course no time to obtain that. We are "too hot to handle" it seems. The Americans do not wish to antagonize the British, or indeed anyone else now that they are at peace. This is the gratitude we receive from the Americans for our support, for doubling the size of their country!" He paused, adding "and we have lost the Saale and the Meduse on the orders of Louis".

The significance of these statements hung in the air. The full realization that they were helpless rats in a swiftly closing, probably lethal, trap impressing itself on each of them.

Las Cases was the first to speak. "Sire, your only option is to surrender your person voluntarily, to give your parole to the British, to the Commander of the nearest Royal Navy ship. The British are the most likely to treat you as men of honour. Asylum in Britain is the only realistic choice. Time is running out. You must not fall into the hands of Louis, the Austrians or the Prussians. I beg you to act, or anything may happen."

De Montholon protested "We have discussed this before. The British Government hates you. They will parade you as a trophy of Waterloo." Their debate raged. Bertrand, finally, agreed with Las Cases.

The Emperor, who had listened but not taken part in these exchanges, said quietly "I cannot abide the idea of living among my enemies."

A sparrow flew into the room through the open window. Once it had settled and ceased its fluttering, Gourgaud caught it swiftly but gently in his hands, "a portent of good fortune, your Majesty", he said, stroking its head with a forefinger and proffering it to the Emperor. The Emperor looked at the small bird empathetically and pointed toward the window – "there is enough unhappiness about, at least we can free this little one - release it". They all watched, as the bird seemingly determined their fates.

After it had set off in the direction of the open sea, and the British ships, Napoleon turned and said "Las Cases, you and Savary will approach the British Captain today to make the arrangements. Bertrand you will write a letter to the Captain and will also write down a private letter from us to the Prince Regent, which Gourgaud you will deliver, as Las Cases and Savary will arrange. The letter must be delivered into the hand of the Prince Regent by you personally. We will entrust ourselves to his care and generosity. Perhaps they will treat us with the same hospitality offered to Lucien.[ii] Now that Louis has returned there is a vacancy in England. Gentlemen, we have much to do." With that the matter was decided.

An Emperor of France, even one who has abdicated, cannot be seen to wilfully adopt the life of a fugitive.

Napoleon wrote to the Prince Regent:

"Your royal highness, confronted with the various factions that divide my country, and with the enmity of the greatest nations of Europe, my political career has come to an end, and here I come, like Themistocles, to sit at the hearth of the British people. I put myself under the protection of its laws, which I request to your royal highness, the most powerful, the most constant, and the most generous of my enemies. Ile d'Aix, 13 July 1815. Napoleon"[iii]

Not far distant, Maitland was in a nervous state of excitement. He did not have time or the means to consult higher authority if he was to secure his quarry before his other, foreign, pursuers. His orders (as given to his fellow blockading captains along the Atlantic Coast) were to prevent the escape of Bonaparte. He knew that by taking him on board, accepting his parole and taking him to England by agreement he was interpreting those orders liberally. Surely that was initiative? Better than refusing him and turning him away to a more uncertain fate, more difficult reports and explanations?

Maitland agreed to dispatch HMS Slaney, a 20-gun sloop, under Captain George Sartorius, with General Gourgaud aboard to Plymouth urgently and thence to London to the Prince Regent to deliver Bonaparte's letter, a firm pre-condition of his surrender. Sartorius would also bear a letter from Captain Maitland to the Admiralty, reporting his actions. Gourgaud left France on 13 July.

During that last day on Ile d'Aix the Emperor met with his advisers, preparing for what was ahead. He spent a long time closeted alone with Schulmeister, who departed as quietly as he had come. A now notorious man whose effectiveness depended upon operating unobserved in the shadows.

As best he could, the Emperor had arranged his affairs, prepared and despatched letters and messages for his family, his supporters, his agents, his bankers and others. He was a renowned master of planning and logistics, with an exacting eye for detail. He enjoyed this familiar activity. Planning and preparation were key, he knew of old.

It was a frantic day of comings and goings, planning, packing and preparation. Time was running out and all felt the imminence of their pursuers. Strangely, the British had come to represent a welcome source of refuge. A foe more predictable and less vengeful than their immediate pursuers hunting them on land, the chase inexorably drawing in upon them.

It was uncertain that they would see France again, or when, as they were acutely aware, most particularly the man who had brought them to this moment.

A message was delivered to Captain Graham – his valuable cargo would not be coming on this voyage; the Pride should sail. He might be called upon again and should keep the deposit against the day.

15 July 1815

In the early morning Napoleon boarded the French brig Epervier, which made its way slowly toward Bellerophon. The wind conditions proving unfavourable, Captain Maitland sent the Bellerophon's barge to intercept and transfer the Emperor.

At 7am, the great man, wearing his famous green Chasseur's coat, preceded by General Bertrand, was received respectfully and with ceremony - including a 21-gun royal salute - aboard HMS Bellerophon, to the obvious excitement and curiosity of its officers and crew and all ashore who had seen him depart. Ever mindful of the moment, the erstwhile Emperor of France, this meteor, the man who had become a force that crashed into, sometimes terrorized, modernized and ruled over much of Europe and excited, terrified and enthralled the remainder, raised his hat, bowed and said in French to the Bellerophon's proud captain, "Sir, I am come on board and I claim the protection of your Prince and of your laws". Maitland greeted his remarkable guest with formal politeness and courtesy and ushered him below to his own cabin, the great cabin, vacated for the purpose. Shortly thereafter, at Napoleon's request, Maitland introduced the ship's officers, following which the great man, mindful of the evident respect and courtesy shown to him, of his effect on others, and again demonstrating his capacity to engage with fellow military men, said "Gentlemen, you have the honour of belonging to the bravest and most fortunate nation in the World." He had made a very good first impression, as he intended.

Matters did not proceed as they had hoped. Life on board the Bellerophon was agreeable enough, but his hopes of a comfortable retirement in the English countryside were soon dashed. News of his capture and intended landing, along with General Gourgaud, reached London before the Bellerophon arrived. Napoleon had placed great trust in Gourgaud – a man who had fought with or for him bravely in many battles, who had been among the first to rally to his cause after his return from Elba and who had twice saved his life – in Moscow in October 1812 where he had himself found and put out the fuse lit by Russians to explode some 500,000 pounds of gunpowder and again at the Battle of Brienne, in January 1814, where he had intercepted a Cossack's lance bearing down on Napoleon.

After Waterloo Napoleon had appointed him, already his "Premier Officer de Ordnance", Brigadier General and his personal Aide de Camp.

Charged with delivering his master's letter solely into the hands of the Prince Regent, Gourgaud failed in his mission. The British would not allow him access to His Royal Highness – and he would not release the letter other than to him. He was returned to the Bellerophon, with the letter.

Napoleon would have been very disturbed if he had known of what was developing.

De Montholon was wrong. Maitland had also misjudged. His Britannic Majesty's Government wished for no such trophy. The Cabinet were very concerned over the uncertain consequences of bringing the most famous man in Europe, the World, their greatest enemy, alternately feared, loathed and admired, but most certainly an object of widely held curiosity, into the country. There was radicalism and unrest about after many years of costly wars with France and in America. Anything could happen, as the 100 days following Bonaparte's escape from Elba had so recently demonstrated. It had been a "close run thing", as they were acutely aware, and the Duke of Wellington had reportedly remarked after Waterloo. But for the late but nevertheless timely arrival and intervention of General Blucher and his Prussians and untimely delay in French reinforcements arriving on the field of battle, Europe would be facing a different future and Bonaparte would be dictating terms to his over-stretched and fragile enemies.

The Prime Minister, Lord Liverpool, who had steered the Britannic Ship of State to this point of victory, wrote to Lord Castlereagh, the Foreign Secretary, who was in Vienna discussing the future of the European Continent in conference with the representatives of the other great powers: "We are all very decidedly of the opinion that it would not answer to confine him in this country.... He would become the object of curiosity immediately, and possibly of compassion in the course of a few months, and the circumstances of his being here, or indeed anywhere in Europe, would contribute to keep up a certain degree of ferment in France...St Helena is the place in the world best calculated for the confinement of such a person...the situation is particularly healthy. There is only one place...where ships can anchor, and we have the power of excluding neutral ships altogether... At such a place and such a distance, all intrigue would be impossible; and, being so far from the European world, he would soon be forgotten."

Aboard HMS Bellerophon, while these matters were being debated and resolved urgently onshore, Napoleon had demonstrated his remarkable capacity to win over the affection of even his recent enemies. He had inspected the ship, showing considerable interest in her running and management. Each day he had walked the deck at about 5pm, followed by dinner taken promptly at 6pm. His habits were regular. He had, for such a senior prisoner, been amiable with both officers and ordinary ratings, showing interest in their activities. In turn the ship's company had warmed to their guests and sought to host and entertain them as best they could aboard a ship of

war. So much so that on 18 July, two plays, The Poor
Gentleman by George Colman the Younger (first
published in 1802) and Raising the Wind by James
Kenney (1803), were performed by junior officers of the
ship's company before Napoleon and his party.

Plymouth

They arrived off Plymouth on 26 July and dropped
anchor in Plymouth Sound. Soon they learned that they
were to be isolated, incommunicado, even the crew were
to remain on board and no private letters were allowed to
be sent ashore from anyone aboard the ship, crew
member or passenger.

For days they were marooned awaiting instructions from
London. News of his arrival having preceded him, there
gathered large crowds of sightseers paying to gaze
through telescopes from the shore, many hiring rowing
boats to take them out for a closer look, which Napoleon
had obliged good humouredly, promenading on deck,
taking the air, raising his hat to those ladies who caught
his eye. He hoped to win over public opinion and it
helped to relieve the boredom. So many were in
competition to come up close that Maitland deployed
boats and crews to keep the overly inquisitive at a
distance. These were uncomfortable and anxious days for
the party aboard. Such a public welcome boded well,
raising their fragile hopes.

On 31 July, in the mid-morning, Napoleon graciously received Major General Sir Henry Bunbury, who introduced himself as His Britannic Majesty's Under Secretary of State for War and the Colonies, and Admiral Lord Keith, Commander-in- Chief in the Channel, an old, no-nonsense Scotsman. Both were received with naval formality and then with all of the decorum and ceremony that the Emperor's entourage could muster in their reduced circumstances. It was far more than either of the envoys was comfortable with; Boney was a defeated prisoner, their long-standing enemy, a self-made tyrant and in no position to bargain or cavil, let alone hold court!

They were serious men come about a serious matter, in determined mood. The sight of hundreds, maybe more, sightseers and maybe even well-wishers in the harbour and around the vessel day-tripping in a carnival atmosphere had served only to irritate them. Being greeted on deck by Bertrand, Gourgaud and de Montholon in the uniforms of French generals was perhaps to be expected, and their entitlement, but their deferential references to "the Emperor" and "His Majesty" were too much. Without obvious rudeness, but nevertheless brusquely, they declared that they had arrived to speak with "General Bonaparte". By the time they were ushered into the great cabin to meet this unique curiosity, for even they were intrigued and undeniably, grudgingly excited to meet him, they were confirmed in the justification for their nation's sentence. They were also girded for a reaction.

Once all had entered, the cabin was crowded, airless on this warm July day. Following introductions, as their host motioned them to do (which also served to irritate them – damn it, this was a Royal Navy ship-of the-line and he their defeated prisoner!), Sir Henry and Lord Keith sat at the dining table together facing Napoleon. Bertrand, Las Cases, de Montholon, Savary, Lallemand and Gourgaud did not take available seats but stood behind their Emperor. Brandy and red wine were offered to the guests and accepted (Napoleon took wine; he avoided spirits). The initial pleasantries observed, including a toast to The King and The Prince Regent offered by Napoleon, Sir Henry got to the point. The French contingent externally composed, inwardly apprehensive, charged, awaiting sentence. Newspaper reports suggesting St Helena as their probable destination of distant exile had reached them; they still hoped these were incorrect or that, by some miracle of persuasion, their leader could change this unsettling fate. Best to maintain calm. It was a tiny spot at the other end of the Earth. It might as well have been the Moon.

Sir Henry spoke, "General, I am instructed by His Majesty's Government to deliver to you its decision concerning your future situation and maintenance and the restrictions to which you will be subject." There was a pause, silence, save for gulls squawking outside and the now familiar and usual creaking and distant noises of the daily business of a Man-o-War at anchor in peacetime. He was as a judge pronouncing sentence, cognizant of his moment in history, speaking for his nation. This was a solemn moment, calling for deliberate clarity and firmness of purpose and voice.

"You are to be transported to the Island of St Helena, in the Indian Ocean. There you will be housed and will receive an allowance and provision for a small household which will allow you to live out your life in adequate comfort, safely out of harm's way. You may take with you such members of your party as His Majesty's Government may approve and servants of your choosing, limited to three officers and twelve domestics. Generals Savary and Lallemand may not go with you." Once delivered, the sentence hung in the air for what seemed longer but was in reality only minutes. All eyes were on Napoleon, whose facial composure had visibly turned to stern cold anger. We can only speculate at the discomfort felt by Savary and Lallemand – the British (the Bourbons?) clearly had something different in mind for them; retribution[iv]

Napoleon glared at Bunbury and Keith and said tersely, "my blood should rather stain the planks of the Bellerophon than will I go to St Helena. This mean and infamous decision will throw a veil of darkness over the future history of England. After three months in that place I will be dead." With that he stood up rapidly and paced to the large window at the stern of the great cabin, his back to those present, his hands held behind him. The audience or meeting, depending upon perspective, was ended. Bunbury and Keith made their exit. Ceremony was at an end, pleasantries over. On their return journey to London, each lost in thought, they spoke little of the meeting, other than to observe in irritation on Gallic pomposity. They felt a sense of anti-climax. They had been dismissed summarily, but their task was accomplished. What else were they to expect?

When they had gone, Napoleon turned to face his lieutenants. "Well, so it is true", he said. "They fear me even now. They fear their own people more" (he gestured toward the boats and the shore). "They want to punish me but dare not go further. I am to rot and die a 'natural' death in poor conditions at the other end of the Earth or be forgotten, or both, they hope". He paused, "and they may succeed".

Amid protestations of anger, defiance and vehemently anti-English sentiments by de Montholon and Gourgaud (who had rejoined their company, reporting on his reception and interviews in London), Las Cases spoke "Sire, you must send a message direct to the Prince Regent, appealing to his sense of justice. Only he can change this decision. We have only enemies among the English Cabinet."

There was little or no hope, but another letter was written and sent, also without response, as it turned out.

The Emperor spoke in private with each of Savary and Lallemand before they departed. As for the remainder of his party, he generously told them that they were not obliged to join him in his distant exile. He would understand if any of them decided to remain. To a man they protested their willingness to accompany him.

Napoleon later spoke with Maitland, telling him "It is worse than Tamerlaine's iron cage. I would prefer being delivered up to the Bourbons. Among other insults…they style me General: they may as well call me Archbishop!" He then informed Maitland, who did not object, that he would be convening his party, including the servants, to break the news.

Crowded into his cabin (Maitland's erstwhile cabin), Madame de Montholon and Fanny Bertrand (who was English and could choose to remain) seated, the senior members of the remaining party behind him, facing the others, some pressed against the panelled wooden walls, they listened to their Emperor. There were different reactions, from resignation, anger and belligerence ("let's fight and set fire to the ship, then they will have to take us ashore") to barely hidden distress. The Emperor called for quiet and slowly they filed out.

Later that evening Fanny Bertrand tried to jump over the side, stopped only by de Montholon who had remained nearby, having observed her odd and unhappy behaviour.

There was to be no delay. Lord Liverpool wanted this exotic captive and magnet for popular attention safely departed and far from the shores of England, the Continent even more so, as soon as could be arranged. No time could be allowed to give opportunity for any kind of deviation or intervention from any quarter. The next day those who were to travel to St Helena and their baggage were transferred by small boats and re-embarked aboard HMS Northumberland, an 88-gun ship-of-the-line, under the command of Rear-Admiral Sir George Cockburn KCB, Bt.

As preparations for the disembarkation of the French party from the Bellerophon were in train, de Montholon had approached Captain Maitland with the information that his master wished to make a gift to the Captain of a box containing his portrait set in diamonds, in gratitude for his gentlemanly conduct towards him and his entourage. Though gratified, Maitland felt compelled to decline. Later, upon his departure, Napoleon pressed upon him as a memento a tumbler bearing the crown and cipher of Josephine. Saying goodbye, in the cabin he was now relinquishing, Napoleon said warmly to Maitland "my reception in England has been very different from what I expected, but it gives me much satisfaction to assure you, that I feel your conduct to me throughout has been that of a gentleman and a man of honour".

Later, recording this chapter, Maitland wrote "it may appear surprising that a possibility could exist of a British officer being prejudiced in favour of one who has caused so many calamities to his country; but to such an extent did he possess the power of pleasing, that there are few people who could have sat at the same table with him for nearly a month, as I did, without feeling a sensation of pity, allied perhaps to regret, that a man possessed of so many fascinating qualities, and who had held so high a station in life, should be reduced to the situation in which I saw him".

Cockburn was a lifelong naval officer, a highly respected, popular, brave and resourceful 43 year-old veteran of the

French Revolutionary Wars, the Battle of Cape St Vincent, the Napoleonic Wars and the American War of Independence. He had directed the capture and burning of Washington a year earlier. As Second-in-Command of the North America Station, he had patrolled Chesapeake Bay and other areas of the North Atlantic coast relentlessly blockading commercial shipping and attacking ports, seeking to strangle the supply routes to the American rebels and to undermine their finances. Lord Liverpool and the Admiralty knew he was just the calibre of man to ensure the safe and uninterrupted delivery of his charges to their far-flung destination and to remain some months to settle them in, as he was instructed to do, as newly appointed Governor of St Helena and Commander-in-Chief of the Cape of Good Hope Station. Cockburn was altogether a different proposition to the less experienced Maitland. Not a man for suasion. Another warrior.

Cockburn received his guests on board and installed them in their quarters. He observed the arrival and storage below decks of their seemingly vast array of baggage, with polite courtesy and some inward amusement. Napoleon would have the great cabin, where they would dine together. Given the extent and nature of the provisions loaded on board and the astonishing arrival of Franceschi Cipriani (*Franchesky Chipriani*), Napoleon's maître d'hotel, his butler and pastry chef Pieron and Lepage, his cook, despite the limited facilities for preparing food aboard a Ship-of-the-Line, it was clear that simple seaman's fare was unlikely to be on the menu and that even the rather better offerings which an

Admiral might customarily expect on his table would not do. Still, there would no doubt be compensations!

There were, naturally, heightened curiosity and varying degrees of excitement among the officers and crew of the Northumberland and a sense of pride. Theirs' would be an historic voyage in peace time - when many other crews and officers were being laid off or put on half-pay. They would be crossing the Tropics, rounding the Cape, carrying the most famous passenger in the World. Something they could dine out on, tell tall tales about, relate to their children and grandchildren. No-one was unmoved, impressed or not, implacable foe or just plain curious. The ship was abuzz, all could feel it.

In all, Napoleon's entourage comprised twenty-six people, the maximum he had been allowed. A company made up of the probable and the seemingly improbable - all tying their uncertain fates to that of their now fallen hero and leader, the man by whom they had been made, elevated and given purpose. Who can know all of the personal motivations, complex or simple? A small microcosm of a court combined with the vestiges of an army commander's staff.

Gourgaud, initially not on the list of those chosen to accompany the Emperor, pressed his case for inclusion with Bertrand, resulting in Napoleon interceding and putting him on the list, displacing Nicolas Planat.

Among those to decline the questionable honour of joining his patron in exile was the Emperor's private doctor, Louis-Pierre Maingault. This was to prove significant. Aboard the Bellerophon Napoleon had met the ship's surgeon, Barry O'Meara, an Irishman and Protestant, fortuitously, as it turned out. Napoleon had discovered in O'Meara an empathetic, skilled and experienced naval surgeon who unusually spoke Italian, having served in Sicily and Calabria. Napoleon's request that O'Meara should become his personal doctor was agreed to by Cockburn – after all, he surmised, who better to keep a close eye on their captive and his health, itself a politically sensitive issue, as it was to prove?

Napoleon was touched that Paola, his sister, now living in Rome as the Princess Borghese, had offered to accompany him. The British refused to permit this.

En route to St Helena

At first his good humour and internal composure had evaporated totally when he was informed of his destination, his sentence.

Disabused of the quixotic notion of a comfortable retirement as an emigre gentleman of note in England, he at first contemplated the 4,400-mile voyage and his destination alternately morosely and furiously.

The ability to recover, to think quickly, strategically, laterally and to adapt and surprise were, however, hallmarks of his life and success. He could think and take action while others froze or reacted. He took stock.

At least he would have familiar and loyal company, plus some physical comforts. He would have picked and capable lieutenants, in Bertrand, Montholon, Gourgaud and Las Cases. With such men there would be possibilities perhaps. In the meantime, his valets (Marchand and Noverraz), Mamluk Ali (his valet and guard) and others of his loyal household (the brothers Achille, groom, and Joseph Archambault, coachman, the footman Gentilini, the fellow Corsican and usher-barber Santini and Rousseau the lamplighter and toymaker) would maintain his routines and provide for him as he was accustomed. Even so, he thought, he was used to the deprivations of campaigning and the economic ups and downs of life – he had experienced both wealth and great power and paucity of means. He was used to adjustment, used to overcoming new challenges, more than that - it was his trademark.

He was not a natural sailor, however, and rough seas made him queasy and ill. In calmer conditions Napoleon enjoyed the sea air and learning about the workings of this substantial fighting vessel. Sailors were soldiers at sea, as were the complement of Royal Marines aboard and they warmed to each other's presence and curiosity. The atmosphere was friendly. Napoleon had always had a way with such men, both accessible and totally self-assured. This was Boney in the flesh and close by. Who could not be impressed?

Colour was ensured by the inclusion in the party of the attractive and intriguing Albine Montholon, contrasting the wrought, unhappy and apprehensive Fanny Bertrand –

who was making her poor husband's life a misery. They were accompanied by the three Bertrand children and three-year old Tristan Montholon. Children are resilient and more adaptable than adults, given adventure and kindness and soon the children were enthralled by their adventurous surroundings, the strange and constant workings of the ship, the bustle and the sights of the voyage. While the presence of both women and children aboard a Royal Navy war ship was highly unusual and not welcomed by all of the Northumberland's complement, the majority were happy to experience this rare exposure to domesticity, their own homes and loved ones long behind and far away. With children language is no barrier.

The long voyage in the main passed without incident, though nearly all of the French party except Gourgaud suffered from mal de mer.

There were a few high points, such as celebrating the crossings of the Tropic of Cancer and the Equator, anchoring in the harbour at Gibraltar to pick up fresh water and victuals and sighting the North Western shores of Africa. These occasions afforded Cipriani, Pieron and Le Page opportunities to create imaginative treats and surprises for the Emperor, his entourage and chief captors. The most irritating event, however, was the confiscation by Cockburn from the party of some 4,000 gold Napoleons, funds needed to smooth their paths - anticipated though this inconvenience had been (to preserve anything they knew they must be prepared to give up sufficient to avert further suspicion and searches).

Relations between Admiral Cockburn and General Bonaparte, as he called him to his intense irritation, remained cool though civil.

St Helena

After a voyage of ten weeks, on 15 October 1815, HMS Northumberland dropped anchor in James Bay, St Helena's only harbour, set against an impressive backdrop of black cliffs 600 feet high, flanking Jamestown, the only town, of some 100 houses. The ship's arrival and anticipation of their famous new resident had the islanders and the garrison agog with excitement. A new governor was news enough, but the arrival of the Great Ogre was the most significant thing that had ever happened here in their small cut off world in the South Atlantic.

For two days Napoleon and his party remained aboard HMS Bellerophon, as accommodation on shore was not yet prepared. In the early evening on 17 October, they landed.

The transfer by barge to shore and landing of Boney and his colourful, obviously foreign entourage and their substantial baggage and possessions were watched with great curiosity. This infamous but magnetic man walked slowly along a line of spectators standing silently behind soldiers with fixed bayonets (to protect the new arrivals). On first seeing the Great Ogre, a Grenadier exclaimed, within the Emperor's earshot, "they told me he was growing old; he has forty good campaigns in his belly yet, damn him!" The Emperor was amused and recounted this pleasing remark to his companions later that evening.

There was a carnival atmosphere, though on a smaller scale than in Plymouth. The curiosity was mutual – Napoleon and his companions were equally interested (and frankly concerned) to take in their new, obviously limited, surroundings and to observe its inhabitants, the New World which was to be their cage, assuredly his final home if Great Britain and the other European powers were to have their way.

They were informed by Cockburn that they would be installed at Longwood House, on the unhappily named Deadwood Plateau, until recently the Lieutenant Governor's residence, but now being refurbished and extended to house its new occupants. In the meantime, they were to squeeze into the Briars Pavilion, in the grounds of the home of an English family, the Balcombes.

That night Napoleon stayed in a house in Jamestown, his companions spread to other quarters – some, including Las Cases and Gourgaud, housed in a hotel.

The next morning Napoleon was taken on horseback by Cockburn to see Longwood. They called in upon the Briars on their return, where they met the Balcombes. When afterwards Bertrand teased the 32 year-old bachelor Gourgaud that he should marry the vivacious 14 year old Betsy Balcombe – producing a sharp riposte – Napoleon intervened, telling Bertrand not to speak of it again – he would find him a wife in Paris! A notably incongruous remark in the circumstances.

The Briars Pavilion, as they soon discovered, provided barely enough accommodation for their sizeable party. Nevertheless, they found that William Balcombe, his wife Jane and their four children, were interested, friendly and respectful hosts, very sensitive to the needs of their extraordinary temporary guests.

Among the Balcombes, only 16 year-old Jane and the younger Betsy spoke French well enough to bridge communications. William Balcombe, happily a merchant Superintendent of Public Sales for the East India Company, that owned the island, soon became a diligent and most useful purveyor of the substantial quantities of catering supplies, wines, brandies and other consumables and goods required to meet the demanding needs of the French household. Opportunity finds beneficiaries in the most unlikely places.

Once she overcame her initial awe, fear and shyness, Betsy found their visitors to be different, fascinating, warm and friendly. She soon struck up friendships, most particularly with the Great Ogre himself, who won her over with his easy charm. They charmed each other, this man of legend and vast worldly experience and the young girl with touching innocence. She soon came to call him "Boney", which when first spoken brought the reply "but I am not at all bony", looking down at himself bemusedly. This familiarity was allowed to no one else and caused some consternation and jealousy within the former emperor's contingent, forbidden such impertinent familiarity.

She amused him, as did the effect on those around him. She also helped him with his efforts to learn English and to learn about his new surroundings and the occupants of the island. Betsy was a ray of sunlight and very useful. News of their friendship soon reached Europe, where many continued to be fascinated by 'news' of the erstwhile ruler of France. Ungenerously, some speculated that this was a love story.

Almost as soon as they moved into the Briars Napoleon began a campaign of complaining of the conditions on the island. He instructed his companions to do the same.

On 20 November a ball was held at Plantation House by Admiral Cockburn, to which the senior officers, Allied Representatives and Napoleon and the senior members of his entourage were invited. In this far off place it was the most exciting event in the social calendar, and a welcome distraction. It amused Cockburn on the evening to instruct Gourgaud to dance with Betsy Balcombe, but the Frenchman had eyes for another unmarried young English lady, Laura Wilks, though to no avail.

Their time at Briars Pavilion soon passed and on 10 December 1815 they were moved to Longwood, now extended and refurbished.

While larger than Briars Pavilion, Longwood House was not capacious and was afflicted by its miserable location, high in the centre of this generally temperate island, on the pessimistically named Deadwood Plateau, shrouded in cloud for more than three hundred days a year and offering winds, damp and high humidity - which unhealthy combination the Emperor soon decided, as he declared angrily to all, reflected the clear intention of his captors to finish him off in this desolate and remote spot on the globe!

They soon discovered the comprehensive - and expensive - precautions taken by the British authorities to ensure there would be no escape, no rescue, no repeat of the return from Elba and all that had followed. There were still many loyal supporters of Bonaparte, his large and still wealthy family, rumours of rescue plots, and while alive it seemed he would always offer a potent threat to the order of things, as he had so recently demonstrated.

Two Royal Navy frigates patrolled the seas surrounding St Helena, constantly on station, capable of seeing off any vessel likely to attempt a rescue or landing. The paucity of suitable anchorages other than James Bay reinforced the island's sea defences. A coastal landing was very difficult and dangerous, for boats and men, the seas and currents strong and treacherous and the island a rocky fortress.

Sited nearby to Longwood at the Deadwood Barracks was a large contingent of regular infantry. A flag station had been installed so that signals could be sent regularly to the Governor, informing him of Bonaparte's situation (such as "All is well with General Bonaparte") or, God forbid, sending an alarm if he escaped ("General

43

Bonaparte is missing"), and other predetermined messages. All of these measures were soon made known, or otherwise became apparent, to the Emperor and the experienced soldiers in his party, for whom it was a simple matter to reconnoitre and assess their surroundings, under the pretexts of walking or riding.

Cockburn was soon relieved and replaced, as intended, by a man who was even less to the Emperor's taste. Major-General Sir Hudson Lowe, a 46 year-old career army officer of broad experience, who had seen active service and been commended for gallantry by the Prussian Generals Blucher and Gneisenau. He had received his instructions from Lord Bathurst, Secretary of State for War and the Colonies, who wrote to the Duke of Wellington "I do not believe we could have found a fitter person of his rank in the army willing to accept a situation of so much confinement, responsibility and exclusion from society." Dubious compliments, but an apt assessment of his man.

Hudson Lowe assumed his responsibilities as the gaoler of The Great Ogre with the utmost seriousness and determination. He would fulfil his instructions to the letter. There would be no escape, could be no escape on his watch – no blame would attach to him!

Lowe received a warm welcome from Cockburn, who was enthusiastic to hand over and to depart aboard the vessel that had conveyed Lowe, his mission accomplished. Over an agreeable dinner at Plantation House naturally they discussed their Prisoner and his principal companions, their roles and idiosyncrasies – it was soon clear to Lowe that Cockburn had not warmed to Boney. That night he went to sleep in his new home with mixed thoughts and feelings about the meeting to come the next day.

Together Cockburn and Lowe made their way by carriage from Plantation House to Longwood.

Lowe observed from the outset that Cockburn and General Bonaparte regarded and treated each other with a cool detachment, exchanging no more than the necessary polite perfunctory formalities. There was no warmth in their brief goodbyes.

It was a short meeting. One of only a half dozen or so that Hudson Lowe would have with his prisoner, as it turned out.

The pattern of life at Longwood had soon become established. Though offering larger accommodation than Briars Pavilion it was nevertheless a tight space for the entourage, which included families, to live shoulder to shoulder. Little could pass which was not soon known to all. Unsurprisingly, tensions and rivalries simmered. They were provided for, for now, but what did the future hold for them? At the centre of this small hive ruled the Emperor Bee.

It had become quickly apparent since their arrival in the island that the French contingent had extensive and prodigious needs. The happy merchants and shopkeepers of Jamestown competed to provide the foodstuffs, wines, spirits, cloth, other household goods and supplies regularly required. The Emperor, to his great irritation, was not permitted to leave the grounds of Longwood, but the other members of his household, watched closely, were allowed the relief of occasional visits into Jamestown, where they soon ceased to be a great curiosity.

Indeed, due to the incapacity of the Briars Pavilion to hold all of the French party, Gaspard Gourgaud was for a time to remain living in Jamestown at the hotel.

Jamestown was a regular port of call on the merchant shipping routes to and from the Cape. At times as many as fifty vessels were anchored in James Bay, replenishing supplies of freshwater, vegetables and fruit, bringing business to the local shopkeepers, victuallers and their suppliers.

It continued to be the habit of the household to meet for dinner and, often, to gather afterwards while the Emperor read to them.

They all craved news from home, from France, from Europe, the outside world - some new stimulation, and perhaps even hope. Rare, dated, newspapers were scoured for all that could be gleaned. A small window on events, fashions, gossip....

Like many an energetic man who finds himself retired and underemployed towards the end of a busy life, the Emperor had decided it was time to write his memoirs, a long project which helped him to pass the time. Something within his control and which allowed him freedom of expression – the only true freedom he enjoyed. For this purpose, it became his habit to retire to his study. He usually dictated to Las Cases, de Montholon or Gourgaud, an extension of their duties, but it helped to pass the time for all involved. Even O'Meara was an occasional willing scribe. For good measure he also wrote a biography of Julius Caesar, a perspective he felt uniquely justified in offering. It was comfortable territory and temporarily relaxing, taking up much of his abundant time, until now an unknown experience.

He was also enjoying intimate relations with Albine de Montholon. Their close proximity aboard the Bellerophon, continued now on St Helena, had moved their relationship on from dalliance and mutual electricity to a regular sharing of their physical needs and appetites. That her room was opposite his own was more than a coincidence.

As was widely known, Napoleon was experienced in the bedroom[v]. He regarded his sexual needs in much the same way he thought of food, drink, exercise and entertainment. It was necessary for his physical and mental health. A happy distraction bringing to him some joy in this otherwise miserable place. Albine was desirable, experienced, willing and available, enjoying his affection and proximity. She was the compliant mistress to a great man, with which comes a place in history and possibly more tangible and immediate rewards. This was not the anxious, exhilarating love of young novices or the furtive affair of commonplace cuckoos.

What of Charles de Montholon? Theirs was a remarkable situation. Ordinarily he would have been faced with the dilemma of whether to challenge his wife's lover or to take a more mature and liberal view, that of an aristocratic husband whose heir is secured, and to ignore the affair, which in any event, must surely end naturally. He chose the latter approach; after all, the lover in question was unchallengeable, even protected by his captors. What was he to do, however miserable or slighted he might have felt? He could only look ridiculous or experience worse. The cold reality was that a pattern had been repeated. His own liaison with Albine had begun while she was married to another man, their wedding coming only two months after her divorce. Neither had inconvenient scruples, neither was a hypocrite. These were the morals and pragmatic accommodations of the times.

When it had become clear that pleasant retirement in England, North America or another acceptable place was not going to be afforded to the Emperor, he began to plan and prepare for his escape from St Helena to a new life. Even before he had surrendered himself to Captain Maitland careful plans had been made to prepare for such a contingency. Schulmeister had received his instructions, sealed coded letters were delivered to members of the Emperor's immediate family, to his bankers in Amsterdam and Switzerland and to his most trusted agents – the spider's web which would ensure that his wishes would be met, his escape probable.

Even now, after the 100 Days, after Waterloo, after all that he and his family had lost, so much of what he had carved out through conquest and extraordinary ambition and daring, their hidden wealth - much of it in diamonds, sapphires, other precious stones and gold; portable, concealable and exchangeable, usually untraceable commodities - was huge and well hidden from his vengeful enemies. His private treasury was said to have held in excess of 54,000 precious stones! Croesus might have envied him.

Such wealth engendered loyalty, bought aid, influence, services and possibilities not available to other men, especially when wielded by a military genius who only recently bestrode Europe, his agents, their networks and tentacles still active or available in many quarters. The Bonapartes had many friends and there were many who did not welcome the new order in France and in the Italian states; though not all wanted his return and the upheavals that would inevitably follow – few families had not been touched by loss in the recent turbulent decades – across Europe a great many men, husbands, fathers, sons and sweethearts had not come home, or were broken by war, exhausted. Aid and sympathy were available, a resurgence of Bonapartism with all that it would bring about by way of war, was not on offer any more, for the time being.

Escape from St Helena was a serious challenge to even his resourcefulness. Developing and executing his plans for escape and a new life excited him, however, as planning new campaigns always had. He usually won and he believed he would win again. Giving up was not in his constitution, nor was being captive or staying put. He was still a man of energy.

He had soon sized up his adversary, Sir Hudson Lowe. The British had sent him just the kind of man he wanted in a gaoler, a man he could keep at a distance and whose character would not question his froideur, or its causes.

The Emperor knew and accepted that it would not be possible or intelligent to attempt escape in the first few years on the island. The British and their Allies would be at their most vigilant and energetic, ready for events. Europe was arranging itself into its post Congress of Vienna shape. France was reduced by war, adjusting to the return of monarchy, of aristocrats seeking to re-impose themselves and restore their families' former positions, wealth and privileges, with consequent economic and social upheaval. He had resigned himself to this unpleasant fact, though the opportunity to write his substantial memoirs, with the happy and welcome distractions shared with Mme de Montholon, was a worthwhile use of the time while he waited, plans were formed, and arrangements put in place. Plans that had to be as thorough and likely to ensure success as possible – for to be caught attempting escape or even afterwards would most probably result in his ignominious death, shot while escaping, or even by execution. He would be hunted across the globe with all of the resources and vengeful energy his powerful enemies could bring to bear. His companions, co-conspirators and accomplices, could expect no leniency either, whether he was caught or not.

Within days of landing at St Helena, the Emperor convened regular meetings of his core staff – Henri Bertrand, Charles-Tristan de Montholon, Gaspard Gourgaud and Emmanuel de Las Cases. From the beginning, once it was clear that they would accompany the Emperor to his place of incarceration, they knew that, in effect, they constituted the escape committee. Sworn to the utmost secrecy, their loyalty beyond question. Each bringing to the problem their own capabilities and experience, the stakes as high as any could be. The hope and prospect of securing the Emperor's escape motivated each of them for a mix of reasons, not least of which was that it should result in their own earlier departure from the island, their relevance there ended. They were not, so far, themselves prisoners, though that status would no doubt change if they were judged to have aided the Great Ogre's escape. It was not lost on them that there was humour in their situation – like bandits, pirates or common criminals they were planning the escape of the most famous prisoner of all!

At their first planning meeting, in his study at Longwood, the Emperor opened the discussion, "Well, gentlemen, here we are – at the end of the Earth! I have been sent here to rot and die! My enemies dare not kill me themselves, so they send me to be buried in a godforsaken hole in the middle of nowhere, with a miserable climate in the clear expectation it will finish me off in a few years, far away from our homeland!", he said tersely, his face suffused in deep rage and resentment, his eyes seemingly focused far away. After a few moments of silence, he added "and they might succeed." The others waited to see if there would be more, but nothing came for a full minute.

As if he had come to an internal decision, the Emperor's visage cleared, he then asked each in turn for their assessment of the situation. Three generals, experienced campaigners, and an atlas maker, educated in military matters, with naval experience. Tacticians all, their leader the greatest strategist of modern times.

The first to speak were the generals, who between them methodically listed the logistical problems of their escape and location, the list growing, the barriers mounting. No likely force could rescue them, a well-equipped regular military force of some size and a squadron of warships would be required – and their captors might be under orders to finish off their captives rather than lose them.

They were not sailors and had no capacity to seize a ship, certainly one which could escape the harbour and the patrolling Royal Navy, voyaging a huge distance to a safe haven, if one could be found. They were closely watched, with limited freedom of movement, the Emperor not allowed movement beyond the confines of Longwood. Communication lines were complicated, involved huge distances and carried a high risk of intervention, the British vigilant and watching closely, no doubt, all arrivals of ships or new persons in the only harbour, James Bay, anticipating covert activities. The prospects looked bleak, and they were glum. No solution was presented. The British had been thorough.

When it came to the turn of Las Cases, who had wisely refrained so far from commenting on military matters, he expressed in words the shared conclusion of the Emperor's Staff, for such they were, diminished in number but nevertheless, his chosen, proven men for this situation. Capable men. "Sire, the only way you will escape is through death." At these words, there was evident discomfort among his colleagues, but no disagreement was voiced.

A reaction was expected, an angry outburst. None came. The Emperor smiled, looking at each of them in turn. "My friends, it is the very hopelessness of our situation which will be our greatest weapon. As you have correctly assessed, there can be no rescue and escape is seemingly impossible. I am meant to die here. We shall nevertheless escape." With surprised, hopeful interest, they perked up, stiffening their backs, reminded that their leader had thought and done the seemingly impossible before, countless times. If anyone could.

"I see I have your attention. Las Cases is correct, I must die here. Only then will the British and their allies relax their vigilance, return this place to its former obscurity, do their best to forget about us. Only then can we find a place to live a new life, somewhere of our choosing. So, we must die."

Uniformly they began to protest, but the Emperor raised his hand for silence. "No Gentlemen, we shall not actually die here, we must be seen to die, to die so thoroughly and convincingly that there can be no room for doubt, for doubt there will be, examinations there will be. The rulers of Europe will want assurances, certainty, verification. We must make sure they get it. Even members of our family, our loyal subjects, followers, friends and supporters must believe it, must give up hope of ever seeing us again. There can be no repeat of last year's events, no return to France. No more campaigns and victories, I must live quietly, discreetly in exile. Those who recognize me living among them must accept, must believe, that it is not me, but someone who looks remarkably similar, as the Germans say a doppelganger, though obviously not the recent Emperor of France and Conqueror of Europe, after all, I am dead and, if I were not dead, why would I return? Surely I would go far away or hide?"

The Emperor paused, allowing them all to absorb and digest the import of his words. He knew men like few others, able to take their measure and inspire them to his bidding. It was transformational for each of them. They understood the import of what they had heard. Their lives and careers had each been forged in the service of this man. They had followed him into exile across the World to this remote, isolated and unwelcoming spot, uncertain of what the future would, could hold. In most cases their families were restless, anxious and unhappy, fearful for their future. The uncertain length of their sentences depending upon the strength, health and longevity of their leader, or their willingness and determination to abandon him, with all that entailed, an unhappy dilemma for even the most devoted. Already their horizons had closed in to the near intolerable, such interest as their travels and new situation afforded long since enjoyed and replaced by boredom, frustration, fractiousness and personal dislikes, rivalries and petty insults. To a man they leapt at the possibility of action, a way forward, a way out, eager to hear more.

The Emperor continued, "so, if I am to be dead, I must present a body for examination, a body dead from natural causes, which their doctors will confirm is me and that I died in circumstances that close the matter. I must be so dead that it is final, irrefutable and I am gone from the stage." The silence in the room reflected this highly inconvenient truth. Once again, it was impossible!

"Gentlemen, it is the very impossibility, or rather the degree of improbability, which will be the key to our success, to our freedom. Some of you will remember that our good friend Schulmeister has within his circle men who have long been useful to us, precisely because, more or less, they were able to convince others, at least for a time, that they were us. On many occasions these men, there are several of them, picked for this service, have been useful to us in deceiving our enemies about our whereabouts, even protecting our person. We need to find a way to infiltrate one of these men here on St Helena, the most resolute, convincing and loyal among them, to impersonate me, in life and eternally in death. A man willing to sacrifice his own identity and to die as me. In exchange we may escape by the means they have come."

The others took this in, both impressed by the dawning possibilities and by the magnitude of the obstacles and pitfalls that stood in the way of achieving this outcome without interference or detection. Could such a man be found, could he be removed from France and infiltrated onto the island and here assume the Emperor's identity and continue without discovery? These were huge and improbable questions – but that was the scale and strangeness of the dramatic solution that they were being instructed to plan and execute.

The Emperor continued, for he had both their concentrated interest and their thoughtful silence, their minds whirling with activity, assessments. "That is enough for today Gentlemen. Before we break up, these are your responsibilities. Generals Bertrand, Gourgaud and de Montholon will take such steps as you can to learn the details of the defences of the island, of the strength, practices and routines of the garrison and the naval forces here, so that we are fully familiar with our situation, identifying any weaknesses we may exploit, especially to effect communications and a possible exchange - when that can be organized. Las Cases, you will be our head of intelligence. The only way in or out will be through the harbour at Jamestown. You must all study it carefully, the shipping that comes and goes, the operations and routines of the harbour authorities, the businesses on the waterfront, etc. You must look for opportunities to bring agents and messages ashore and to send them away. We will meet each week to develop our planning. Thank you" (and with that they each stood, nodded and left, dismissed). They left with a refreshing sense of common purpose, of relevance. No longer just uncomfortable captives in a self-imposed, indefinite and increasingly intolerable exile.

Over the months that followed, the Escape Committee met regularly, sharing news and information, building the picture of their situation on the island and receiving such information and news as their leader chose to share. They were long since used to this method of operating.

The Emperor had arrived in St Helena in very good health. During his first year on the island, he regularly took plenty of exercise and his health remained excellent. During his first two months there, while at Briars Pavilion (and before the arrival of Hudson Lowe), he had been allowed to walk into Jamestown and to mingle and talk (as best he could) with the townspeople unrestricted.

This is not to suggest there was carelessness, far from it, the British kept a tight and disciplined watch on their prisoner and looked out vigilantly for any suggestion of a rescue bid. A constant lookout was kept for approaching ships, which once sighted, normally some 60 miles off, were announced by the firing of a gun, a reward given to the first man who spotted it. Some 500 guns were then manned, sited around the island to prevent illicit landing or embarkation by small boat.

The transfer to Longwood had brought with it isolation from the islanders and much closer unwelcome scrutiny by his gaolers. Longwood House and its grounds were enclosed by a wall, some four miles in circumference.

Within the grounds was the separate cottage at Hutt's Gate (about 100 metres from the main house) occupied by the Bertrand family. A modest but relatively private abode for the Imperial Grand Marshal and his family.

The garrison at Deadwood Barracks provided 125 sentries to guard and watch over Longwood House by day and 72 at night. In total on the island were some 2,280 troops, including 500 officers. At night a curfew was imposed. An officer was stationed at the house.

During the first year Napoleon regularly took exercise by way of long walks and rides in the Longwood estate, accompanied at a short distance by a British officer. He was truly a prisoner and felt it. He objected to the close proximity of this officer (under standing orders to keep him in sight) - when Lowe refused to budge, Napoleon stopped riding.

From early on the Emperor had concluded that they should maintain some distance between themselves, the Governor and other British authorities on the island. This was in any case, not difficult, as Sir Hudson Lowe was not to his taste, as he soon made clear.

Sir Hudson Lowe tried at first to be on good terms with his prisoner, but this approach was short-lived once he found his early overtures rejected. The sentiment was returned. The two could not bear to be in each other's company, exacerbated by the Governor's insistence (in accordance with his own instructions from Whitehall) on referring to Napoleon as "General Bonaparte".

Hudson Lowe, an experienced quartermaster, soon discovered that Napoleon's entourage enjoyed the finer things in life. Each day from Jamestown came fresh supplies of the best available meats, ducks, turkeys, etc. In fact, Napoleon's personal taste in food was simple for a man of his stature, but he provided for others as befitted him. His well-known personal preference was for the Burgundian red Gevrey-Chambertin (to which he would add a little water) and for champagne. He had also developed a taste for Klein Constantia, a sweet yellowy dessert wine from Muscat grapes grown in the Cape. Lowe concluded that the expenditure of the household at Longwood, met by the British Government, was extortionate and, not without a little satisfaction, cut the allowance. This further soured their infrequent meetings and correspondence, much of which reflected complaints from Napoleon about his living conditions and meagre allowance. The subject became a weapon for them to beat each other with.

Two skirmishes highlighted the developing rift between these protagonists. Marchand, the Emperor's valet, visited a cobbler in Jamestown with a worn-out pair of his master's shoes to commission replacements. On receiving a report of this mundane matter, Lowe saw an opportunity to humiliate his adversary. The cobbler was forbidden to make the shoes without his express approval. Lowe visited "General Bonaparte", to tell him that if he wanted new shoes, he must make the request to him in person, presenting his own worn-out pair. Lowe would then make the necessary arrangements. The erstwhile Emperor regarded him for a short time and said "you are sticking pins into us. You wish to prevent us escaping – there is only one way – to kill us." These words were said for effect. The Emperor was purposely disagreeable to Lowe, who was returning the compliment.

Their short interview ended, Lowe was ushered out by General Bertrand - however much he sought to downplay the formalities, Hudson Lowe found that he continued to be received as if he were attending a superior, in a microcosm of a court. He could not help himself resenting this. This jumped up, self-aggrandized tyrant had lost, but treated him like a supplicant, a junior granted an audience! Exasperated, Lowe remarked to Bertrand that "I went to see General Bonaparte determined to be conciliatory. He created an imaginary Spain, an imaginary Poland. Now he wants to make an imaginary St Helena!"

Bertrand reported these remarks, to their shared satisfaction; the plan was working – few of their captors had direct sight of or access to Napoleon; of these the Governor was the most dangerous, the most vigilant, the one who could insist on access and proximity, the most consistent, who therefore could most readily recognize change. Contact had to be discouraged, as much as possible. They had to get under Lowe's skin and make his visits to Longwood as infrequent as strictly necessary, their duration kept to a short perfunctory and distant minimum.

Bonaparte's words were effective; however, Lowe felt increasingly uneasy. These words did nothing to soothe his thoughts, as he returned to Jamestown and in the subsequent days. Surely it was a futile challenge, a statement of intent, or was it? The chances of his prisoner escaping were, or should be, near to nil, but this was the Great Ogre, the man who had turned the World on its head more than once, having escaped from Elba and reignited the flames in very recent memory. The thought that he should be in command of his gaolers and responsible should Bonaparte escape was intolerable, nerve racking for a man of his serious disposition and circumstances, a career army officer of no special background, privilege or sponsorship. He would be cashiered, held to account and ignominy by his superiors, his government, his nation, his king – a laughingstock in the eyes of the world, with nowhere to hide, his name forever tarnished, infamous – it was too dreadful to contemplate, except that he was forced to, by the nature of his posting and of his charge – a man who had never been contained before.

Lowe ordered that the perimeter and sentry postings around Longwood must be reduced further and that sentries on night duty must take up position in the garden at 6pm, instead of 9pm, as before. The message was clear. The prisoner must feel his incarceration, the hopelessness of rescue or escape. If he would not behave himself, he should understand there were consequences, reduced privileges. The hitherto man of action who cared so much for freedom, who had been the master of his own destiny and that of millions of others was a caged bird of prey.

Lowe decided to go a step further, he insisted that the senior members of Napoleon's household each sign written undertakings that, in exchange for being permitted to remain with General Bonaparte, they personally undertook not to leave the island other than in the event of his death or by the Governor's consent. Resentfully, they each did so. Lowe had correctly surmised they would not leave their master; if they were to begin do so it would set alarm bells ringing at Plantation House long before they could depart St Helena. As the Escape Committee recognised, this was an additional complication to be overcome.

In another, somewhat petty, act Lowe ruled that of the not infrequent gifts and packages that arrived on the island addressed to his prisoner from well-wishers, only those that made no reference to his former imperial status should be delivered – therefore only a minority got through. All were examined for hidden messages or other items.

Napoleon complained regularly that "of all my privations, the most painful, the one I shall never get used to, is being parted from my wife and son."

He had known many women. Josephine had long and famously been his passion, but in time, through absences and affairs, their relationship had cooled and, ever mindful of his legacy and need to cement the position of his family, his newly crowned imperial dynasty, among the rulers of Europe, after his victories had finally crushed the Austrians, the Emperor Francis had paid a high price to keep his throne.

In 1806, after a long series of campaigns between revolutionary France and the Holy Roman Empire, Napoleon had forced the end of the empire that had ruled over much of Europe since Charlemagne was crowned in 800. A humiliated and resentful Francis retained the status of Emperor of Austria. More fighting, more victories followed, until at Wagram in 1809 he had himself inflicted a crushing defeat, with substantial losses to the forces of Francis and his allies. The terms he had exacted from Francis in Vienna under the Treaty of Schönbrunn were the toughest yet. Hardest of all for Francis, head of the mighty and ancient Habsburg Dynasty, was to have to agree, at the initial suggestion of his own Foreign Minister, Count Metternich and after as much resistance as he could muster, to proposing a marriage between this upstart Corsican nemesis and his eldest daughter, Marie Louise, a great prize. A prize Napoleon very nearly was unable to claim – while he stayed at Francis's Palace of Schönbrunn, overlooking Vienna, a young knife-wielding German assassin had only just been prevented from his lethal mission by the vigilance of one of his aides.

Across Europe there had been amazed reactions to these events, in France celebrations. In Britain, which continued to be at war with France, The Gentleman's Magazine commented:

"This Treaty is certainly one of the most singular documents in the annals of diplomacy. We see a Christian King, calling himself the father of his people, disposing of 400,000 of his subjects, like swine in a market. We see a great and powerful Prince condescending to treat with his adversary for the brushwood of his own forests. We see the hereditary claimant of the Imperial Sceptre of Germany not only condescending to the past innovations on his own dominions but assenting to any future alterations which the caprice or tyranny of his enemy may dictate with respect to his allies in Spain and Portugal, or to his neighbours in Italy. We see through the whole of this instrument the humiliation of the weak and unfortunate Francis, who has preferred the resignation of his fairest territories to restoring to his vassals their liberties and giving them that interest in the public cause which their valour would have known how to protect. O, the brave and loyal but, we fear, lost Tyrolese!"

Napoleon having divorced Josephine had married his new bride with great pomp, himself placing the crown of the Empress of France on her head. He had planned strategically, dynastically, not expecting that he would fall in love with his new bride, who had agreed to the marriage out of duty, prepared from childhood for an arranged match, though certainly not this one (with the hateful Frenchman) or in these circumstances. Nevertheless, she knew her duty, her obligations to her father and her family. Such had for centuries been the lot of Habsburg daughters.

Napoleon had relished the prospect of his bride to be. Reports and a portrait of Marie Louise told him she was young, fresh, charming, beautiful, alluring, altogether delightful in her inexperience – everything Josephine could no longer offer, in fact. He was eager, the more so at the prospect of begetting the heir that he and Josephine had together failed to produce, to their mutual sadness. An heir essential to cement his dynastic ambitions, to inherit his achievements. A symbol of his great victories and recognition into the highest rank.

Napoleon showered her with gifts. A wonderful Parisian trousseau, diamonds and other jewels fit for an Empress, his Empress. Napoleon had sent his sister Caroline (Queen of Naples) and Marshal, Louis-Alexandre Berthier, his outstanding Chief of Staff to prepare the way. Berthier stood as his proxy at the wedding service held in Vienna before Marie Louise left for France to meet her enthusiastic new husband. Caroline and Berthier spent a fortune on balls and firework displays – Vienna was alight, with dancing, operatic performances and galas!

Francis had genuine affection for his eldest daughter. For an ostensibly stiff, aloof man, hidebound by the customs of his own court, he did all he knew how to soothe her nerves, to reassure her, but his hands were now tied.

Finally, in a train of carriages, the young bride had left Vienna behind to join him in France. Never a patient man, he had found it impossible to wait calmly for her in Paris. At heart he had hoped for something more romantic than a political union – a coupling of States. He had insisted that her Austrian companions must leave her at the border with France - from there only her new French companions would travel on with her. She continued her daily progress toward Paris, across the slow unpaved roads of the day.

A fretful Napoleon could wait no more. He set out for the Chateau of Compiegne, some sixty kilometres from Paris, where they were to meet for the first time. There he decided to press on – fresh horses were harnessed to his carriage and, with night descending, in lashing rain, they pushed on to Soissons, where Marie Louise was due to dine. He found she had not yet arrived – on he went, into the night, again with fresh horses. At Courcelles he met the outrider who foretold her imminent arrival. Soaked head to toe in water and mud, he stood waiting, pacing excitedly in the doorway of the church. When the procession of sodden horses and coaches emerged, it was halted by one of his officers. The door of the carriage was opened, and Napoleon's presence heralded by a chamberlain. "L'Empereur", he announced (through the wet night air).

Napoleon entered the carriage. Behind the closed door he soon bestowed all of the pent-up passion and ardour of an experienced impatient middle-aged man and conqueror upon his prize. Napoleon ordered that there should be no stop at Soissons (as planned) – the train pressed on to Compiegne. There the couple had dinner, and all were dismissed, careful arrangements set aside. She became his wife that night.

More grand formalities of marriage and the coronation took place in Paris later with great fanfare and pomp – he himself placed the newly minted crown of Empress on her head. That first urgent, overpowering devouring greeting, however, had set the tone for their relationship. He fell in love; she, overwhelmed, observed her duty.

Louise (as he called her) had quickly won her new husband's heart. He felt proud and protective of her, moved to tenderness. Soon she had, thankfully, wonderfully, given him the son, the heir, that he so badly needed, descended from among the noblest houses of Europe. This son, born in March 1811, Napoléon François Charles Joseph Bonaparte, styled the King of Rome, was his greatest treasure, rightfully heir to a new empire – soon nicknamed "L'Aiglon", the Eaglet.

A new era of peace with Austria had followed, his young wife loyally taking her husband's part, France's part, not always to the pleasure of her father or her family, Count Metternich and other powerful players at her father's court. As Napoleon now knew was a miscalculation, he had then assumed, hoped perhaps, that marital, family ties would bring Austria onto his side, as Louise had loyally tried to bring about, or at least make it neutral in the wider European theatre. Life was rarely so simple, and the rulers of Austria did not share this sentiment, long enmity with revolutionary France and memories of their recent humiliations and his leading role fresh in their minds. He might marry a Habsburg, a prize exacted under duress, but he could never be accepted into that proud family – in fact they hated him the more for it, were that possible.

After his first abdication, his wife and their son had returned to Vienna to her father. He had written to her regularly from Elba, hoping for warm replies, for news, missing them profoundly, asking his wife to join him. His letters were intercepted, falling into the hands of

Metternich and Emperor Francis (who made it clear to his daughter that she must not return to her husband). Louise was being led to believe that her husband was grieving for another, Josephine, who had recently died. Although now at Schönbrunn, Louise rarely saw her father and stepmother. Louise had never felt secure in the belief that her husband's close relations with Josephine were not continued during her marriage, as Napoleon had remained close to his former wife and mistress, never a comfortable feeling for a young second wife (and not helped by reports from Francis's spies and other 'wellwishers' at court).

Once back in Paris, retaking the reins of power, Europe reawakening to the prospect of the renewal of conflict and upheaval, Napoleon had written urgently to his father-in-law, Francis, asking him to permit his wife and son to return to him. He had sent his Minister of Foreign Affairs, the trusted and faithful Armand de Caulaincourt post haste to the Austrian Court to persuade them of his peaceful intentions, toward Austria and in general, with the private request for the return of his family and with the message that should he again have to abdicate, his son would reign under the regency of Louise. He had hoped that tired of war, Austria and in turn the other powers, would prefer the path of peace and, however reluctantly, accept the reality of his restored regime in France, a regime no longer threatening conflict and one the heir to which was part Habsburg.

Napoleon had soon written to Louise that he had had their apartments (maltreated during their recent enforced absence) redecorated and that "all that is missing now, my good Louise, is you and my son. So, come and join me at once by way of Strasbourg." Again, this was a forlorn hope. They had had enough of him and wanted him gone – there was no favourable sentiment towards this new familial connection.

Weeks later Napoleon received a blow he had felt profoundly. He heard from his long-standing faithful companion and First Secretary, Claude Méneval, on his arrival from Vienna a report that his wife had openly declared to him that she and his son would not be returning to Paris. He felt betrayed and deeply frustrated, alternately angry and sad. He was also well aware of the political and strategic significance of this clear physical statement to him, to France and the wider World – he was being very publicly snubbed, taunted and humiliated by Francis.

Méneval had faithfully accompanied and served his master on his campaigns and travels and been present to witness many of the seminal events of his career since he became First Consul. He had accompanied Marie Louise and the young King of Rome on their difficult journey to Vienna in March and April 1814 – so as to hide it from being looted by Tsar Alexander's roaming Cossacks he had broken the blade of the Emperor's sword (the Regent diamond affixed to its pommel) and hidden it in his greatcoat. There he had stayed, sending reports to his master on the meetings taking place there of the representatives of the Great Powers on the future of Europe and the comings and goings there – the Congress of Vienna. A whirl of balls, galas, concerts, operatic performances, theatrical and other entertainments, amid complex bedroom diplomacy, manoeuvrings and one-upmanship, featuring the Emperor, Tsar Alexander and various other crowned heads, foreign ministers and ambassadors of nations great and small (and even those hoping for revival, like the benighted Poles), plus endless spies and hangers on.

These reports had been delivered to Napoleon by the Carabelli brothers, merchants from an old and influential Corsican family, long familiar with the Buonapartes, and who assisted Napoleon and his family with many unofficial tasks, sharing both common heritage and customs (themselves also steeped in the history and sometimes troubled and violent internecine quarrels of that colourful island).

Worse than that, the screw had been turned further by the rumours, soundly based, that had reached him (and many others) of a blossoming romantic relationship between his young and lonely wife and Count Adam Albert von Neipperg, a man who, though far below him by most measures of status or success, had shadowed him, a malevolent presence who had previously crossed his path.

Neipperg was a handsome man, a man of intrigue – adventures and misadventures that could only be guessed at - enhanced by a dramatic black bandage over his empty right eye socket, covering a wound received from a French sabre in a fiercely fought action as a younger man. A mature romantic figure, with an air of danger and a reputation as a soldier, diplomat, duellist and womaniser, with a trail of female conquests in his wake. Years earlier, Napoleon himself, fruitlessly, had sought to win him over, awarding him the golden eagle of the Legion d'Honneur, when Neipperg for a time was attached to the Austrian Embassy in Paris.

This ambitious, unscrupulous, indomitably anti-French and anti-Bonapartist, Austrian aristocrat and army officer had caught the attention of and become a confidant and agent of Count Metternich. Metternich was pleased to observe a mutual affinity when the French Empress Marie Louise and Neipperg were introduced, as he intended, on the glittering occasion of the meeting of the two Emperors at Dresden in May 1812, her husband then at the zenith of his power, surrounded by those kings and princes whom he had made into his vassals or even appointed.

Metternich's agent provocateur had once again fulfilled his mission – to gain the romantic notice of the Empress in this fellow Austrian man of mystery and masculine charms.

Metternich had long since recognised the usefulness of Neipperg and employed him – a ruthless and resourceful man. He had been sent to neutral Sweden, as Ambassador. Due to the lack of an heir from his own old dynasty and seeking stability in the royal succession, in 1810 the King, Charles XIII and the Swedish Parliament (Riksdag) had chosen an heir presumptive whom it was thought would meet with the approval of the then de facto ruler of Europe, Napoleon - Jean Baptiste Jules Bernadotte. Having learned that relations between the two men were not as warm as supposed, it was Neipperg's secret and successful mission, as events bore out, to encourage the separation of strategically influential Sweden from the Bonapartist cause. Neipperg had been kept busy, criss-crossing Europe (overthrowing Murat in Naples, elsewhere persuading allies to abandon Napoleon's cause), stirring up problems for France, for Napoleon, as his own spies reported.

Neipperg's ruthlessness extended to the treatment of his lovers. He was known to have swept his married Italian lover, Teresa Pola off her feet, persuaded her to leave her cuckolded husband, and then, she having borne him five children, to have married her in order to legitimise them. This inconvenience was not allowed to get in the way of his new mission.

As Napoleon now suspected, Marie Louise's return to Vienna in 1814 had been a decisive step in a larger plan to separate him from his wife and his son. Francis, the Habsburg family and their servant Metternich would prevent their return to him. Neipperg's role was to be Marie Louise's chaperone, guard and mentor. If something more romantic were to ensue, while scandalous, it would serve to drive a wedge between her and Napoleon from which there could be no return. A final insult to him, to his honour and to that of France!

Neipperg was instructed by Metternich to accompany Marie Louise, then at Aix-les-Bains, to keep her entertained and to prevent her from joining her husband on Elba. Abandoning the devoted Teresa Pola, he had assumed the role with relish. He had been given licence to woo a still young and attractive Habsburg princess and empress, the wife of his arch enemy – a delicious prospect, even his patriotic duty. He resolved to himself that within six months they would be lovers and that he would in time make her his wife! He was not the type to be put off by impediments.

Marie Louise set off with her new and constant companion on a tour of Munich, Baden and Geneva. This was a vacation, a distraction for a young woman who had recently experienced great events. Undisturbed by messages from her husband (intercepted by her Father's secret service), in romantic surroundings, Marie Louise was soon enjoying the attention paid to her by the dashing Neipperg, who would sing to her when they were alone in the evenings. On one such evening she yielded and theirs became an enduring relationship.

News of their closeness had spread widely, causing offence and upset in France and in Austria; the honour of both countries impugned. Méneval reported on this affair at first hand, worse he had brought with him a message from his wife: "I hope he will understand the misery of my position…I shall never assent to a divorce, but I flatter myself that he will not oppose an amicable separation, and that he will not bear any ill feeling towards me…This separation has become imperative; it will in no way affect the feelings of esteem and gratitude that I preserve." Their personal relationship was ended, she was his wife in name only, but also the mother of his beloved son and heir and a significant piece on the chessboard.

He knew her to be shy, timid and persuadable, in the manipulative hands of his enemies. It had been an affair of state, not a love match. He did not feel enmity; she had wanted to accompany him to Elba – it was he who had sent her to her father, to intercede for him and their son, hoping to preserve the Empire for his heir.

Now, here on Saint Helena, he was sustained by some few words etched into his memory. The faithful Méneval had reported that when, before leaving Vienna, he took his leave of Marie Louise and the King of Rome, saying to the boy: "I am going to see your father. Do you have anything to say to him?". The young prince had replied sadly: "Monsieur Méva, please tell him that I still love him a lot".

News had reached him that the Congress gathered at Vienna had, as a final act, appointed the 24 year-old Marie Louise as Duchess of Parma, where now she ruled with her ever-present companion, Count Neipperg, beside her. He did not begrudge her happiness. His son, however, had been held in Vienna, in effect a hostage, no longer styled the King of Rome but dubbed the Duke of Reichstadt. It was not lost on him that even Marie Louise would be freed by his death - free to marry again. A tidy solution for his Austrian enemies! Freedom comes at a price, he mused.

What most upset him now, thousands of miles away, was that he could not see his son, share in his upbringing and development, could not teach him all that he would need to know, all that he should impart to him, as his heir. Worse, brought up at the Austrian Court, surrounded by his father's enemies, prohibited from even learning to speak French, the boy was being alienated from his father, his family and his country, his destiny denied, stolen or destroyed. His education and circumstances designed to ensure he could not follow in his father's footsteps.

Napoleon, nevertheless, wrote to Francis requesting that his son be permitted to travel with his mother. The subsequent ongoing resounding silence was clear; he was not to be permitted contact with his child, his greatest, most heartfelt and frustrating punishment. Francis, the Habsburg family and Metternich, after so many humiliations, finally had a knife in their hands to twist and twist it they would.

From the firm of Beaggini in Italy he received the gift of a marble bust of the King of Rome. He had it placed prominently in his bedroom at Longwood and pointed it out with pride to visitors. Lowe had initially confiscated it, preventing its delivery to him because it was sent secretly (he was worried that it might contain a message), but reluctantly he had eventually allowed it to be delivered for fear of negative publicity – as an obvious act of spite.

The discreet benefit of the developing standoff between Napoleon and Lowe to those at Longwood was greater privacy and less familiarity. In time these factors would become crucial to the fulfilment of their plans.

In the meantime, the complex domestic arrangements in operation at Longwood saw Albine de Montholon delivered of her fourth child in June 1816, a daughter, who was named Napoléone Marie Hélène Charlotte. She soon bore a striking resemblance to the Emperor and rumours spread.

Many factors contribute to success or give rise to failure in a campaign or battle. None knew this better. There could only be one attempt at escape, and it had to succeed, they knew, or they would all suffer the consequences.

Amongst the greatest challenges to overcome was to develop a reliable, trustworthy and secure means of communication with those in Europe who would help them. Even so, the time it took to exchange messages was frustratingly long and imposed its own limitations.

The English, Hudson Lowe in particular, were fully alert to the possibility, almost certainty that there would be attempts at secret communication, whether inward or outward bound. Everything and everyone that came from or was destined for Longwood and its residents was meticulously examined or searched.

It being inconceivable that there would be no such illicit communication had been anticipated by Napoleon. Before leaving France, he had made arrangements for messages, sent by a variety of correspondents, including family members and some of his former aides and supporters, to be delivered to him, wherever he would end up, by different methods, arriving in packages, dressed up in varying guises, through the intermittent post and cargo addressed to him, now at Longwood.

Finding such items would keep his captors busy and would go some way to satisfying them of the effectiveness of their watchfulness. Such messages could usefully serve to misdirect his enemies and, as it now turned out, to unsettle Hudson Lowe. It typically took some two to three weeks for a message to be sent and received in either direction, reflecting long voyages to and from European or American ports and onward transmission.

Nevertheless, communication there was, 'real' coded messages and his instructions confirmed by the inclusion of a key word, pre-agreed with Schulmeister and known only to the very few most trusted persons in their circle, including his brother Joseph. A system they had long used to conduct their most private affairs.

For secure delivery they had a selected a relatively reliable and regular method. False-bottomed casks of wine, with a thin hidden chamber, packed solid, which did not echo a tell-tale hollow sound when tapped, as invariably they were by the vigilant English sentinels. The substantial consumption by the Longwood household and its regular orders for French and Italian foodstuffs, wines and other goods maintained a constant supply, consigned from Marseilles, carried by merchant ships. Coded orders sent outwards, concealed letters returned, the emptied barrels, their contents consumed, chopped up and used for firewood. Simple, but effective.

In addition, letters were sent by other means. As a 'disaffected' Gourgaud would later confirm to Lowe over dinner at his table, before departing the island, Dr.

O'Meara had operated as a conduit, as had even British merchant naval officers, willing to accept reward. Of course, some of these communications had been intercepted, as anticipated. It was inconceivable that there would not be attempts at correspondence outgoing and incoming.

Schulmeister was a renowned master of disguises and a consummate actor. He had first met Napoleon in 1804 in Strasbourg, in the Great Hall, where he asked to be employed as an agent. When asked for his references, he had replied "Sire, I have no recommendations but my own", to which the reply was "you may go. We have no work for men without references" and Napoleon had risen and departed behind a screen. Schulmeister had adjusted his dress, puckered his face and, when the Emperor came back, he thought this person was a different candidate. In reply to Napoleon's demand of "who are you?" he had said "I am Karl Schulmeister. You interviewed me a moment ago. Now that I have demonstrated my ability to change my personality completely, perhaps you could find me a job in your service?" Within a year, the French took Vienna, and he was made Commissioner of Police there, responsible for maintaining law and order. In time Napoleon would say that Schulmeister was worth an army division.

There were many stories of Schulmeister's daring and seemingly impossible exploits. As a secret courier of a letter from one of Napoleon's Ministers to a spy in the Austrian Army, Schulmeister had disguised himself as a jewel merchant. He was arrested and searched by the

Austrians. The letter was found, and he was sentenced to be shot the following dawn. He was guarded by six Austrian soldiers. When wine was brought to them, he managed to introduce opium that he had hidden in his clothes. He donned one of their uniforms, found the person the message was intended for and recited it to him word for word from memory, before making his escape through Austrian and French army lines.

On another occasion, at the Battle of Wagram, he was pursued into a house by Austrian soldiers chasing him. As the Austrians burst into the house, they were met by a barber coming down the stairs with razors, soap and towels. The Austrians demanded "we are chasing a spy, have you seen him?", to which the calm reply was "a man ran upstairs". The soldiers ran upstairs and Schulmeister made himself scarce.

Napoleon was served well by Schulmeister and enjoyed hearing of his exploits. On two occasions he had done the seemingly impossible – with incredible audacity.

Schulmeister had even managed to attend an Austrian Council of War, dressed as an Austrian general, in place of the true general whom he had bribed with one million francs. Even the Emperor Ferdinand, overseeing the meeting, did not spot the fraud – the debate was reported by Schulmeister in person to Napoleon.

He had achieved something even more remarkable, having gone to Vienna and presented himself to Marshal Karl Freiherr Mack von Leiberich, Commander of the Austrian Army, declaring himself to be a Hungarian nobleman, who had lived in France for many years, but who had been banished on suspicion of being an Austrian spy. He asked to be allowed to exact revenge by truly becoming a spy for the Austrians. Mack, an experienced general, arranged an Austrian Army commission for him, got him in as a member of the leading military clubs in Vienna and appointed him chief of intelligence on his own staff.

One day he entered Marshal Mack's office bearing a French newspaper and saying that "we have just had news that the French are about to revolt against the tyrant Bonaparte. Most of their army is being withdrawn from our border to deal with the expected uprising". Setting the newspaper on Mack's desk before him he added, "this was smuggled from France. You will see it says civil strife is spreading across the country. This confirms information from our spies. France will soon be torn by civil war".

Mack grasped the situation quickly – "this is the time to attack, when the French are at their weakest!" He ordered the advance of his 30,000 strong army to Ulm (in South West Germany) – there he was surrounded by a much stronger forewarned French Army under Napoleon and obliged to surrender. The newspaper was a contrived forgery.

Taken prisoner by the French, Schulmeister was 'interrogated' by Napoleon, made his escape and got back to Vienna, continuing as Director of Intelligence for the Austrians.

Schulmeister supplied his French master with a steady stream of information on the movements and state of the Austrian forces, contributing to their defeat at the decisive battle at Austerlitz. Suspicions were already circulating, and he was in danger of exposure. An order was issued for his arrest, but he was rescued just in time by a French army under Joachim Murat which overran Vienna.[vi]

In 1816 three Allied Commissioners landed in Jamestown tasked with seeing for themselves that Napoleon was safely secured there, which they confirmed to their masters.

It had been obvious from the outset that their exfiltration would have to be long drawn out, with no discernible pattern, no sudden departure for the exit by any members of their party, no changes in the outward demeanour of the lead players or those close to them. Nothing that could alert their captors to optimistic changes of circumstance. Nevertheless, the process must begin. The substance of their plans to bring about the Emperor's escape could not be set down in writing and left to chance discovery, with untold dire consequences. Their circumstances and intentions needed to be relayed by someone trustworthy with inside knowledge – it was concluded that one of them must leave the island and return to Europe, to prepare the way. Emmanuel de Las Cases was chosen by Napoleon. The others did not demur – neither de Montholon nor Gourgaud, especially, liked him or would miss him. He would take his son too, who was fretting over his own future.

A contrived infringement of regulations secured Las Cases' expulsion from St Helena by an indignant Sir Hudson Lowe who had had him arrested on 25 November 1816 for attempting to smuggle out a letter from Napoleon. Lowe told Las Cases that he would permit him to remain provided he met conditions – Las Cases refused these, and Lowe ordered him off the island. He was shipped first to Cape Town, thence, after a delay, to Europe.

Barred from entering France by the government of Louis XVIII, he made his way to Brussels. It was there that Schulmeister's chosen man (the spymaster could not come himself and thereby cast inevitable suspicion) found and debriefed him, his vital mission then accomplished, his freedom restored. Subsequently confirmation of his safe arrival was communicated to those at Longwood. Thus, they knew their plan was in motion, preparations would be made as instructed.

Schulmeister's own fortunes had seen dramatic changes. The Austrians had taken revenge on his properties in 1814, though he had managed to evade capture and probable execution. Thrown into prison by the Prussians after Waterloo, he had paid a huge sum for his release. Back in France he knew he was followed and watched everywhere, limiting his freedom of movement, necessitating constant watchfulness, subterfuge and the selective employment of trusted (and well rewarded - and therefore expensive) lieutenants.[vii]

The most visible consequence of Las Cases' mission was that in 1817 Joseph Bonaparte, Napoleon's elder brother, formerly King of Naples and Sicily (1806 – 1808) and King of Spain (1808 – 1813) embarked for the United States. There he sold jewels and installed himself in New York and Philadelphia. His home soon became a magnet for other French emigres and francophiles.

Joseph, a lawyer, politician and diplomat, experienced in dealing with the Americans – in 1800, as Minister Plenipotentiary, he had signed a treaty of friendship and commerce between France and the USA at Morfortaine – was entrusted with commencing negotiations to secure permission for his brother to be permitted to come to live in quiet retirement in the USA, if he could be brought there.

In this, it soon became clear that he would fail. There was still no abiding appetite amongst the Americans to house a man who would upset relations with the major powers. Neither lavish entertainment accompanied by eloquent persuasion nor substantial offers of money could sway the decision. This was a serious setback, one that denied Napoleon a secure home, free from being hunted by his vengeful, fearful former enemies, but it was not a surprise. It took time to relay this disappointing message to Longwood.

Joseph remained in America, acquiring an estate at Point Breeze, Bordentown, New Jersey, where he received many figures of the day.

On St Helena relations between the chief gaoler and his prisoner remained frosty. Bonaparte was much the stronger character and intellect, easily able to play the cat with this simpler mouse. Winding up Sir Hudson Lowe was not difficult; made easier by his adversary's fear of consequences, most particularly of losing his prisoner.

Lowe had taken to visiting Longwood on surprise inspections, testing its security. He was doing just this one afternoon when he came across an islander, of Indian origin, in the grounds. It was explained that he had been hired as a servant to Napoleon. Lowe had him arrested and dismissed.

Lowe's mood was not improved by Napoleon's obvious friendliness towards other British officers and their families. In particular Napoleon held long and friendly conversations with Admiral Malcolm, who had arrived to take over the Naval contingent. Napoleon even played chess with Lady Malcolm, taking pains to be charming.

Lowe took Malcolm with him to visit Napoleon, so that he might see for himself how he was treated by the Frenchman. Lowe returned to a bête noir – household expenses, informing Napoleon that these were too high. He said that he had tried to deal on the matter with Bertrand, who had declined to discuss the matter, which showed disrespect to the Governor.

After a long silence, Napoleon replied, addressed Admiral Malcolm: 'General Bertrand is a man who commanded armies, and he treats him like a corporal…He treats us all like deserters from the Royal Corsican Regiment. He's been sent out as a hangman. General Bertrand doesn't want to see him. None of us do. We would rather have four days of bread and water.'

Shocked and angered, Lowe replied 'I am perfectly indifferent to all this. I did not seek this job - it was offered to me and I considered it a sacred duty to accept it.' Napoleon replied, 'then if the order were given to you to assassinate me you would accept it?' 'No Sir' replied Lowe.

Lowe then said money must be saved and therefore supplies would be reduced. Napoleon replied 'who asked you to feed me? Do you see the camp there, where the troops are? I shall go there and say, "the oldest soldier in Europe begs to join your mess" and share their dinner'.

Napoleon accused Lowe of reflecting the blind hatred of his master, Lord Bathurst, the Colonial Secretary. Lowe exclaimed 'Lord Bathurst, sir, does not know what blind hatred is'!

Napoleon went on 'I am Emperor. When England and Europe are gone, when your name and Lord Bathurst's are forgotten, I shall still be the Emperor Napoleon. You had no right to put [Bertrand] under house arrest – you never commanded armies – you were nothing but a staff officer. I had imagined I should be well treated among the English, but you are not an Englishman!'

Lowe replied tersely 'you make me smile sir'. 'How smile?' Napoleon replied. 'Yes sir, you force me to smile – your misconception of my character and the rudeness of your manners excite my pity – I wish you good day!' With that Lowe walked out.

Lowe followed up on this heated exchange by making the security arrangements even more visible from Longwood – posting sentries in plain view - and by informing General Bonaparte that His Britannic Majesty's Government's contribution to Longwood's household expenditure on provisions (running at some £20,000 per year – a huge sum) must reduce to £1,000 per month, with any difference paid for by the French. Lowe confirmed this in person to de Montholon when he told him that French Government funds were used up and they would have to foot any extra themselves.

The response from Longwood soon came. Marchand and Cipriani were despatched to Jamestown on three occasions with large baskets full of the Emperor's table silver, which they were to break up, removing all symbols first. The substantial hoard of silver was sold in plain view to Gideon Solomon, a Jamestown jeweller. Sailors, officers and merchants bound for England and other destinations saw this and asked for an explanation. Sir Hudson Lowe, whom, having heard of this event had gone to investigate, challenged Cipriani to explain 'why do you need so much money?' 'To buy food, Excellency' came the reply. Napoleon, ever a master of propaganda and the dramatic, let it be known that "the next thing I must sell will be my clothes!'

The master tactician had achieved a seemingly pyrrhic victory – however he had managed, in plain view, to convert silver he knew he must one day leave behind for cash that would be needed – and strangers would not dine off his silver, his eagle. These funds would supplement what remaining money and jewels they had smuggled onto the island concealed on their persons. The increasingly unsettled Hudson Lowe had missed a key clue – both practical and symbolic – pointing to what was afoot. It was a public statement of intent, cloaked in huge improbability.

December 1816 and January 1817 witnessed visibly deteriorating relations between Gourgaud and the de Montholons and between Gourgaud and Napoleon. These persisted through 1817 and were reported to Sir Hudson Lowe.

Ostensibly because he resented the required constant presence of a British officer, Napoleon ceased to ride and began to remain in or close to the house. The man who had been seen to arrive on the island in rude good health seemed to be suffering from the damp and cold conditions on the Deadwood Plateau to which he had been consigned.

One regular visitor to Longwood was always welcomed and admitted. Young Betsy Balcombe had become a firm friend of the erstwhile Emperor. He was charmed by her fresh inquisitiveness, her playful innocence. She was fascinated by this man of great charm, vast experience and twinkling eyes. Often Cipriani would prepare for her a treat and she was a firm favourite amongst the household, always bringing good cheer. This warm and apparently unlikely relationship had been noticed, of course. Reports in Europe, written about in newspapers, had even gone so far as to speculate about a romantic affair, but this was untrue. Friendship and joy in each other's company is possible between the most apparently unlikely and unequal of partners.

Betsy's father had done very well out of his role as procurer and supplier in chief of goods and supplies to Longwood's residents, in effect 'By Appointment...'.

The comings and goings of the Balcombe's had excited the suspicion of Hudson Lowe and others. Perhaps there was even a degree of jealousy over the obviously warm and friendly relations. Ever vigilant and suspecting that secret messages were passing between Longwood and the outside world, Hudson Lowe concluded that the Balcombes must be involved as couriers. He intervened to cause William Balcombe's dismissal by the East India Company and their removal from the island. Their leave taking in March 1818 was sad, all knowing they would not meet again. Betsy's and her parents' departure removed regular and now familiar sources of amusement, and friendly faces. Their world was smaller.

The departure of the Balcombes, however, came with a silver lining – the removal of a potential problem for the Escape Committee. Their regular contact with the Emperor and, especially, Betsy's close friendship with him put them in a unique position – they could not but notice changes in his person or circumstances. Changes which were essential to the success of their plans. The Balcombes had become a problem, not just for Hudson Lowe – in fact unwittingly he had done himself a disservice, having removed a possible source of alarm.

Another regular intimate at Longwood was Barry O'Meara, who not only looked after the health of the Great Ogre, but that also of the members of his entourage. It might have been expected that O'Meara would become the most effective of spies and rapporteurs on the Prisoner at Longwood in the employ of the British, but that is not how things turned out. In practice O'Meara was placed in a very awkward spot – as a doctor he owed care and confidentiality to his patient, as a servant of the British Crown he owed fealty. He was put under pressure by both sides. Hudson Lowe, a fellow Irishman, at first expected to find a willing friend and agent – ready to report on all he found and observed during his regular visits and examinations. He demanded regular reports. The occupants of Longwood - in particular Napoleon - impressed upon him the importance of reporting to the Admiralty and to the outside world the poor and unhealthy conditions and climate at Longwood and the negative impact these were having on the Prisoner's health. The objective was to garner public sympathy and political pressure in Europe, especially in London, to demand Bonaparte's return to Europe for the sake of his health. Press reports, encouraged by Bonapartists, including Napoleon's family, supported in England by liberals such as Lord Byron, the poet, were emphasising the poor climate, poor quality of food and risk of tropical diseases, with their consequent impact on the Emperor's health.

Lowe had discovered that O'Meara was corresponding with a well-placed friend at the Admiralty, John Finlaison, who was passing these letters on to his superiors, including the Secretary at the Admiralty and Lord Melville. These letters described matters both concerning Napoleon and Sir Hudson Lowe. Lowe decided he had to get rid of O'Meara, who had become both a bridge and a buffer between himself and Longwood's occupants, but an unreliable one with friends in awkwardly high places.

By early 1818 relations between Lowe and O'Meara – who had found himself intolerably squeezed between the French and British contingents – were breaking down entirely, with O'Meara refusing to cooperate further. It was clear to Lowe, at least, that O'Meara had been suborned by Boney and was now useless, dangerous and probably actively conspiring to help his prisoner. He also suspected him of facilitating communication between those at Longwood and the outside world. O'Meara offered his resignation, which was refused; Lowe feared a trap and knew that London had to be squared first.

At Longwood the complement grew by the addition of yet another baby daughter born to Albine de Montholon.

Soon, however, matters developed further. The Escape Committee 'moved' another piece on the chess board. It was the turn of Gaspard Gourgaud to leave St Helena. It had not been difficult over the past year to manufacture a simmering and visible disagreement with de Montholon, treated as his superior (itself a cause of actual irritation to him in their confined world), an exchange of 'intolerable' insults and a challenge to a duel, satisfaction demanded. The Emperor of course stepped in, issuing rebukes to his subordinates. At this Gourgaud had requested an urgent audience with Sir Hudson Lowe, a meeting that resulted in significant consequences. Gourgaud, who made it clear that his relationship with de Montholon had broken down irretrievably, was allowed to leave the island for Cape Town and then England (a duel could not be allowed – newspapers at home and across Europe would have a field day) and Hudson Lowe was left even more certain in his belief that Bonaparte was masquerading ill health and conducting a propaganda campaign, in which O'Meara was complicit, and should stay put at Longwood.

In early February 1818 Gourgaud submitted a letter to Napoleon seeking to be relieved of his duties, so that might return home, citing ill-health. He received a written confirmation and an award of a pension of 12,000 Francs for life. The next day, 13 February, he departed Longwood, with Lowe's permission, and moved into Bayle Cottage, near Plantation House, together with Lieutenant Basil Jackson (also a veteran of Waterloo). The two had already come to know one another as Jackson had been tasked with overseeing repairs at Longwood, including to Gourgaud's own room. Jackson had seen the ill-feelings at work at Longwood with his own eyes and reported as much to Lowe.

That evening they both dined as Sir Hudson Lowe's guests. Lowe was a solicitous host. Nevertheless, Lowe asked Gourgaud point blank whether he was on a mission for Napoleon and whether, if he were to search him and his belongings, he would find anything of importance? Gourgaud assured him, as he might, that he would not.

Indeed, he was carrying no such items. All he needed was in his head!

The next day Lowe instructed his military secretary, Major Gorrequer, to examine Gourgaud's papers and belongings ('but you need not be too thorough – he has assured me there is nothing"). This was done in Jackson's presence. Nothing was found. Jackson remained close to Gourgaud until he left the island. Gourgaud and Jackson were regular dinner guests at Plantation House – perhaps Lowe hoped Gourgaud would let something slip as he relaxed in their company? Maybe he did – one evening he both confirmed that it had been easy to exchange letters with correspondents in England and even that O'Meara was implicated.

On one such evening Gourgaud said that Napoleon had had to be persuaded not to commit suicide, as he had threatened more than once. Thus, presumably, Lowe could take assurance that his prisoner considered his situation hopeless. He also concluded that Gourgaud was "a foolish, vain fellow, without sense enough to conceal his weaknesses". Nevertheless, he loaned him one hundred pounds from his own funds.

Before Gourgaud departed St Helena, Baron Sturmer, the Austrian Commissioner on St Helena (there to observe the prisoner and keep Metternich and his Emperor informed), who lived nearby to Bayle Cottage, invited the General to see him. Asked by Sturmer whether Napoleon spoke of his future? Gourgaud replied (as Sturmer reported and Gourgaud later recorded) "He is convinced that he will not stay at St Helena." Sturmer asked "Do you think he can escape?", to which Gourgaud said "He has had the opportunity ten times, and he still has it at this moment." The startled, then thoughtful Sturmer commented "I confess that does not seem impossible", to which Gourgaud responded "What is not possible when one has millions at his disposal? He can escape alone and go to America whenever he wishes."

Another member of the Longwood household, familiar with the Emperor, was encouraged to return to France. This was the cook – he was not of a standard to be labelled chef - Michel Lepage, who having married Jeanette, a Belgian who had previously worked for the Governor's household at Plantation House, was potentially a risk. The couple left St Helena in May 1818. The price was that the remaining residents of Longwood had to eat Chinese food (to Lowe's amusement, when he learned of it) until replacements (for Jeanette had assisted Lepage) could be found and sent from Europe. Gradually those at Longwood in close proximity to the Emperor were leaving or being whittled down, in each case for 'good reason'.

Gourgaud arrived in London in early May 1818 and was taken to see Henry Goulburn, the Under-Secretary of State for War and the Colonies, a deputy to Lord Bathurst, for 'de-briefing'. Gourgaud departed this meeting leaving two clear impressions. Bonaparte was in good health (better than reported) and O'Meara, William Balcombe and some other Britons who had visited him were involved in furthering the secret correspondence between Longwood and Europe. This meeting sealed

O'Meara's fate. Lord Bathurst wrote forthwith to Hudson Lowe instructing him to expel O'Meara from St Helena. O'Meara was ordered to leave Longwood on the day this letter arrived in Jamestown, 25 July 1818. He was arrested and put aboard a ship in early August 1818.

In London Gourgaud came across the French Ambassador, Marquis d'Osmond, to whom he declared it was possible for Napoleon to escape. When the Ambassador replied, "easily said", the General said "no, easily done and in all kinds of ways. Supposing for instance, that Napoleon were placed in one of the barrels that are sent to Longwood full of provisions and returned to Jamestown every day without being inspected. Do you believe it impossible to find a captain of a craft who for a bribe of one million francs would undertake to carry the barrel on board a vessel ready to sail?"

The Ambassador was, of course, entitled to assume that one so close to the subject would not be so rash, foolish or disloyal as to give away his master's plans. Rather he would sow uncertainty and insecurity among his enemies. Even so, it was well known that at Rochefort, when it would have been easier to get away amid the aftermath of Waterloo and the prevailing disarray, Bonaparte had disdained a proposal to be hidden in a specially made cask and loaded onto a Danish vessel, to escape to America, on the grounds it did not befit his Imperial Dignity – a cause of some mirth in the revivalist royalist circle in Paris! Of course, were he to escape, he could not simply embark as the 'dignified' former self-styled Emperor of France, but as a hidden or disguised fugitive

– surely his own impossible vanity would imprison him!
A consoling (and amusing) thought.

For a time Gourgaud was vocally anti-Napoleon,
however once the British authorities had intercepted a
letter from him to Empress Marie Louise in which he
wrote of her husband as a martyr in his remote and bleak
place of exile they decided he had fooled them; he was
seized and shipped to Hamburg in November 1818.
There he remained until he was allowed to return to
France in 1821. He was helped by receipt of 12,000
Francs from Napoleon's brother, Eugene (as Napoleon
had promised).

Gourgaud fulfilled other private and more open aspects of
his mission. His role was communication; his reward his
release and return to Europe. Letters were written to the
Emperors of Austria and Russia and to Marie-Louise, as
before, and as expected, falling on deaf ears.
Nevertheless, a purpose was being served – they were
evidence of the increasing desperation of their captive.[viii]

On a number of occasions Napoleon himself was heard to
say that he regarded his prospects of escape as five out of
a hundred, or near impossible. There were always
rumours, both on the island and elsewhere. There were
plots too – some serious ones uncovered by the British
authorities, whose network of agents and others currying
favour or reward was extensive. In particular such
rumours emanated from the Americas, where there
existed pockets of sympathy for the captive former
Emperor and where Joseph Bonaparte was actively

plotting his brother's freedom, as the Allies' intelligence services regularly reported.

Opinions generally took the view that if Napoleon were to escape it would be to a new life in the Americas, where he could expect a warm welcome. Many of his former officers and supporters had found sanctuary there, building new lives in the New World. Of course, all of this rumour and activity served to create a febrile atmosphere of anticipation. Would he, when, how, where would he go? Even in exile across the World this man continued to fascinate and create expectations of events. It was impossible to ignore him, to forget him, while he lived.

After the departures of the Balcombes and O'Meara's forced exit from Longwood, Napoleon's absences from view became regular. British officers were instructed to peep and to listen in, in the hope of seeing or hearing their prisoner, who was, they were now told, too ill to show himself. No British officer or official – especially anyone who knew him - had seen Napoleon at close quarter for quite some time - with the result that an apprehensive and suspicious Hudson Lowe visited Longwood, demanding to see the prisoner. Lowe, uncharacteristically, accepted an assurance from de Montholon that the prisoner was still there. At one point the Emperor was not seen for two months.

An officer posted to Longwood was under orders to see General Bonaparte twice each day with his own eyes and to report his presence, which was then confirmed by the telegraph to Sir Hudson Lowe, in Jamestown. The

Prisoner made it difficult; he would have the shutters drawn and observe the officer through a telescope. One resourceful officer returned the compliment, using a telescope himself. Another hapless officer, mindful of his duty, crept up to the window for a peep inside – there he saw the Ogre in his bath and, when spotted, provoked the naked bather to charge at the door – the startled officer turned tail and ran off in full retreat!

Many years earlier Schulmeister had offered to Napoleon a stratagem that had saved his life on occasion, had confused his enemies and had helped to maintain the morale of his troops. It was a simple but effective deceit. The employment of doubles, a small, handpicked number of chosen men, trained to affect the Emperor's stances and mannerisms and whose appearance, when dressed suitably and put in the right context, could convince those who were not from the Emperor's immediate circle that he was present. These men were well rewarded for their loyalty and silence, but it was dangerous work. One 'Napoleon' had been shot dead, one was crippled after a riding accident and a third was poisoned before the Battle at Waterloo, a victim of an assassination attempt.

Francois Eugene Robeaud assumed his peculiar services would no longer be in demand after Waterloo. It was difficult to hide from Schulmeister, however, and there was always the question of funds. Loyalty was important, but money was a necessity – and Schulmeister had funds at his disposal. When the instructions came via Gourgaud, Schulmeister knew exactly whom to summon. A man was needed who could be the Emperor in the eyes of all but those who knew him best, who had been tested and succeeded confidently in this deception many times before, who was totally trustworthy, known to Napoleon, and who would be willing to swap his existence for that of the life prisoner on St Helena.

Robeaud, who had been found living at home with his sister at Baleycourt, near Verdun in North East France, readily agreed, after all such conditions might be intolerable for an emperor, but they held attractions for an ordinary man of the people, who had discovered that his greatest asset was his capacity to be, for a time, a convincing mimic of a colossus. He and his sister would want for nothing – though she would have to move to a town where no-one would ask about her missing brother. He was not slow to see the benefits of a life cared and provided for as only the former Emperor of France would be, a much better alternative to the uncertain future in the new France he could otherwise look forward to. Besides, he had enjoyed masquerading as an emperor, so surely, he would enjoy being an ex-emperor also?

Robeaud explained to his sister that he would be away on a secret mission (she was long used to his comings and goings and limited explanations) and that they must move to Tours, in the Val de Loire (West Central France), where he installed her. Thenceforward she received a regular income, her bills paid. She never met her brother's employer, but she had learned not to question Good Fortune.

In time she gave up hope of seeing Francois – that was the saddest part of life - losing hope. When asked about her brother, she would simply reply that he had gone away to sea – that is as much as she knew. It was the truth.

Flight

The ship's crew was comprised of a mixture of Frenchmen, Genoese, Sicilians, a handful of Corsicans, Spanish, Portuguese and even a few Irish. It was a tight-knit hardened group who had experienced much together, both the lethal challenges of the seas and the onshore and offshore vagaries of coastal trading down the West coast of Africa. They looked out for each other and for themselves – both at sea and when on leave in port - and all knew the value of silence. Profitable trade and survival in seas and coasts frequented by occasional pirates and others willing to take what they could and to whom life was cheap required resourcefulness and watchfulness. The ship's master, Pietro Mariani, was a resourceful Genoese, a taciturn weathered short solid seafarer, more than capable of handling the type of men who choose a life at sea for reasons good or ill. The vessel was owned by a Genoese mercantile house, with a long history of trade in the Mediterranean and beyond, associates of the resourceful Carabelli brothers.

On this trip a passenger had joined them. Shortly before they had set sail from Genoa on the outward leg of their regular voyage, the Capitano had welcomed aboard

Signor Bianchi, letting it be known to those aboard that he was a supervisor and agent for the ship's owners, making the voyage to observe their route and assess opportunities at the ports they were to visit and to report. He was to be treated with respect and it was important he should form a good impression of them. They must behave themselves.

From the outset it was understood that their visitor was not a loquacious man, nor did he welcome unnecessary conversation. The crew, while initially interested to observe the new arrival, soon became used to his detached presence and got on with the business at hand – there was plenty to keep them occupied. Bianchi was usually in the Capitano's cabin (who had bumped down the First Officer, and so on) or standing alone, apparently observing activities aboard or looking out, seemingly lost in thought. He often ate his meals alone, though sometimes the Capitano joined him. When they periodically stopped at ports along their route he usually went ashore on his own business, presumably scouting out commercial opportunities, they assumed, those who thought about him, that is. After the initial flurry of excitement and some concern at having aboard someone who could herald changes, they had lost interest; only one other feature of their passenger provoked some humorous comment among the crew – their visitor had an uncanny resemblance to images they had seen of a man famous across Europe. Even that fact became uninteresting with familiarity, the inevitable jokes soon wearing thin.

An old adage is that merchant ships must keep moving. A good master, and the Capitano was just such a one, sticks to his schedule as best as the voyage and port conditions allow. Time spent sitting idly in a port or harbour wastes money (including expensive port fees) and with the owner's agent aboard it was clear that no time would be wasted on this round trip. In many ways that suited the crew, because once they were into the South Atlantic the only port where they could find pleasure was at Cape Town. Jamestown was good for stretching legs ashore, a long evening at a tavern and a square meal of fresh food, but little else. Not a place to dwell for long. It was the Bonaventura's regular practice, weather and winds permitting, to spend no more than one or two nights in Jamestown harbour, offloading and loading cargoes and some water and fresh provisions, before beginning the return leg, eventually to Genoa. This voyage would be no different.

The substantial consumption of wines at Longwood had not only been noted by Sir Hudson Lowe, it was also the subject of much ribald comment and even respectful envy among the officers and troops stationed nearby. Each month a wagon would stop by the jetty at Jamestown and be loaded, under the watchful gaze of a British officer with impressive quantities of fine still wines (some bottled, but mainly in casks) – a mixture of French and Italian vintages - champagne and other supplies of fine goods. This was the usual pattern. The officer on duty was well aware of his responsibility to ensure that this commerce did not conceal secret messages, weapons or other contraband directed for Boney and his group at Longwood.

Sir Hudson Lowe would himself on occasions come down to observe proceedings and even poke around, satisfying himself that nothing had got through, while nurturing his irritation at the largesse in plain view - it made him feel better. He had detected that in an unusual spirit of apparent frugality Longwood had begun purchasing casks of a particular dessert wine from a Cape wine producing estate, Klein Constantia, a muscat (over 1,000 litres each year were being consumed at Longwood), shipped from Cape Town – rather more economical than transporting such wines from France, with the risk they would not travel well. Never before had a prisoner of war been allowed so much luxury!

Through William Balcombe of the East India Company a regular channel had been developed for the sourcing, shipping and delivery from France of wines and other goods. The Bonaventura beat a regular round route from Genoa, via Gibraltar, down the West coast of Africa, with port visits to drop off and collect cargoes and occasional passengers, thence to Cape Town, from where it would make a return trip to Jamestown, before repeating the exercise.

By August 1818 this route was well established, the process well understood and familiar to all its participants, including the watchful British sentinels on St Helena. Nothing had occurred to cause the British authorities to clamp down on or close off this supply of harmless, if expensive, goods to Napoleon, which would,

Sir Hudson Lowe and Lord Bathurst knew, provoke outrage and perhaps even diplomatic and political consequences – Bonaparte still had many supporters, concerned for his welfare and quick to criticize the British government for their treatment of him.

It was a matter of some pride to the crew of the Bonaventura that it was their vessel that regularly carried the consignments of wines and other cargoes addressed to the former Emperor of France. Something they could and did boast of. It made them more interesting.

All visitors to Longwood, all vehicles and all goods delivered there were vetted and examined thoroughly and efficiently by the military guards on duty, subject to strict discipline and well aware of the consequences of a lapse. These guards were familiar with the regular visitors, including those members of the household who were permitted to come and go, in particular to visit Jamestown for supplies and other purchases and chores connected with the household. Frequent among these were Napoleon's valet Marchand and, until shortly before his death in February 1818, the Maitre d'hotel Cipriani and the cook Michel Lepage, often accompanied by, as she became, Madame Jeanette Lepage. The latter two would usually go off to enjoy an outing in the town and to purchase fresh produce. Cipriani would check and then sign for consignments of shipped in supplies as they were unloaded by the dockside in Jamestown, before crew members from the Bonaventura would load these approved items, under the watchful eyes of the British observers, onto wagons for carriage back to Longwood, accompanied by a Sergeant and a small detail of soldiers from the Longwood garrison, for whom this domestic process relieved their usual boredom. After all, a Maitre d'hotel, a valet and a cook and his wife could offer no threat here, miles from anywhere.

The death of Cipriani and the departures of M. and Mme. Lepage had necessitated, hopefully temporary, changes. It had become one of Marchand's duties to ride on the wagons into Jamestown, accompanied by the 'temporary' Chinese cook – who would step off to find meat, fruit, vegetables and other household requirements – to inspect and sign for the consignments delivered by the Bonaventura and other vessels that supplied them. Having occasionally accompanied Cipriani on these missions it was an easy substitution.

Marchand enjoyed his new responsibilities, and it was evident that he took them seriously.

It was clear, to the amusement of the British subalterns who oversaw these events at the harbour side, that he considered himself something of an expert 'nose'. On two occasions, soon after his assumption of responsibilities, having insisted on tapping the casks of wine unloaded and ready for lifting onto his wagons, to the evident impatience of Capitano Mariani, he had denounced one of the casks as 'off', in effect 'corked' or stale, refusing delivery. The Capitano, having tried the wines himself had vocally disputed this, but to no avail – with the result Marchand would not sign for them and the Capitano would not throw away the contents – the casks were reloaded – at the worst the wine could be used for the crew's allowance.

On this occasion, Marchand was in a hurry, he declared. He must load up and return to Longwood as they were short-handed and the Emperor had insisted on his early return. The usual procedures were followed, casks examined by the guards for hidden contents, knocked for hollow echoes, but the tasting did not take place, to the apparent relief of Mariani – who could not resist teasing Marchand about this "so finally you accept I am right!". The reply was short and impolite, though friendly – the two enjoyed their duel of wits. "Don't you worry, you may be certain I will let you know if there is a problem – you have the nose of an ass and the palate of a goat!" and with that the wagons and the contingent set of for Longwood with a sense of some urgency.

The next day Marchand pointed out to the officer on duty that their Chinese cook had not been able to accompany him the day before, they were out of provisions and, what's more, three of the casks of wine needed to be returned – the wine must have suffered in the heat of the transit and was off. One barrel could perhaps be forgiven until the next occasion – three could not! He would make this abundantly clear to Capitano Mariani. The excitable Frenchman got his way – a wagon, Marchand, the Chinese cook, a Sergeant and two privates left for Jamestown within the hour, with three barrels of 'stale' wine and various empty baskets aboard.

There was quite a scene at the dockside, the excitable French valet and the normally implacable Genoese ship's captain exchanging sharp words in a combination of French and Italian, watched on by a British subaltern, a Sergeant and two amused privates, to say nothing of the passing citizens of Jamestown, assorted Naval personnel and, until he peeled away to fulfil his tasks, a silent Chinese cook. There was elaborate tasting by the two protagonists, but with diametrically opposed conclusions declared firmly. The conclusion was that three barrels – their stale contents having been offered for independent tasting by the British officer (but declined – it was before midday and the barrels had, it seemed logical to assume, been checked before leaving Longwood) – were reloaded aboard the Bonaventura. Within an hour she had left Jamestown with the tide, embarked on her return route.

That same day the attention of the harbour authorities and the Governor were focused upon unusual visitors. Painful indelible memories of the rebellion of the American colonials, the incomprehensible and humiliating defeat of the British Army, its ignominious withdrawal, the losses, death and injury to comrades and friends were recent. The arrival in Jamestown harbour of an American merchant vessel, its captain and crew could not but create a stir. Reactions were mixed, ranging from the curiosity of the indigenous population – largely untouched by the past troubles, used to receiving travellers of many colours and cultures – to the outright hostility and suspicion of the older officers, officials and enlisted men posted to the island, not least of all the Governor, Sir Hudson Lowe. Hudson Lowe, on hearing of the arrival of an American merchant vessel, the "Pride of Charleston", himself came down to the harbour from

Plantation House to see it for himself. Rumours of plots to free his captive involving perfidious Colonials and flight to the newly formed United States for sanctuary had reached him from London. The arrival of Boney's brother Joseph and his conspicuous cultivation of influential figures was being watched and reported on.

A subaltern, a Sergeant and three privates, by rotation of watches, were instructed to position themselves at vantage points and to keep watch, reporting anything unusual, especially the identity of anyone other than the crew going on board. Obviously, no one from Longwood should be permitted near the vessel.

The Pride's captain, Henry Graham, was summoned to meet Lowe. Their exchange was formally polite. Asked to state his business in St Helena, Captain Graham explained that he had been instructed by his ship's owners to investigate the possibilities for using Jamestown harbour as a stopping off point, for replenishment of fresh-water provisioning and light repairs and a safe harbour against Atlantic storms, if necessary. Lowe eyed him carefully, impressed by the quiet strength of the man before him, suspicious that this plausible answer could not be the full story, knowing he could not extract more, without cause. Lowe replied "Well, Captain, I imagine our friends of the East India Company will take great interest in your plans - you must know that you are unlikely to be made welcome. My interest, however, is in ensuring the peace and governance of this island and, as you must be aware, the security of my prisoner here. My eyes are on you and your crew. Behave yourselves, or I will know, and I will do my duty, whatever that may require." The meaning was clear – they took leave of each other.

Lowe relayed the substance of this conversation to Admiral Malcolm. The Royal Navy would escort the Pride out of St Helena's waters - it was only two years earlier that a captain of an East India Company vessel had reported sighting an American vessel, a schooner, apparently holding station off St Helena. When approached by Royal Navy warships she had put on an impressive turn of speed and outrun them, again taking up station before finally leaving without explanation. Another American ship, a rare thing in these waters, had put into Jamestown harbour pleading shortage of fresh water – a dubious excuse, as Lowe had reported in despatches to London.

Meanwhile, aboard the Bonaventura, Signor Bianchi, who had been unwell with a migraine during their visit to Jamestown, felt well enough to emerge with Capitano Mariani to take the air on deck that night and at intervals during the following day. The crew of the Bonaventura toasted Marchand, with profound irony, the next day when their wine allowance proved to be of a noticeably improved quality – but what can you expect from a valet they laughed! A story that amused them for days, as did two barrels of Gevrey-Chambertin. Even their passenger permitted himself a cup or two.

When under close observation the Pride sailed the day after its arrival, there having been no disturbance, no reports of untoward comings or goings, Lowe was both relieved and left with a nagging concern – what were they up to? What had been missed? He was uneasy.

At Longwood the Prisoner had taken to his bedroom, unwell again, and would see only Bertrand and Marchand for the next few days. The telegraph signalled to Plantation House that Bonaparte was at Longwood. All was well.

That Autumn, an indiscreet Mme Bertrand, no doubt without her husband's approval, wrote in a letter from St Helena to a friend "Success! Napoleon has left the island!" This news was not broadcast.

The Bonaventura slipped into Genoa's bustling harbour unremarkably. M. Bianchi was seen to thank Capitano Mariani warmly and spoke briefly to thank his officers and one or two others. He went as quietly as he had come and, as soon it became clear that his report had not changed their lives, the crew thought no more of him and continued with the cycle of their existence. If, in their cups and telling tales of their voyages, they had thought it interesting to mention the ship owner's agent who bore a resemblance to images of the erstwhile Conqueror of Europe, or the amusing tale of the barrels of stale wine and the foolishness of an Emperor's valet, this was not recorded, but how many such stories are?

Our story now moves to the ancient and picturesque city of Verona in the Veneto, straddling the River Adige, in the North of Italy, part of the Kingdom of Lombardy - Venetia, again under the Austrians since the fall of the French Empire, which had earlier prised it away from, first the Venetian Republic and, later, the Austrian Empire. For some time, it was part of Joseph Bonaparte's Kingdom of Italy, a kingdom carved out for him by his brother.

Verona has since ancient times been at the junction of important cross-roads, in effect a hub. Its Roman amphitheatre and fine buildings, many paid for by rich merchants of the City, make it a characterful and comfortable place to live and to visit, then as now. Travellers have long been through there.

That the Veronese merchant Signor Petrucci took on a partner, a Signor Revard, newly arrived from Genoa, a merchant and occasional dealer in diamonds and other precious stones, was interesting to his rivals, but unremarkable. In any event Revard, who so resembled old images of that famous Corsican now imprisoned on St Helena that his neighbours were amused to calling him "Napoleon", was a quiet, friendly soul who generally went about his business discreetly and politely – always with a ready joke, playful gesture or smile if teased about his ridiculous resemblance to the famous general. He spoke excellent Italian, if with an accent and soon settled into the careful quiet life expected of a dealer in precious stones. In practice it was clear, to those who occasionally dealt in these things, that most of the process of negotiating a sale was handled by Petrucci. Presumably Revard was the buyer, and his occasional absences were for this purpose. Diamonds, of course, were not only very valuable but also highly portable, readily concealed and untraceable – qualities appreciated by all.

Signor Petrucci acquired a cook and housekeeper, a cheerful woman of the town and a valet, who looked after his person and ran errands for him. As always happens in such situations, those of a prurient disposition, vivid imagination or just a brand of realism, speculated that the relationship between the cook/housekeeper and the still handsome and personable (and rich) widower, Signor Revard, were more than commercial. Tongues will always wag, gossip being common currency and entertainment. Nevertheless, the shopkeepers of the town were grateful for their custom. After all, everyone knows that a diamond merchant lives well. It was a comfortable life, for a time.

On St Helena the Emperor had rallied. He had developed a determined interest in gardening, in particular in growing vegetables in the grounds of Longwood beside the house. This new outdoor activity was more appreciated by his captors than by his fellow occupants of Longwood, whom he roped into the exercise, willingly or not. The British took comfort from seeing General Bonaparte again in plain view for hours of each day. He was seen wearing a sun hat, working in the garden and even overheard singing, clearly in improved health. The perimeter around the house was extended, as the area covered by the garden grew, pushing observation further away.

There would be more departures. Early in 1819 Albine de Montholon struck up a fast friendship with the much younger lieutenant of the 20th Regiment of Foot, Basil Jackson, the erstwhile overseer of repairs at Longwood

House and recent companion of Gaspard Gourgaud. Tongues wagged and the apparent closeness of the Englishman and the colourful Frenchwoman was remarked upon by the Russian Commissioner on the island Count Aleksandr Balmain to Bertrand – Jackson had been seen leaving her quarters late in the evening.

Albine was an experienced manipulator of men. When Jackson next visited her, she insisted they walk in the grounds, in plain view of the house, but out of earshot. In distressed tones she told him that Napoleon had insisted they could no longer meet – he had confronted her alleging an affair and that Jackson was Lowe's spy, there to use her to spy on him!

Jackson protested his innocence and devotion and their friendship continued, enjoyed with regular walks (when it was dry enough – Longwood experienced rain on most days) – they would arrange to meet so that he need not call at the house. The following month, a tearful Albine told Basil that Napoleon had forbidden further contact! They discussed what could be done – she decided that her only option was to leave; to remain at Longwood in the unhappy jealous atmosphere prevailing in the house and unable to see him would be intolerable. Of course, he understood and agreed; she must go.

Sabine wrote to Sir Hudson Lowe, explaining that she was ill with liver problems and requesting that she be permitted to return to Europe, together with her children (Napoleon wished her husband to remain), so that she might seek treatment and healthier conditions. Dr Stokoe, who now attended to the Longwood party, examined Sabine. Lowe (who considered her a complication) decided to agree to the departure of Sabine and her children, including the three-year old Hélène and they embarked in July, witnessed by a tearful Napoleon.

Basil Jackson followed her one week later, under orders from Lowe to follow her and report – Lowe was suspicious. Jackson was happy to oblige – they would meet in Brussels, where they continued their liaison for a time. She had successfully drawn the intelligent, watchful Jackson from St Helena.

It was noticed by observers that the Emperor's time in St Helena could be divided into two halves; the first, the active period of his introduction to the island, his visible participation in social activities and exercise, an active man in good health, occupied in dictating his extensive memoirs and other works and the second half, one of withdrawal and decline.

On 26 December 1819, however, a British orderly officer recorded that "I saw General Bonaparte this afternoon in one of his little gardens in his dressing-gown. They are doing nothing but transplanting trees. Even this day, though Sunday, they are moving peach trees with fruit on them. They have been moving young oaks in full leaf, and the trees probably will survive, but the leaf is falling off as in Autumn."

After his long self-imposed retreat into his rooms at Longwood, the emergence of the prisoner into plain view was a source of relief to Lowe. Over the next year or so there continued to be rumours and reports of escape and rescue plots, even false sightings as far away as America, but nothing came of these.

On St Helena it became clear to the authorities, however, that the previously robust health of General Bonaparte had begun to decline, he took less exercise and spent increasingly more time indoors. In February 1821 his condition deteriorated, and he soon became an invalid. A known atheist, the patient, as he had become, was reconciled with the Catholic Church. It was reported that on the 5th of May 1821, having confessed, received Extreme Unction and after Viaticum, administered by Father Ange Vignalli (*Vinyally*), General Bonaparte died. His last reported words were "France, l'armee, tete d'armee, Josephine".

Days later news from St Helena reached Europe and spread rapidly – Napoleon Bonaparte, the Corsican youth who had turned the World on its head and crowned himself Emperor of France, Master of Europe before his eventual catastrophic fall, had died in that far away, hard to imagine, lonely and windswept place. Many celebrated, many wept. It was a romantic tragedy, an end of an era.

After various examinations, which concluded death was due to natural causes (stomach cancer[ix]), and contrary to the Emperor's wishes, Sir Hudson Lowe (presumably acting on the orders of London, agreed with its Allies, not wanting the problems associated with a funeral in Britain or in France) arranged a simple burial on St Helena, in the Valley of the Willows. There were soon rumours that the Prisoner at Longwood had died from poisoning.

The few remaining members of the party that had voluntarily set sail with their Emperor from Portsmouth in 1815 could now return to Europe. To the end de Montholon served his master.

Napoleon Bonaparte was gone, and the World could move on, finally. The British authorities, especially Sir Hudson Lowe, and the other Allies would make no fuss – death closed the matter very satisfactorily; St Helena lost its over large and expensive garrison. The Royal Navy re deployed its ships and Sir Hudson Lowe and the Allied Commissioners had fulfilled their duties and could return to their grateful masters.

The long-suffering Bertrands were also now free to return to Europe, though Bertrand was at this time under a death sentence should he return to France (he was later to be pardoned by Louis XVIII).

Marchand too could return home. As the chosen executor of the Emperor's last Testament, bearer of those most personal artefacts that he had been charged with distributing according to Napoleon's express wishes. Napoleon, in his last hours, ennobled Marchand with the status and title of a count, leaving to him 400,000 francs, with the words "the services he has rendered me are those of a friend." He instructed Marchand to wed the daughter of an officer of the Old Imperial Guard[x].

In Verona another man knew he was liberated – finally, though a death of a loyal servant is always regrettable.

In the subsequent hours, days...years, there would be many stories, rumours and opinions as to the Great Man's demise – forests would be turned into print – did he die of natural causes, as reported by the British and other Allied authorities, or, more sinisterly, was he murdered? Either was possible, believable, probable, improbable – who knows? Who could be believed? Some cannot accept a prosaic end for their hero; others believe themselves more realistic. About such a man in such a situation it is not possible to be sure and to secure consensus. The great strategist himself understood that – always the master tactician and propagandist.

In Rome, living with her brother, Joseph Flesch, in their home, the Palazzo D'Aste-Bonaparte, in piazza Venezia, a mother was inwardly untroubled, albeit that outwardly and visibly she mourned the loss of her most famous son. Madame Mère had shared in her son's first exile on Elba. She had suffered for his banishment to St Helena. She was now content that he was free and well. Only a small handful of the most trusted family members and a very few necessary others knew the true identity and whereabouts of Signor Revard.

PART II - THE EAGLET - "not a prisoner, but in a very special position"[xi]

On 22 July 1821, at Schonbrunn Palace, on the outskirts of Vienna, in his apartment on the third floor, with fine views overlooking the Kahlenberg, in the early evening a ten year-old boy was informed by his tutor, Jean de Foresti (deputed this sad task), that his father, whom he had barely known, but whom he loved and revered, was dead. It was a profound shock, Foresti wrote to Neipperg that "I saw more tears flow than I would have expected from a child who did not see or know his father".

Francis, so advised by Metternich, determined that the Court would not mourn, only the boy was permitted to do so. In Parma three months of official mourning were observed by Marie Louise and her household.

Marie Louise wrote to her bereaved son:

"I have learned, my dear, that you have been very much moved by the misfortune which strikes us both, and it is for my heart, I feel, the best consolation, to write to you on this subject and to talk to you about it. I'm sure you felt a pain as deep as mine; for you would be an ingrate if you forgot all the goodness he had for you during your young years. You will strive to imitate his virtues, while avoiding the pitfalls he encountered." There was no recorded reply, and it was noticed, that for quite some time after, the boy did not speak of his father.

This boy, known within his mother's family circle as Franz, was being brought up in the formal environment of the Austrian Imperial Court. Already his short life had seen significant adjustments. Born the son and heir of an emperor, grandson of another emperor and great historic dynasty, the Habsburgs, first entitled as the King of Rome, he had succeeded his father briefly as Emperor

Napoleon II after his father's abdication in 1814. Taken to Vienna after his mother returned to the safety of her father's care, his grandfather (and his mother) had ignored his father's requests for the return of his wife and son after his return from Elba. Defeat at Waterloo had led to the loss of his inheritance; he was stripped of all titles and rights to inherit from his father. In the eyes of his grandfather, by breaking his bonds in leaving Elba and once again threatening peace in Europe, this boy's father had become an outlaw.

Nevertheless, the boy was the son of his eldest daughter, his own flesh and blood. For a Habsburg, family and the position and security of the family came first. Francis was not vengeful toward this innocent. His determination, in consultation with Klemens Metternich (*Metterrnih*), his chief counsellor, was that the boy should be brought up at court under close supervision and in the manner of a Habsburg prince.

Marie Louise had been joyful to learn of her husband's defeat at Waterloo. She had considered it final confirmation of her freedom - freedom to remain under her father's aegis, freedom to pursue her relationship with von Neipperg, her relationship of choice, her duty done. She had written to her father:

"Dear Father, I hope that we will have a lasting peace now since the Emperor Napoleon will never trouble it again. I hope he will be treated with kindness and clemency, and I beg you, dear father, to contribute to it. This is the sole prayer I can dare to pray for, and this is the last time I will deal with his fate; I thank him for the quiet indifference in which he let me live instead of making me unhappy."

His mother's attitude towards Franz's upbringing was explained in another letter (to Mme. de Montebello):

"I want him raised in the principles of my country, and I will explain it to you. I want to make quite a German prince so loyal, so brave, I want, when he grows up, that he serve his new homeland. It will be his talents, his spirit, his chivalry that will make him a name, because the one he has from birth is unfortunately not beautiful."

Napoleon (and Bonapartists generally) would have been apoplectic to read this confirmation of his worst fears for his son's future. Two contrasting and opposed forces of love and nurture, indoctrination, envisaging irreconcilable destinies.

Marie Louise was in step with her father. This grandson was the product of a union forced upon them both by the man whose armies had ended his tenure as Holy Roman Emperor (naming Franz King of Rome had confirmed this humiliation), had defeated his armies with great loss of life, territories and prestige and had endangered the future of his house. She had paid the price for dynastic survival. On one issue they diverged; Francis (supported in this by Metternich) was determined that the prince should not leave Vienna. When Marie Louise, recently styled Duchess of Parma, sought to take her young son there with her, Francis ordered that the boy could not accompany her. He was nervous of the consequences of Napoleon's son arriving in Italy. He also needed to assure his Allies, especially England, that Parma would not end up in the hands of this boy; a highly secret pact was made between Austria, Russia and Prussia to adjust the Treaty of Paris of 1814, under which Franz would succeed his mother. Of course, the boy was not told of this.

Francis had decided that arrangements should be put in hand for his grandson's education. Everyone in the prince's circle was forbidden to mention or discuss his past with him. Francis had written: "it is necessary to dismiss everything that can remind him of the existence he has led so far." He was to be raised as a German, a descendant of Austrians. The Emperor had selected Count Maurice Dietrichstein to oversee Franz's upbringing. He could be counted upon to be a reliable guardian of the interests of the Habsburg House[xii]. Dietrichstein was to draw up a programme of education and to appoint tutors. The Emperor remained in close touch with these arrangements.

Napoleon had sought to surround his son with a small group of trusted French carers, loyal to him. People he could rely upon to remind his son of his father, of his future role and destiny. It was a forlorn hope, as he probably knew, but he had had to try.

This small group comprised Claude Meneval, Mme. de Montesquiou, Mme. Marchand (mother of Napoleon's valet, with him on St Helena) and Mme. Soufflot, her daughter. One by one they had been sent away. The last to leave had been Mme. Marchand - ostensibly for sending a lock of his son's hair to Napoleon, on far away

St Helena, in response to a request that had reached her from her son. If she was in communication with Napoleon's valet, what else might be conveyed by these means?

Pressed by his daughter to outline a future for her son, Francis had responded. In 1817 a treaty had confirmed that on his mother's death Parma would pass not to him, but to the Duchess of Lucca. Francis granted property in Bohemia to young Franz, properties generating some 500,000 francs per year. He was patented as Duke of Reichstadt, his arms, rank and income awarded by Francis. There was no mention of his father.

His mother lost no time in tying the marital knot with her lover, von Neipperg, once she was legally free to do so. Her husband's death was timely - she was expecting Neipperg's child. Mourning over, they were soon married, on 8 August 1821, in a quiet ceremony presided over by Father Giovanni Tommaso Neuschel[xiii]. She had already borne Neipperg two children, Alberta (in May 1817) and Guillaume Alberto (or Wilhelm Albert) in (1819). Treason in the eyes of the ardent Bonapartists. Franz, however, felt affection for von Neipperg, who treated him well.

Napoleon's death left Franz as his only legitimate heir. Heir to a great legacy and heir to a great fortune. Before Napoleon had last departed from Paris in 1815, he had deposited almost US $6 million (worth vastly more today) with Lafitte, the banker, against a double receipt. Napoleon's last Will and Testament had charged Lafitte,

Montholon, Bertrand and Marchand with its distribution. His banker and three of his closest confidantes.

Austria and France were angry with Britain for permitting the Will to be made public. This presaged infighting. Lafitte refused to accept his fellow executors as of sufficient standing and would not release the funds. Neipperg (encouraged by Marie Louise) pressed Metternich to intervene on Franz's behalf and Marie Louise nominated Count Dietrichstein (*Dyetrihstein*) as her attorney to act for her son's interests. Metternich considered whether to mount a challenge for half of the property of the boy's father?

Napoleon had not designated these funds for his son (perhaps realising that they would fall into the hands of his gaolers - but he might also have had other good reasons). Instead, he designated for him to receive his most personal items - his Austerlitz epee, his camp beds, spyglass, watches, guns, silverware, library, necklace of the Legion d'Honneur and sword as First Consul. His most valued personal treasures. These items, however, were not received by Franz.

A total of US $9 million was the official sum of Napoleon's legacy. Lafitte returned only $3.5 million of the funds deposited with him. Substantial sums were paid to the French Treasury.[xiv]

Once Marie Louise and he had obtained a copy of Napoleon's Will, Neipperg challenged the British Government to explain why it did not disclose those funds Napoleon was believed to have deposited with

Baring Brothers & Co., the London merchant bank, for safekeeping?[xv]

Austria pressed Paris to recover some of these monies, but the Will was valid and the Duke of Reichstadt (and the Bonaparte family as a whole, including their descendants) had been dispossessed of all civil and property rights in France under a law passed in 1816.

Franz was an intelligent, natural and gifted student of military matters, mathematics, German and Italian and was taught chemistry, physics and biology. Contrary to rumours, he was not forbidden to learn French, the lingua franca of diplomatic Europe and the elite. He was taught to play the piano (not well) under the direction of a M. Eybler. Francis, sensitive to accusations of neglecting his grandson's education, established commissions of academics, the court prelate, senior army officers and other advisers to oversee the development of his education and training.

Franz was brought up in solitude, educated alone, often without other children to play with and then they were his Habsburg cousins. His mother was often away in Parma, which he could not visit. He was treated well as a member of the Imperial family and the Emperor Francis was fond of him. He liked his comfortable, if chilly at times, rooms on the third floor at Schonbrunn Palace, with their fine views - of the square in front of the Palace and of the Kahlenberg, reaching to Dornbach. A coterie of some 20 - 30 persons were responsible for his welfare, development and security.

As the boy became a teenager, he became a focus of interest by those in France, Italy and in Poland who saw in him a possible leader or figurehead, a successor to his father, who could once again unite them and lead them back towards the glory, independence or other bright future they had associated with his father, and in many cases sacrificed for, hopes of which had been extinguished or suppressed along with his flame once the Allies had regained control. There were various attempts by such groups to reach out to him, to gain his attention and to gauge his awareness and interest.

Paris, Berlin and Moscow were determined to ensure that the prince was incubated from infection by these causes, neutered. Francis and Metternich both understood and shared these concerns. They had no wish to see the balance of power upset once more. They were well aware of the building pressures of nationalist and anarchist causes. The prince was guarded and watched closely.

When from France came news of a plot kill to King Louis, in order to restore Napoleon II, the French ambassador, M. de Caraman reported to Paris that:

"I am assured every day that the subordinates around the Duke of Reichstadt have been put there by the police and report directly to the administration. Count Sedlinstky, head of the department, applies a religious conscience to it. The Emperor charged him with the selection of these individuals and he is responsible for anything that occurs in the inner circle of the young Duke. The Count has assured me that everyone surrounding the Duke has been placed there by him and is answerable to him."

In the years after Waterloo and the restoration of the Bourbons and many returning ancien regime aristocrats, reclaiming lands and privileges, settling scores nurtured in exile, memories of the Revolution still recent, France experienced exhaustion from war, foreign occupying armies on its soil, unemployment, mechanisation (with consequent effects on the countryside, workers and their families paid meagrely and living in poor declining conditions), a bourgeoisie enjoying the products of industrialisation, but fearful of radicalism and social discontent. The Army felt disenfranchised, officers unhappy in peacetime, their own finances dwindling. These were circumstances ripe with discontent; that caused many to look back favourably upon the days of Empire and the regime of Bonaparte - a new cult of Bonapartism developed. Images of the Emperor and of the Eaglet began to appear, sometimes disguised craftily, on canes, inside snuff boxes and elsewhere.

Art, music and literature picked up on the Bonapartist theme, a romantic, seductive theme, offering a better world to the oppressed and disappointed, the downtrodden and, elsewhere in Europe, those feeling the weight of the yoke of power, conquest and subjugation.

The news of Napoleon's death on St Helena in 1821 produced a massive literary and artistic reaction, with huge public appetite in France and elsewhere for the Napoleonic genre. This was the death of the modern Alexander, Julius Caesar, or Hannibal - the great commander and conqueror of modern times. A man who's most enduring legacy, transcending his many and great victories and devastating defeats, was the product of his visionary, ambitious, energetic breadth of concentration and innovation on more peaceful matters - on the legal system (the Napoleonic Code), governance, education, commerce, science and culture. A legacy that lives on. He changed our world, irrevocably and in many respects, for the better.

Cries of "Long live the Emperor! Long live the King of Rome!" were heard in France. There were uprisings, mainly led by former junior Bonapartiste army officers, but all failed or were suppressed. They were organised or supported well enough to carry realistic prospects of success. It was a romantic notion, a tragic one for those few who gave their lives or liberty.

In late November 1823, in Verona, Signor Petrucci, the diamond merchant and 'business partner' of Signor Revard, after an increasingly anxious wait of 90 days, prepared to do as he had been bidden - should Revard not have returned or contacted him - travel to Paris to deliver into the hand of King Louis ("only the King himself") a sealed letter.

On 23 August 1823 the quiet and comfortably private way of life of Signor Revard was transformed when a visitor arrived with an urgent message. His son was seriously ill. Revard had packed a valise and left that day, leaving his remarkable instructions with Petrucci.

Napoleon was dead, as the World knew. Revard was able to travel by coach to Vienna armed with the usual good humoured, if worn and weary, ripostes of a doppelgänger of a famous person. When pressed, he would say that he found life both easier and safer now that the Tyrant was dead. Jokes of his escape from St Helena were offered and turned aside comfortably. None could or did seriously suspect.

At an inconspicuous address in Hietzing, in the vicinity of Schonbrunn Palace, arriving in darkness, he met with two of Schulmeister's trusted agents, recruited years ago when he was Chief of Police in Vienna. Briefed on the exact location of his son's apartment in the palace nearby - a palace with which he was familiar of course - indeed he had once narrowly escaped assassination here - preparations were made. He would enter Schonbrunn Palace under cover of darkness. He could not enter via one of the guarded entrances; it would have to be done by ladders on each side of the wall. Although armed Guards patrolled the grounds at all times, these were very extensive and wooded around the perimeter, affording the cover of darkness on a cloudy night. A member of the household would meet them on the other side of the wall, to smuggle him into the palace through the back passages used by servants and (amusingly) those on amorous clandestine missions. Servants, those who were not asleep, tired at the end of their day's labour, who came across strangers in these dark narrow undecorated corridors, were used to not challenging such visitors or asking questions, long knowing that discretion was an essential attribute; they minded their own business, to interfere could only bring trouble and possibly summary dismissal. Of course, it was interesting to know whose rooms they went into.

Revard was both excited and anxious. It had been some nine years since he had last seen and held his beautiful little boy, his heir. He had longed for him and fretted over his absence and captivity in the hands of his enemies these long years. Those trustees whom he had sought to place around the boy to nurture and develop him, to cause him to remember his father with kindness and understanding and to influence him towards becoming the French Imperial prince that should have been his destiny had long been chased away. This excitement was tempered by his worries for the boy's health (his life was at risk, had been the report, emanating from a reliable and well-placed source close to the prince's tightly managed circle), concerns as to how the boy would react on meeting his father clandestinely, appearing in his rooms (raised from the dead, itself a shock), and of course the risk of discovery, capture and all that might follow - incalculable consequences, an unprecedented situation. Francis and Metternich might simply murder him and bury the evidence. See his boy again, he must, however; it was a compulsion and his new life in Verona, while a comfortable enough but dull existence, was only that; he had faced danger and death many times in many situations. It would be better than dying in bed. A slow, horrible end that reduces everyone, high or low. This boy now mattered more than anything else.

It was a long day of waiting. There was little risk of discovery and capture, provided his subordinates maintained his security - for which they were paid very handsomely.

That night, 4 September 1823, in the very early hours of the morning, a patrolling sentry, used to the mindless task of patrolling his designated beat inside the palace grounds by the perimeter walls, where the only night sounds were those of nature, was astonished to see a ladder and the dark silhouette of a man dressed in a dark cloak dimly lit by moonlight outlined in contrast against the whitewashed stucco walls of the Palace grounds. The Guard thrice shouted his challenge to halt, or he would shoot. The intruder responded to this challenge by climbing the ladder faster, seeking escape - the Guard did as he was trained, he fired and did not miss. With a yell, the body fell to the ground. The Guard approached the limp lifeless body - his mind reeled when he saw the face of his kill, lit by the moonlight. He just stood there, in shock.

The shot brought commotion, followed by more Guards and officials and others from the Palace household. The officer of the watch swiftly assessed the situation and had the presence of mind to cover the body and to place Guards in a perimeter to prevent curious onlookers from learning more. Marie Louise, who, together with von Neipperg, was staying at the Palace, was called to the scene, where they took charge. All but a handful of those Guards on the scene were sent away and ordered to keep quiet about the situation. There had been an intruder, possibly a misguided assassin or thief, but he was dead, and the police would now take charge of the matter, they were told. After the excitement they went back to bed.

Police activity in Hietzing discovered another ladder on the outside of the perimeter wall, evidence of footprints of more than one person and, the next day, after enquiries, an empty house, recently vacated, as confirmed by neighbours - the accomplices were gone. It was not lost on the authorities that someone close to the prince was likely to have been involved - an investigation was begun. Napoleon's name could not be mentioned.

The covered body was stretchered into a cellar in the Palace and guarded. No-one was permitted access by order of the Emperor. The French Ambassador was summoned and, to his astonishment, informed. He readily agreed to preserving the utmost secrecy - if news got out in France and elsewhere that Napoleon had escaped St Helena somehow, lived as a free man until now and had been shot by the Austrians as if he were a common thief or assassin it could have incalculable consequences. It was mind blowing! The lid on this information had to be airtight.

On that night an unmarked grave was dug in the Palace grounds and into this hole in the ground was laid to rest the erstwhile conqueror of Europe and Emperor of France. Another conspiracy was born; the conspiracy of silence of those who knew of this explosive secret. Not least, Franz must not be told or find out. He had not seen his father and was not aware of how close he had been to meeting him again.

Days later, in her salon in Rome, Madame Mère wept real tears.

This time there would be no official mourning, no outward manifestations, only a profound sense of loss. Mothers should outlive their children.

Elsewhere, in Europe and in America, as the news reached them clandestinely, those few most trusted family-members and former subordinates who had maintained their devotion to her son and his cause, and who had been aware of his secret existence, also felt the true loss of a loved one, a powerful life force finally and truly extinguished.

Franz was now not only the publicly acknowledged heir to his father; he was so in their eyes too. Long live the King of Rome! Long live Napoleon II!

In December 1823, having insisted that he see the King himself, with the message that he had in his possession a letter to the King from Napoleon Bonaparte, the faithful Signor Petrucci was eventually permitted to fulfil his commission. The letter was placed into the King's hand - the hand of a man who had heard an extraordinary tale from Vienna. Signor Petrucci had known the true identity of his former partner.[xvi] He returned to Verona, where the illusion was maintained - his partner had left. Petrucci was suddenly a wealthy man - but then what could you expect of a diamond merchant?

By the age of 17, in 1828, Franz was six-foot tall, unusual for the time, a young adult and a very promising soldier –

too promising. It was his chosen career. His progress was a matter of interest and developing concern, especially in France, where social unrest provided fertile ground for political interference and memories of the boy's father and his glory days were still quite recent, Bonapartists were influential – with eyes and hopes turning towards this emerging young challenger.

Austrian Chancellor Clemens von Metternich received regular reports (police updates, compiled from informants, and reports from Count Dietrichstein) on the young Bonaparte, monitoring his development, activities and inclinations and keeping a record of with whom he met and who made up his circle. This young man was to be kept on a short rein and forbidden any political activism, out of reach of those who would encourage him to ambitions of pursuing his father's legacy. He was nevertheless a useful piece on the chessboard in Austria's relations with its neighbour France.

As Franz grew up it became clearer that he was increasingly determined to be his own man.

From an early age the prince would question his entourage and Francis himself about his father and about his own former title as King of Rome. He insisted on having and regularly studying a copy of 'Les Fastes de la France', an historical work in which were described details of his father's victories.

Metternich and Emperor Francis began to observe the young man's growing frustration with the tight reins on which he was being controlled and the denial of his

French, Corsican, family and imperial heritages. Francis ordered that the boy's questions should be answered openly and truthfully.

Franz found solace in studying military matters, developing his career in the Army and in a burgeoning friendship. Antoine von Prokesch-Osten was 16 years his senior, born the son of a provincial administrator in Gratz, Styria. He was not born a noble, but this able man, as a young law student, fought against France in 1813-14 for German liberation, again in 1815 as an ordnance officer under Archduke Charles, subsequently teaching mathematics at the Olmutz Cadet School, where he came to the attention of Prince Schwartzenburg. His climb was rapid. It was the publication of his written piece on the Battle of Waterloo, complimenting Napoleon's generalship, which appeared in the Österreichische Militärzeitschrift in 1819, that first caught Franz's attention. Franz himself translated this work into French and Italian.

They were to meet in 1830 in Gratz, when the Emperor's court came to visit the town. Prokesch was invited to dine at the Imperial table and placed next to Franz - they were unable to speak much on this occasion, beyond the prince saying to him "you have known me for a long time".

On the following day Prokesch was summoned by Count Dietrichstein to meet the Duke of Reichstadt. Eagerly the prince approached him with greetings and said "You have known me and I have loved you for a long time. You have defended the honour of my father at a time when everyone slandered him at will. I read your memoir on the Battle of Waterloo, and to better penetrate each line, I translated it twice, first in French, then in Italian".

Prokesch later recorded that "I answered in words inspired by the desire to bind myself closely with this handsome young man, so deluded in this world".[xvii]

No one was allowed by Dietrichstein to have access to the prince who was not first vetted and then sanctioned by Emperor Francis, in consultation with Metternich. The Neipperg stratagem had succeeded spectacularly (maybe too much so) once, with the lonely mother (recently widowed and much affected by her loss of this husband whom she had loved demonstrably). It succeeded again with the lonely son. The prominent publication to the whole Army, to the elite, of an article unfashionably praising the generalship of the boy's late father, was rich bait, manna to to him. Editorial control made its appearance questionable, but the boy, though intelligent and wary, needed empathetic support. Prokesch was nothing if not ambitious - in the eyes of his critics an energetic social climber. A very successful one, as time would tell.

Dietrichstein introduced the topic of Greece, where a ten-year war of independence had been fought against Ottoman rule, with interventions by the other Great Powers, the British, the Russians and the French. On the previous day, following dinner, in conversation Prokesch had ventured the opinion that the the time was ripe to install a king drawn from a suitable European dynasty to settle the situation.

Prokesch later wrote "In the presence of the Archduke John, Count Maurice [Dietrichstein], [and] Colonel Werklein, Steward of the Archduchess Marie Louise, I had, taking advantage of a moment when the Duke of Reichstadt was occupied elsewhere, slipped into the conversation the idea that the throne of Greece, lacking pretenders since the refusal of the Prince of Coburg, could not be given to a more worthy than the son of Napoleon. This proposal had, to my great surprise, received general approval. The Imperatrice [Caroline] herself who, during this conversation, had approached us, did not seem opposed to it... Now, Count Maurice [Dietrichstein] having provided me with the same morning once more the opportunity to speak of Greece, the Duke would soon guess my thoughts and catch fire at my words."

Their conversation was interrupted by the arrival of a young female visitor (Melanie Kostrowicka perhaps?) the Duke excused himself for a few minutes. When he returned. he impressed upon Prokesch and Dietrichstein that rather than a Greek adventure he wanted to become a soldier, to follow in his father's footsteps, to become a great general, a commander of armies. A commander who wished it to be clearly understood that he did not want to be or be seen to be a threat to Europe or to act contrary to the interests of France or Austria, of his French family or his Austrian family, most particularly his grandfather.

Their enthusiastic discussion of his father's military manoeuvres and strategy, convinced Prokesch of the aptitude, intelligence, skill and penetrating capabilities of this young man. They were interrupted again by the same young lady with a summons to Prokesch to attend upon the Archduchess Marie Louise. They went to her together.

Over the course of subsequent conversations, Prokesch tells us, the boy unburdened himself to him: "my heart is far from being ungrateful to Austria; but it seems to me that, once seated on the throne of France, I could lend my country a more effective support than by confining myself to following in the footsteps of Prince Eugene[xviii]. If I opted for this last role, it is in order to commence the career of arms, the only one that suits the son of Napoleon. And if ever I come to acquire the slightest military glory, it will be one more step towards the throne. I cannot be an adventurer, nor do I want to become a toy. The situation must clear in France before I consent to set foot there. For the moment, my task is to make myself able to command an army. I will not negotiate anything that can lead to this goal. We do not learn war in books, they say; but is not every strategic conception a model for awakening ideas? Does not getting familiar with historical narratives establish real and living relationships, not only with writers, but with the very actors of the great drama of history?"

Prokesch related that at that moment the prince pointed to a newspaper that lay on his desk, at an article reporting on events in Poland, saying "if the general war comes to burst, if the prospect of reigning in France vanishes for me, if we are called to see the unity of Poland arise from the heart of this cataclysm, I would like her to call me, and it is time to repair one of the greatest iniquities of the past."[xix] [xx]

We may be confident that Prokesch reported this conversation. The Prince was nineteen years old - a young man, beginning to know his own mind, to seek his path and destiny, one that would reflect well in the shadow of his great father, very aware of the responsibility attaching to his name and legacy. His grandfather, Metternich and other observers, who included the leaders of France, Russia, Prussia and Britain were watching carefully. He must not be allowed to become a problem.

In the febrile atmosphere in France, in Italy, in Poland and elsewhere in 1830 the Prince was a piece on the chess board, if he could be brought into play.

The death of Louis XVIII in 1824 prompted a crisis. Charles X, his successor had made an unpopular monarchy even more so, by his attempts to reassert the ancien regime, to roll back the changes for which so much blood of his compatriots had been shed. It was untenable and, in July 1830 produced a revolution. Charles' abdication (and flight to Britain[xxi]) could have been an opportunity for the triumphant reinstatement of Napoleon II, as some Bonapartists hoped for, but there was no prospect of his grandfather permitting this and no realistic chance of exfiltrating the prince and setting him on the throne.

Into this opportunity stepped Louis-Philippe, from the Orleans branch of the Bourbon family, supported by a mixture of the government in London, English bankers, the wealthy bourgeoisie and some former Bonapartist army officers.

Meanwhile, the Bonaparte Family were keenly aware of their lack of contact with the scion of their House. This presented many practical problems. One of which was to even assess the young man's orientation and capabilities. What could they hope for from him? How could they reach out to him? Who could be relied upon?

Another Bonaparte was chosen. Napoleone, daughter of Elisa Bonaparte, Grand Duchess of Tuscany, and Felix Bacciochi. Napoleone was married to a man rather older than her, Count Philippe Camerata Passionei of Mazzolino (from Florence). She was a game girl, who enjoyed horse riding, hunting and fencing.

In October 1830 the Countess Camerata travelled to Vienna alone, staying there in an hotel. She hoped to approach her cousin discreetly in the Prater Park, where it had become his known custom to walk. The prince was rarely seen in public and was always escorted. Napoleone soon realised that she could not go up to the prince and speak with him alone without being tackled by his protectors and gaolers.

The resourceful young woman made the acquaintance of Baron Oberhaus, a member of the Prince's entourage, who invited her to his home to a gathering, where she might meet her cousin.

Franz was excited to meet his cousin, this lively young woman who so obviously wanted to speak with him. He felt keenly the starvation of news from his father's family. When she suggested they meet alone in a corridor, leaving the room separately, he was happy to oblige, intrigued. Baron Oberhaus was no fool and followed them; when he challenged the Countess with "what are you doing, Madame?", Napoleone quickly replied "who will refuse me to kiss the hand of the son of my sovereign?", and did so, a useful double entendre. The event was soon over.

Another means had to be found. Napoleone knew that she was now being watched and not trusted; she would not have another opportunity to speak with the Prince, certainly not alone. She resorted to bribing a servant of Oberhaus' to deliver a letter to her cousin - it was passed to Oberhaus and on to Dietrichstein and thence to Prokesch, who showed it to the Prince. According to Prokesch, Napoleone had written:

"Vienna, November 17, 1830

Prince, I write to you for the third time. Please let me know by word if you have received my letters and if you want to act as an Austrian archduke or a French prince. In the first case, hand over my letters. In giving me up, you will probably gain a higher position, and this act of devotion will be attributed to you. But if, on the contrary, you wish to profit by my advice, if you act like a man, then, prince, you will see how much obstacles yield to a calm and strong will. You will find a thousand means to speak to me, that alone I cannot embrace. You can only believe in yourself. Put out of your mind any idea of entrusting yourself to someone else. Know that if I asked to see you, even in front of a hundred witnesses, my request would be refused, that you are dead for all that is French or of your family. In the name of the horrible torments to which the kings of Europe have condemned your father, thinking of this agony of the banished, by which they made him expiate the crime of having been too generous to them, remember that you are his son, that the sight of him in death rested on your image, [let it] penetrate you with so much horror, and inflict on them no other punishment than that of seeing you seated on the throne of France. Profit from this moment, prince. I may have said too much: my fate is in your hands, and I can tell you that if you use my letters for my downfall, the idea of your cowardice will make me suffer more than anything else they can do to me. The man who will give you this letter will take care of your answer. If you have honor, you will not refuse me.

Napoleone C. Camerata "

Prokesch was sent to warn the Countess to leave Vienna and not return. He told her that he came on the prince's behalf. The prince wanted her to leave, to cease any activities that could embarrass him and even affect his liberty. Prokesch questioned her about the Bonapartist party. Who had put her up to this, he demanded to know? Napoleone said that she was acting alone. She was bundled out of Vienna. Metternich's security cordon around the prince had worked, as he reported to the Emperor.

140

Questioned by the police, her husband claimed he had no knowledge of the affair - his wife was a strong-willed independent woman.

In January 1831 Francis concluded it would be safe to permit his fretful problematic grandson greater latitude to go out into society. This would cheer the boy up, hopefully distract him from his lonely brooding existence, fixated on his father, his future and military matters and would go some way to answering accusations that he had imprisoned his own grandson. By this time things were looking more promising, from Francis's perspective, in France and in Poland, where grip was being applied. It seemed unlikely that the boy could get into trouble and, in any event, he would remain on a leash, just a slightly longer one. If he enjoyed himself too much that could even be helpful!

Franz's first official event in the social round away from the Court was at a ball held by the British Ambassador, Lord Cowley, on 25 January 1831. The prince took to social life with gusto, attending salons and becoming a regular at the theatre.

Of course, the prince's guardians and the police continued to be watchful, to compile and submit reports and to keep the Emperor and Metternich abreast of developments. Franz was very well aware that he was under constant surveillance. He knew that very little surprised his grandfather. Franz understood that in many respects this was for his own protection - a necessary concomitant of his parentage on each side. The Prince was a split personage in many respects, part heir to

Napoleon and part Habsburg prince, with opposing weights pulling on his conscience, loyalties and love - an intolerable position.

For the time being, the focus of the reports being received by Metternich and the Emperor was increasingly on the handsome young Duke's growing interest in and effect upon the ladies. Of itself this was in the normal course of things and even a potentially helpful source of distraction. Some suitably compliant girl of good enough family. Or even just a discreet maid or two - problems could be contained, resolved, after all it had happened with princes of the house before and would again. It was in part what the secret police were there to deal with, protecting the Imperial Family, even from itself if need be. No other dynasty in Europe had advanced and protected itself so effectively for so long. The Emperor put family and the future of his House above all other considerations. Scandal had to be avoided, contained if not anticipated, and dealt with.[xxii]

In his memoirs of his relationship with the Prince, Prokesch would tell us that he sought to procure a relationship for the Prince with a singer, a Miss Peche (peach!). The Prince declined. Count Esterhazy wanted to arrange an affair with Countess Naudine Caroly but, according to Prokesch, this also came to nothing. He would later assert that "nature was awakening in this young man of twenty. He often spoke to me of his impressions with the tone of the purest innocence. Never would he have so expressed himself with such frankness if he had had more intimate relations with the fair sex - he

would have betrayed himself by his embarrassment".
That would have been too convenient - a young man who
dies a virgin can have no heirs, no consequent problems.

Once again, we have to remember the extent to which
Prokesch's remarkable career advancement owed itself to
his usefulness to the Habsburg Court, a court that sought
to create a cordon sanitaire around the prince and his
legacy.

There were rumours at the time and soon after. One of
these spoke of an affair between Franz and his cousin,
Archduchess Frederique-Sophie, daughter of the King of
Bavaria, who was married at 19 to a dull boorish
husband, the Emperor's son Francois-Charles-Joseph.[xxiii]
On 11 July 1832, eleven days before the death of Franz,
the Archduchess would give birth to a boy, Ferdinand
Maximilian Joseph, who would later become the ill-fated
Emperor Maximilian I of Mexico whom, before departing
for Mexico[xxiv], with the support of Napoleon III, declared
himself the son of the Duke of Reichstadt. This was
consistent with rumours in circulation at the time of the
boy's birth. Rumours of a son to the Duke having been
born.

Unquestionably the prince and his cousin were close, and
she was a regular visitor and companion toward the end
of his short life. It was also a convenient and not
incredible segue to the rumour doing the rounds of
Vienna (and beyond) at the time of the prince's death, a
rumour based in fact as we shall learn.

Already there was set in motion an elaborate mechanism of wheels within wheels. As we watch one wheel turning, our attention is taken by another, and so on it went.

Two Viennese sisters, Therese and Fanny Elssler, following on the heels of successes in Naples and Berlin, had captivated audiences with their balletic skill and beauty, most especially the younger, Fanny. This was to be the beginning of what would become a long and successful international career. Her most famous character dance would become the Spanish La Cachucha ("The Cap"), so much so that it would not be attempted by ballerinas who came after her.

A beautiful, voluptuous brunette with a perfect youthful complexion, Fanny captivated hearts and inspired men's passions wherever she went. At 16, performing in Naples, Fanny caught the roving lustful eye of the elderly heir to the throne of the Two Sicilies, Leopold, Prince of Salerno, brother to the King and married to a Habsburg Archduchess. Leopold, a ruthless man used to imposing his will, was determined to have her. He pressed his case on her mother with offers of money so insistently that, in fear of what he might do if she turned him away, she assented. This was no love match. It was later said that Leopold was "Fanny's first purchaser, who had her body without touching her soul!"[xxv]

Of course, the eyes of many were on them and their relationship caused tongues to wag - the news soon reached Vienna. Scandal touching on the Imperial Family was to be avoided and Prince Leopold was

144

instructed to present himself in Rome, where he found himself newly appointed to the Papal Guard of Honour. The Imperial Family and the Roman Catholic Church looked after their own - themes repeated throughout this story.

Released, a pregnant Fanny returned to Vienna, where she bore Leopold a son, Franz Robert Essler. Fanny could not keep him close and continue her career and so he was removed discreetly to be brought up by her relatives.

Fanny's fame continued to grow – and her admirers were many. In December 1829 she captured the heart of Friedrich von Gentz, more than three times her age, then a famous political writer (a critic of Napoleon), respected Imperial Counsellor and friend and adviser of Metternich.

However unlikely, even pathetic, a figure the physically unprepossessing 60 year-old Gentz might cut (stooped, bewigged and bespectacled), that he became smitten by Fanny was beyond doubt.

On 25 November 1829 she put in her first performance in the leading role (Viviane, the fairy) in 'The Fairy and the Knight', an acclaimed performance - one that the renowned Gentz attended, seeing her for the first time. On 5 December he watched again as Fanny performed as Emma in Horschelt's 'Der Berggeist' (The Mountain Spirit) - it turned his head. He arranged for four lovely camelias to be delivered to the theatre for Fanny, with his card. He contrived a meeting - on 4 January 1830 they coincided at a musical soiree arranged by Countess

Gallenberg. More visits to the theatre followed and more gifts too. By the Spring, aided and abetted by Count Robert von Gallenberg (then Director of the Vienna Opera), matters had progressed to the point at which Gentz was a regular visitor to the Elsslers' home.

That Summer their relationship, between a foolish smitten old man enjoying a totally unexpected last flourish of romantic ardour and a young, beautiful and increasingly famous woman, saw them together each day. Gentz wrote to Fanny "I never knew such bliss on earth. How can I thank you for this my Fanny? 'My'! In this single syllable more than heaven lies, and you have written it and your eyes have strengthened it". To Countess Fuchs he remarked "Her beauty alone cannot explain the fire she has kindled in me. There must be another mystery above that. Supernatural things come to pass." A note from Fanny on 3 July can only have encouraged him "I will keep the kisses until this evening, but then I shall kiss you so as to drink in your soul."

Fanny's reputation was spreading, her star ascendant. She was contracted to appear in October and November 1830 in Berlin. The Viennese '*Bäuerles Theaterzeitung*' remarked on her departure "Because her every movement is born of a natural grace her talent develops freely and spontaneously. She can portray the most diverse characters, but best of all the simple, mischievous ones, for she has an inner sympathy with the Italian character. We have indeed never known her to fail, never seen her make a false step. Fire and precision are at the heart of her portrayals. We see her depart from her native city, convinced that the fame which she has won here and takes with her, she will bring back twofold."

The unlikely lovers parted company with heavy hearts on 18 September.

Fanny was a great success in Berlin, appearing on 8 October as the heroine in a triumphant production of 'The Swiss Milkmaid'. Meanwhile Gentz pined for her, supported by friends, such as Prokesch. In Berlin Fanny was drawing full houses. In December Fanny returned, via Prague, to Vienna and to Gentz.

Over the following months, in which Fanny's career continued to blossom, their relationship became increasingly one of warm friendship, companionship. Gentz himself was increasingly feeling and showing his advancing years. Another invitation to perform in Berlin in mid 1831, a contract for Fanny and her sister, brought with it a looming separation, felt keenly by Gentz, who wrote to a friend (Rahel von Varnhagen) "even now my heart bleeds at the thought of this parting, and I really do not know how I shall bear it this time."

Gentz took to bringing along his friend Prokesch on evening visits to Fanny's apartment in Karntnerstrasse, Hietzing, close to Schonbrunn Palace. Prokesch later wrote that 'we had a room there called 'Portici', reserved for our communal readings and our work, pleasantly furnished and full of flowers, the most delightful place imaginable. Between ten and eleven o'clock Fanny brought us coffee, and with full confidence in one another we read or talked among ourselves." Discussion was on diverse subjects and their reading covered Goethe, Schiller and other influential writers. We may reasonably assume that the topics discussed included matters relating to the Duke of Reichstadt. It would also be reasonable to assume that Fanny learned many things in the course of these evenings. Gentz and Prokesch continued their visits to Portici even after Fanny and her sister had again departed for Berlin on 14 November 1831.

This time Fanny would be away for three months. Gentz wrote in his diary "I often think I might be happier, more at peace perhaps, if I loved her less, but can you hold back the waters from flooding your house and vineyards in their preordained course or the consuming fire from destroying your home? Work and repose, pleasure and suffering, only have a meaning for me through her, and freedom itself would be a burden to me if I had to dream away my days far from her, for I am in chains even if they are chains of roses. That blissful roguishness, that enchanting smile, from which one drinks and drinks until one is completely bewitched, and all without any artifice or striving for effect, not a breath of coquetry in it! But if it were artifice, the magical smile would not come from the soul, it would simply be one more proof that women are fearful creatures. One should never, even under the most painful circumstances, believe in the impossible, for it can always happen. When a great sorrow darkens everything around us, and the last ray of hope and peace, which only Heaven can send, fades away, no one should believe that the everlasting stars have been extinguished. They are still shining above the clouds, and every sorrow is but a cloud. It disperses and disappears. Why in this world should there ever be a last time? The only way to find salvation and comfort is by an effort of will to turn the last into the first and make a new beginning."

More success greeted Fanny in Berlin, where Fanny appeared in a succession of different productions. On 1 February 1832 Fanny appeared in 'La Fille mal gardee', a comedy, that she co-produced with Anton Stuhlmuller, her dancing partner, also Viennese.

Metternich was well aware that his old friend Gentz was making something of a fool of himself over this girl and was worried. His friend's initial obvious happiness with this lively beauty (with something of a colourful reputation, he knew - as of course Metternich had been involved at first hand in resolving the affair of Prince Leopold) was astonishing, and he hoped he would not be hurt. Fanny attracted highly placed male attention wherever she went and required watching, he had decided.

By mid-February Metternich was receiving intelligence reports from Berlin of developing intimacy between these two dancers, Fanny and Stuhlmuller, partners on and off stage, it seemed. There were also reports of a dalliance with the King of Prussia, who had shown obvious interest in her performances and showered her with expensive gifts. Metternich warned Prokesch - they agreed that such news would devastate their mutual friend, Gentz, increasingly fragile and emotional. They were very concerned for him.

Fanny was soon back in Vienna, however, where she found Gentz ailing. Though attentive to him, her balletic performances continued, while in the background Gentz began to fade. He passed away on 9 June 1832.

Metternich wrote to inform Prokesch, who was in Italy: "The real reason for his death was a complete exhaustion of his strength, the fuel was used up, and it is to this that the increasing irritability of his nervous system during the last eighteen months may be attributed. Everything which brought him tranquillity had vanished, and at the same time his own sensitivity was increasing...Gentz was a man who dissociated himself from any kind of romanticism, yet for some five or six years a kind of romantic feeling awoke in him and it developed to a high degree from his acquaintance with F. Romantic love in an old man soon exhausts his spirit, and the end is not long delayed." He blamed Fanny for the loss of his friend.

Fanny herself was very sad. She had loved this man as a true devoted friend and mentor, one who had opened her mind and experience to an intellectual world of which she had known very little, lacking in education as she did. She was used to the attention and temporary passionate interest of powerful men; in Gentz she had found an influential and highly intelligent man who genuinely was fascinated by and cared for her, who was himself happy to be the object of her affections and to find such love at the end of his life. Theirs' had been something of a bargain.

Fanny's close friend Betty Aioli would later record that "even when [Fanny] was old, she used to recall the days she had spent with Gentz, and until her death she held the tenderest memories of her dear friend". This should be tempered by what Fanny explained to an English friend, Harriet Grote, when asked by her about the relationship. Fanny replied that she did not love Gentz as such, rather "he fascinated me by his manner of talking, by his delicate attentions, and by his adoration of me: besides he was so influential in Vienna that I felt it a great compliment that he should be at my feet. I often felt, however the restraint which his monopoly of my person and the vigilance with which he looked after my actions imposed upon me.... I used to envy my Opera companions when they got a chance holiday and went out junketing to parties in the environs on a Sunday with other young folk, whilst I was debarred from all such enjoyments. On the days when I was at leisure, Gentz used to take me in his carriage to Weinhaus, a suburban villa belonging to him, about a quarter of an hour's drive from Vienna, and there we used to stay all afternoon, dining there, and in the Summer walking in the garden, until 10 o'clock, when he would bring me home again. We were usually alone, but sometimes Gentz would invite a friend or two to dine with us. Baron Prokesch not infrequently came to Weinhaus. My mother was extremely desirous that I should continue under Gentz's protection, for she thought that so long as I was in his hands no risk was to be apprehended to my professional career being interrupted by my having children, for the earnings of my sister and myself were the chief support of my family. Gentz gave me few presents, but paid the current expenses of my father's and mother's housekeeping over and above what Therese and I earned by our dancing…. He told me again and again that when he died, the house and everything in it should be mine, but on his death everything was seized by his creditors and I got not even a legacy, for he was heavily in debt." Their bargain had been broken, it might be said. Gentz's creditors were closing in on him when he died. A miserable end to a distinguished life.

Metternich, ever the cold realist, saw Fanny as an opportunist, but a useful one, as it would turn out. This small circle of Fanny, Gentz, Prokesch and, in the background Metternich (and, when necessary, even the Emperor), crossed over with two others of significance.

Franz was both living close by the Hietzing apartment and was also, since his grandfather had permitted him to go out in public, a regular in the audience for Fanny's performances, where he made it obvious that he found her fascinating. Through Prokesch and Gentz he came to know Fanny. There were in time rumours and gossip of an affair spread in Viennese society. As we have seen, however, the jealous Gentz kept a very tight leash on Fanny and she, in later years, would in private consistently deny that she had been the lover of the Duke of Reichstadt. It was a "made up tale", she would say.

Helen Grote would later write that Fanny told her that "Gentz was terrified at any indication of Fanny's preference for anyone else. In particular he was desperately jealous of the young Duke of

Reichstadt...whose admiration for the charming danseuse was publicly known, and to no one more unmistakably than to Fanny herself. Never was His Royal Highness known to miss a ballet wherein she appeared, and his earnest gaze was always directed to her movements during the evening. Fanny used to peep through the slit in the drop curtain before the performance began, and would exclaim "Ah, voila mon petit Prince! toujours a son poste!" He was constantly to be seen walking on the fortifications near to which the Elssler family lived in the hope of seeing Fanny as she went to the theatre...I have more than once questioned Fanny on this point, and her replies convinced me that that she had been effectively prevented from encouraging the passion of her royal admirer. Her mother exercised a watchful control over her daughters, never leaving them unattended when out of the house, and when in it, little danger was to be apprehended. They occupied a flat some three stories up with a single door of entry so that no one could come in unobserved."

Mrs Grote related that she had asked Fanny "So you never really had the curiosity to make the Prince's acquaintance?" to which Fanny replied to her "I should have liked to do so, but I was so closely guarded that it was difficult. My mother trembled as to what might befall her, if the higher powers suspected that the Duke had formed an acquaintance with me, and accordingly I dared not so much as look out of the window. I might perhaps have liked to have a Napoleon as a lover, but it would have been the death of Gentz. I knew that. I could not bear to cause his death. He was after a manner too dear to me." Fanny and her family were well aware of the realities of their situation.[xxvi]

Nevertheless, the rumours of an affair with the Duke were promoted, for which there were driving forces at work. It was a plausible, colourful and intriguing story - the Prince and the Showgirl, a romantic story of two young, beautiful and interesting people, both in the public eye - a hackneyed cliche - and one that sold theatre tickets.

In 1834, after further successful performances in Berlin (where another old man, Friedrich Wilhelm III, King of Prussia, was said to have been smitten) and London, Fanny and Therese were invited to Paris by Dr Louis Veron, Director of the Paris Opera, who had travelled to London to judge them for himself. They agreed on a three-year contract. Back in Paris Veron set about organising advance publicity, stoking up interest in his new signings.

The owner of the daily theatrical newspaper 'Courrier des Theatres', Charles Maurice, and he had often helped one another. The paper announced that "Something which has no bearing on the question, but will nevertheless do her much good, will add to the anticipated success of the Paris debut of one of the Mlles. Elssler. When this artist was appearing on the Vienna stage, people were curious to know whether she interested a prince who was very dear to the French nation and who died in the flower of youth to the sorrow of our age. Whether this rumour is well-founded or not, it is certainly one that will stimulate interest and curiosity in Mlle. Elssler. Whether it is seen only as an excuse for poignant memories, as a thought associated with so many cruelly disappointed hopes, or as an occasion...to express feelings which people who have not renounced their principles have for the illustrious dead, the opportunity will be seized to see and applaud her, and ponder."

Other writers and critics picked up on the theme and the legend took hold. Fanny made no public comment on this subject - she could not if even she had wished to; there were powerful forces at work. Nevertheless, we know that she was firm in her private denials to those few she trusted. Prokesch later affirmed this, writing "what gave rise to these rumours was that the Duke's huntsman had sometimes been seen entering the house where Fanny Elssler was staying, but the huntsman was coming there because Herr Gentz and I had at that house a room which served us as a study or reading room, and this servant, certain of finding me there most often, brought me the short missives of the Duke, or came to request me to visit him".

It was nevertheless a useful legend, useful to highly placed persons. Its promotion in Paris, soon after the death of the Prince, at a time when to many French men and women he had become a romantic figure cloaked in some mystery, reinforced by the powerful legacy of his father's achievements and his own captive lost potential, was both commercially astute and politically effective. It distracted from underlying realities, highly problematic ones. It had been no accident that Fanny and Therese were invited to Berlin, to London and thence to Paris.

Fanny was sent away from Vienna and purposely exposed to the French public as the probable lover of the lost prince. Strategic moves, made by puppets whose invisible strings led ultimately back to Vienna, to Emperor Francis and to Metternich. They were part of something elaborate, screening something simple, but significant.

Fanny's parents had remained in Hietzing, de facto hostages to her good behaviour.

A short distance from the Elssler home, inside Schonbrunn Palace, other dramatic scenes were being played out.

In the wider background the upheaval in France that had seen the overthrow of Charles X and the opportunity seized by Louis-Philippe to seize the throne had also been, perhaps, a missed opportunity for Franz to return as Napoleon II. As his father foresaw, his absence from France and captivity in the hands of Metternich were near insurmountable handicaps. The French people (and other nations) did not want war, as memories of loss were still raw, even though many felt keenly the disaster of 1815. The inability of Bonapartists to communicate directly and effectively with Franz negated his opportunity. Metternich concluded that even placing a pro-Austrian Napoleon II on the French throne would upset the recently established balance of power in Europe.

Metternich was also becoming convinced that Franz could not be relied upon to do as bidden, especially once he held the reins of power. Metternich wrote "at the end of six months the Duke of Reichstadt would be surrounded by ambitions, demands, resentments, hatreds and conspiracies; he would be on the edge of the abyss…the Emperor [Francis] is too fond of his principles and his duties toward his people, as well as the happiness of his grandson, to ever lend himself to such proposals". He also wrote that 'to make Bonapartism without Bonaparte is an absolutely false idea. When with his genius, which will not be found easily, Napoleon managed to tame and subjugate the French Revolution, he needed a set of circumstances that favoured his projects" and, finally, "greatness seldom passes from father to son".

Franz, growing up fast and seeking his destiny, was politely, but firmly, pressing his grandfather and sometimes Metternich, whom he sought to reassure. In September 1830 he told Metternich that "the essential object of my life is not to remain unworthy of the glory of my father: I think I can achieve this high goal if, as much as I can, I manage one day to appropriate some of his high qualities, striving to avoid the pitfalls that befell him. I would fail in the duties his memory imposes on me if I became the toy of factions and the instrument of intrigues. The son of Napoleon can never descend to the despicable role of an adventurer".

Unrest in France was followed by a riot in Belgium, which proclaimed its independence from France. The possibility of the Duke becoming its king was mooted but not encouraged in Vienna.

The November Uprising in Poland proclaimed a provisional government under the (brief) presidency of a former Napoleonic general, a veteran of the Russian campaign of 1812 and other actions, General Józef Chłopicki (*Hwopitski*).

It was a hopeless and tragic affair. Tsar Nicholas' uncle, the Grand Duke Constantine, Governor of Poland, had demonstrated his disregard for the Polish Constitution, upsetting many Poles, including large segments of the Army's officer corps. It was the discovery of a Russian plan to employ Polish troops, in clear violation of the Polish Constitution, to put down the July Revolution in France and the revolution in Belgium that triggered revolt. Napoleon had offered a pathway to freedom and the restoration of an independent Polish Kingdom - many Poles and Lithuanians had served and fought valiantly and died in his ranks to further this cause - and once again there were cries for a Napoleon in Warsaw - "Long live Napoleon II, King of Poland". It was not to be.

Franz was well aware of these events, that were of course widely discussed at Court and to be read of in the newspapers. His brief contact with his cousin and namesake, Napoleone, Countess Camerata, had at least assured him of the ongoing interest of his father's family. That he could not expect his grandfather or Metternich to allow him to become embroiled in these events was, however, made clear to him. The realpolitik of the fragile economic state of Austria-Hungary, its dependency upon London bankers and therefore not upsetting Whitehall, the growing military ascendancy of its Russian and

Prussian neighbours all stood in the way of it. He understood their position; but it was not his position, rather it was his circumstance, and he did nothing overtly to be seen to encourage these factions.

At Lord Cowley's ball on 25 January 1831 Franz was excited to meet one of his father's marshals, Auguste de Marmont, Duke of Ragusa[xxvii] (whom many, including Napoleon, regarded as a traitor, for his secretly negotiated surrender of his troops in 1814, precipitating the end). Marmont recorded that "my eyes went eagerly on him. I saw him for the first time from near and with ease. I found in him the look of his father...." The Prince invited the Marshal to visit him to discuss his father's campaigns and, having first obtained Metternich's permission, Marmont did.

Marmont wrote that the Prince impressed upon him that "if the policy of the sovereigns of Europe determined them to put me forward, I would solemnly protest. The son of Napoleon must be too great to serve as an instrument, and in events of this nature, I do not want to be a vanguard but a reserve, that is to ... arrive as a help in recalling great memories." Franz wanted it understood that he was not looking to stir up trouble, had no wish to put his revered father's legacy at risk, but that he was open to invitation. It was a prudent message to deliver to Marmont, who could be relied upon to relay it. Franz still had hopes that he might yet have a role to play. He knew also that he could not trust a man who had so significantly betrayed his father, whatever his earlier value to him.

Three weeks later Franz's patience was tested too far. Distressing news reached him that the rebellion in Modena, that had spread within the Romagna, had extended to Parma, where a popular uprising had resulted in his mother being imprisoned in her own palace.

Franz went quickly to his grandfather to urge him to send him with his regiment to his mother's aid. This was something that he could do, it was his duty, and it could not conflict with the interests of his grandfather and even Metternich, surely?

Franz knew only so much. Metternich had received reports from his secret police agents in Italy. The insurgency had been encouraged by another Habsburg kinsman, the Duke of Modena, Francis IV of Habsburg-Este, ambitious to increase his domain. Learning that he had been rumbled and seeking to recover from his gambit, the Duke of Modena had done an about face and arrested the ringleader, but the revolt continued and spread. Its objective was to establish a kingdom of Italy, taking lands from the Pope, as a constitutional monarchy - with Franz as king! So briefed by Metternich, Emperor Francis refused his grandson permission to go to his mother's aid. Italy was a powder keg and his grandson's arrival could set it off. In so doing they would lose control of this region and of Franz. Anything could happen.

Franz wrote "I am rather unhappy, here I am obliged to lose the first opportunity that was presented to me to show my mother all my devotion to her. I was so sweet to help her and in such circumstances I am reduced to offering sterile consolations, this is the first time I have been in pain to obey the orders of the Emperor." He did not write, "my grandfather".

Franz's realisation was more fundamental, crushing - he truly was a captive, and he would not be allowed any slack on his gilded chain; others could not be trusted, and he could not give assurances that would satisfy them, whatever he might say or do. No meaningful role would be found for him and none allowed. He was to live out a pointless existence. His grandfather had so resolved. It was the breaking point. He was watched too closely for this not to be anticipated, perhaps reluctantly by his grandfather, more coldly by Metternich.

Watched closely, but not closely enough.

Count Dietrichstein, who continued in his role of guardianship, would later claim that he had intercepted a passionate letter "from a lady of the court, a Pole and a canoness[xxviii], also very pretty, intended for the Duke of Reichstadt, "hero of romance", "eagle raised in a henhouse"".[xxix] We may speculate as to why Dietrichstein would later leave us this helpful confirmation, when so much else was done to cover over or divert from what occurred. Perhaps his conscience was at work. Perhaps he was once more seeking to deflect the eye or perhaps he wanted posterity to judge that he had not failed in his duty.

As we will come to learn in the pages that follow, this intercepted letter was certainly not the beginning or the limit of the correspondence between Franz and this young lady, Melanie, the 18-year-old daughter of Graf (Count) Samuel Kostrowicki (or "*Kostrovitzky*" as it was phonetically spelt in German).

More than a century later, in a letter dated 28 November 1958, Jan Kostrowicki, great nephew of Melanie (the grandson of her brother Lucjan (*Lutsian*)) would write (in Polish)[xxx]:

"It is understood that I fully comprehend the importance of explaining the lineage of Apollinaire - Kostrowicki and his relationship with the family and through him with Poland, however, what I can communicate to you will be only to report information that in 1903 or 1904 my father[xxxi] told me when I was 15 and so it is very much what is still in my head. Nevertheless, I remember this story quite well, and I remember some fragments almost literally. I cannot, unfortunately, support my current statement with any material evidence, because all the family memorabilia in the form of documents, files, letters, memoirs, engravings, etc., was lost during the First World War; so my story will only allow speculation and supposition... and this will not constitute any historical value, unless you manage to obtain your direct or indirect evidence from the Austrian archives [and] access the material regarding the [Austrian] Court from the period covered by my story and an explanation of certain facts in the Vatican archives. Then it would be possible to see a lot of ambiguity about Apollinaire's pedigree.

Now to tell [about] my father and the events of the story [above].... A dozen or so years before the day when my father related this to me and my older brother, he visited his aunt..., Melanie Kostrowicka, already an old woman, living in Vienna in her own home on one of the main streets, the name of which I do not now remember. When my father inquired about this house, he was told that it was the palace of the Kostrowicki family, and that there lived not Frau Kostrowicka, but "die alte Grafin" (the high Countess). It surprised my father a little because he did not pretend to any title himself. However, my great aunt, Melanie, may have had grounds for using the title of countess, because soon after the death of my father, I received from my sister and my aunt a number of family documents, and among them the family tree. It was made on parchment a few hundred years earlier (the date that I saw on this document, today I do not remember) and it contained the signatures of Tsarina Catherine and Repnin[xxxii], stating the family's right to the title of nobles and coat of arms (Bajbuza)(*Bybuza*). On this document there was an inscription declaring that "because the Kostrowickis were *comes* [xxxiii] obviously, now they have the title of counts", then the date was visible (above the signature of Catherine) and the signature was illegible, though sweeping. This detail is given to you because it could have influenced the fact that my great aunt, Melanie, found herself at the Austrian court.

After this digression, I return to relating the story of my father's visit to his aunt in Vienna. His aunt received my father in a religious outfit, in a black habit with a large cross on her breast hung on a massive chain and with a red cap on her grey head. My father visited Aunt Melanie for a few days, they visited the cemetery [at Hietzing], where the Kostrowicki family grave was located. Melanie's parents and her sister were buried there. Also buried there was Fanny Elssler, a famous Viennese ballet dancer, but about her later.

The house - the palace where my father's aunt lived, was richly furnished, my aunt Melanie had numerous servants, such as a porter, a butler, several ladies' maids, she had to be wealthy. One can guess that the visit of my father was aimed not only at family responsibilities, but also at hopes of inheritance.

Aunt Melanie bestowed upon…my father several portraits of her, her father and sister and her grandfather and some of ancestors in armour with shaved heads[xxxiv]. The portraits were well brushed, I can confirm this, because I studied painting for several years. There was also a well done painting of St. Francis, the face of this saint gave an impression that was similar to the likeness of Fanny Elssler, with the expression of the eyes and lips clearly betraying an irreligious smile. My father's portraits were placed in a few old-fashioned trunks, oddly shaped, covered in leather and intricate ironwork and copper. The trunks contained a mass of correspondence, documents, several items with engravings, drawings, watercolours, and quite a lot of oil paintings not bound, but rolled on wooden batons; on many of them on the reverse side were the inscriptions "King of Rome" or "Duke of Reichstadt", there were also copies of paintings from The Sistine Chapel, especially the head of St. Peter, which was probably the best copy of the original. There was some lace in the trunks, pretty shawls, and even shoes similar to those worn by dancers today. By donating these things, Great Aunt Melanie expressed her desire to remove from her eyes what she associated with the world that reminded her not only of the joyful past, but also of ill-fated experience. Beside this, my father's Aunt Melanie blessed him with the words: "God bless you, my angel," but she did not make any more concrete wishes. After her death, it turned out that both her capital and the palace were designated for St Peter's [in Rome].

Father brought home the gifts he had received. The portraits were hung in the rooms of the house in the Koscieniew[xxxv] property (*Koshcheniev*) in Wilenszczyzna (*Vilenshchina*), and the trunks with their contents were stored in a special locked space in the attic of the house.

Koscieniew was the property of my Uncle Samuel, father's brother, who lived in Riga permanently (he was the chief architect there), and my parents (my sister and brother) spent our holidays there[xxxvi].

When I and my brother asked my father about the lives of our great aunts Melania and Julia and our grandfather (and their brother) Lucjan and their parents, my father told us the following stories. Our great-grandfather Samuel, the father of the above-mentioned Melanie, Julia and Lucjan, was the son of Ignacy Kostrowicki (*Ignatsy Kostrovitski*), General of Artillery in the Polish Army, participant in Napoleon's Moscow campaign.[xxxvii] He had the following properties in the Vilnius region: Kowale, Papiernia and Koscieniew (*Kovale*), as well as some properties in Polesie, but I do not remember their names. He married a lady from the Volynskaya region[xxxviii], Miss Zaleska, a wealthy and intelligent person.

Political accidents that occurred in Poland at that time probably caused my great-grandparents to travel to Vienna, where they acquired the house where my father visited my great aunt.

My great-grandparents had three children - two daughters, Melanie and Julie, and a son Lucjan, my grandfather. They gave all of their children a careful and comprehensive education, and therefore knowledge of foreign languages, literature, music, painting, and my great aunt [Melanie] demonstrated many talents. When my great-grandfather's children reached the appropriate age, my great-grandfather sent my grandfather to France, to the Higher Military School[xxxix], and his daughters were accepted at the Austrian Court, where they entered the circle of Marie Louise, wife of Napoleon I, who after the French Empire fell had returned with her son, the Duke of Reichstadt, to her parents....

My great aunts, besides being well mannered, were, based on their portraits, very beautiful and handsome, especially Melanie. Here the secret of her life and fate begins. According to my father's words, my great aunt at the age of 18 became pregnant[xl]. This accident befell not only her parents but also the court of Vienna; however, the affair was not exposed, and Melanie was secretly sent to Italy, where the birth took place. She gave birth to a son who wore her name, and his given name my father did not want to disclose, nor did he want to reveal the supposed father of that child. When we asked him about this, my father answered that we were too young to understand the situation properly; he hinted that it was a high-ranking person associated with the throne of France.[xlixlii]

That he was not a regular mortal, can be inferred [from the fact that] my great aunt's son grew up in the care of the Vatican, and the mother of the child often stayed in Italy. It is from that time that her paintings come, copies of paintings to be found in St. Peter's Basilica in Rome."

Jan Kostrowicki first learned of this story from his father in 1903 or 1904, living in what was then a dominion of Tsarist Russia.

Far away, in Paris, in 1916 the poet Wilhelm Albert Włodzimierz (*Vwodzimierz*) Apolinary Kostrowicki, known simply as Apollinaire, published *Le Poète assassiné* (The Murdered Poet), a collection of autobiographical poems, and incorporated *La Chasse à l'Aigle* (The Hunting of the Eagle), written in his twenties. In that year the elderly Emperor Franz Joseph I of Austria died, WWI was raging and Apollinaire, a soldier in the French Army, was hospitalised and in convalescence due to a head wound, contemplating mortality.

Apollinaire wrote (in French):

'I had been in Vienna a week. It never stopped raining, but the weather was mild, midwinter though it was.

I made a special point of visiting Schonbrunn, and felt full of emotion as I walked in the dripping, melancholy park, once the haunt of the tragic King of Rome, fallen in rank, to be mere Duke of Reichstadt.

From the "Glorietta" - the name struck me as an ironic diminutive, one that must have made him dream of the glory of his father and of France - I stared a long time out over the capital of the Hapsburgs, and when night fell and all the lights came on I started to walk back towards my hotel in the centre of the city.

I lost my way in the outskirts, and after many false turnings I found myself in a deserted street that was wide and dimly lit. I caught sight of a shop, and dark though it was and seemingly abandoned, I was about to go in to ask my way, when my attention was attracted by another pedestrian, who brushed lightly against me as he passed. He was short, and a capelet of the kind worn by army officers floated from his shoulders. I quickened my steps and caught up with him. His profile was turned to me, and as soon as I glimpsed his features I gave a start. Instead of a human face the creature beside me had the beak of an eagle, curved, powerful, fierce, and infinitely majestic.

Concealing my agitation, I continued to walk ahead, staring attentively at this strange personage with the body of a human and the head of a bird of prey. He turned toward me, and as his eyes stared into mine a trembling, old man's voice said in German:

"Have no fear. I am not a bad man. I am an unfortunate."

Alas! I could make no answer, no sound came from my throat, it was so parched with anguish. The voice resumed, now imperious and with a hint of scorn:

"My mask frightens you. My real face would frighten you more. No Austrian could look at it without terror, because I know I look exactly like my grandfather...."

At that moment a crowd rushed into the street, pressing and shouting; other people came out of the shops, and heads peered from windows. I stopped and looked behind me. I saw that those who were coming were soldiers, officers dressed in white, lackeys in livery and a gigantic beadle who was brandishing a long staff with a silver knob. Some stable boys were running among them, bearing flaming torches. I was curious to know the object of their chase, and I looked in the direction they were headed. But all I could see before me was the fantastic silhouette of the man in the eagle mask, fleeing, his arms outstretched and his head turned as though to see what this danger was that was threatening him.

And at that instant I had a vision that was very precise and immensely moving.

The fugitive, seen thus from behind, his short cape spread wide over his arms, and his beak in profile above his right shoulder, was exactly the heraldic eagle in the armorial bearings of the French empire. That marvellous effect lasted barely a second, but I knew that I had not been alone or mistaken in what I had seen. The crowd pursuing the Eagle stopped, amazed by the sight, but their hesitation lasted no longer than the vision.

Then the poor human bird turned his beak away, and all we had ahead of us was a poor unfortunate, making a desperate effort to escape from implacable foes. They soon caught up with him. In the gleam of the torches I saw their sacrilegious hands catch hold of the cornered Eagle. He screamed some words that so filled me with panic and so paralysed me that I was incapable of even thinking of going to his help.

His last desperate cry was: "Help! I am the heir of the Bonapartes…."

But fists rained blows on his beak and on his head, and cut short his plea. He fell lifeless, and those who had just murdered him promptly raised him up and hurriedly bore him off. I tried to catch up with them, but in vain; and for a long time, at the corner of the street they had taken, I stood motionless, watching their flickering torches fade away in the distance….

A short time after that extraordinary encounter I attended an evening gathering at the home of a great Austrian nobleman whom I had known in Paris. There were marvellously beautiful women, many diplomats and officers. For a brief moment I found myself alone with my host, and he said:

"Everywhere you go in Vienna just now you hear the same strange story. The newspapers don't speak of it, because it is too obviously absurd to be believed by anyone with common sense. Still, it is something that cannot help interest a Frenchman, and that is why I want to tell you about it. People are saying that in a secret ceremony the Duke of Reichstadt married a daughter of one of our great families, and that a son born of this marriage was brought up unknown even to those in attendance at court. The rumour is that this very important person, the true heir of Napoleon Bonaparte, lived in concealment until an advanced age, and that he died barely two or three days ago in particularly tragic circumstances, though precisely how is not known."

I stood there silent, not knowing what to answer. And in the midst of the brilliant party I had a vision of the old Eagle who had spoken to me. Condemned to be masked for reasons of state, wearing the superb sign of an august race…. Perhaps I had seen the son of the Eaglet."

We do not know whether records of their secretive correspondence still exist, hidden in some dusty box or file in a locked away archive, perhaps, waiting to be revealed or not. We can imagine the excitement and private passion of a young man of 20 years and a girl of 18, both attractive, one the caged son of a foreign hero to many Poles and Lithuanians, her countrymen, a symbol of hope that their nations could regain their past independence, self-determination and even glory - a romantic notion shared by many compatriots, at home and in exile. Brought together by Fate in the gilded surroundings of the Imperial Court, they were innocents sharing an impossible love, risking discovery at any time.

It must have been a tour de force for Melanie and we may wonder at whether Franz, for a short time, found love, not in the arms of an actress or ballet dancer, but in those of a young, fresh, accomplished, beautiful and lively[xliii] noblewoman, who was able to come and go to and from the Palace without, at least initially, gaining unwelcome suspicious attention?

Perhaps this relationship with the daughter of a Polish and Lithuanian patriot was the spark that gave rise to the Prince's interest in Poland - as recorded by Anton Prokesch - "if the general war comes to burst, if the prospect of reigning in France vanishes for me, if we are called to see the unity of Poland arise from the heart of this cataclysm, I would like her to call me, and it is time to repair one of the greatest iniquities of the past" - a view surely instilled in her by Melanie's patriotic family? Perhaps he did briefly entertain speculative thoughts of a future there - if so, these were desperate thoughts, as both his doomed relationship with the beautiful Melanie and the realpolitik of Poland - Lithuania's situation, captive, carved up between its old adversaries (Austria, Prussia and Russia), each determined not to see it free and restored, would demonstrate.

There is a notable and very significant difference between what was written by Jan Kostrowicki, relating what his late father, Marcin, Melanie's nephew, told him and what Apollinaire wrote - Apollinaire tells us there was a secret wedding, to repeat:

"People are saying that in a secret ceremony the Duke of Reichstadt married a daughter of one of our great families, and that a son born of this marriage was brought up unknown even to those in attendance at court."

The position of the son of this union would have been fundamentally different if it was legitimate, the true and legitimate heir to Napoleon I and Napoleon II, the King of Rome, or Duke of Reichstadt, as you will, but in any event the rightful Bonaparte claimant to his grandfather's legacy and also legitimately of Hapsburg descent. Had news of the birth of such an heir to Franz and his father reached the public in the early 1830's or at any time before 1870, when the disaster of the Battle of Sedan in the Franco-Prussian War resulted in the abdication of Napoleon III, and the final end of Bonapartism in France as a potent political force, it could have had unpredictable and material consequences.

In Poland, so soon after the failed Uprising, it could have contributed to relighting the flames, offered hope, this child of the heir to Napoleon and a daughter of Poland - Lithuania from an old noble family. Unquestionably none of this would have been lost on Emperor Francis or Metternich, or indeed, the Tsar and the King of Prussia. They were dealing with enough fires without adding more potent fuel. The Vatican would have shared this view. None wanted conflagration and the destabilisation of the balance of power that was both fragile and only recently recovered.

Is it possible that Apollinaire had an even better source of information than did Jan Kostrowicki? It is, as we shall learn.

The revelation to the Emperor and to Metternich, when it came, that, despite surrounding Franz with persons responsible for safeguarding him and preventing embarrassment or worse, he had conducted a secret (?) liaison (and marriage?) with this young Polish countess, producing the prospect of a child, a grandson or granddaughter (preferably) of Napoleon and the

Emperor's eldest daughter, was shocking and presented another very unwelcome problem.

Did Marie Louise, who had herself had matrimonial peccadilloes to resolve with the aid of the Catholic Church, in which she was assisted by Father Neuschel, her loyal confessor, intercede at Franz's request and arrange this? We do not know how the secret was revealed or who by - perhaps only once Melanie found herself pregnant, disclosing this to Franz and in confession to her parents? Was his grandfather informed by Franz or Marie Louise, or by Metternich or another informer, having discovered the secret liaison? Did Marie Louise arrange a wedding, officiated in camera? It was a family problem requiring a solution.

We also do not know the exact date on which the child, a boy, was born in Rome, but we know that this took place in 1831. We also know that Franz never got to see or to hold his baby son.

Metternich devised a strategy of containment. There were rumours of Franz having a liaison with a beautiful woman. Franz himself had relied upon the distraction of his widely noted fascination with Fanny Elssler, the ballerina, to keep the gossips' attention on her, rather than on what went on behind the scenes at Schonbrunn. This rumour was promoted. It was not difficult to oblige Dietrichstein (who had clearly failed in his oversight duties), the elderly Gentz and, Franz's closest male companion, Prokesch, to join in this theatre. In any event, none would wish to oppose the Emperor's will on such a matter, and all were servants and dependents of the House of Habsburg.

Another rumour that circulated related to the Prince being unusually close to the 19-year-old Archduchess Sophie, the Emperor's daughter-in-law. When a child, a son (later Maximilian I of Mexico) was born in July 1832, these rumours even suggested it might be the child of Franz. After all, the two had been close, indeed, as Prokesch would later tell us, it was she of all of the Imperial Family to whom he was closest in his last months. Most probably they simply were of an age and she was sympathetic to this interesting young man. That he would risk an affair with his grandfather's daughter-in-law and Melanie at the same time (let alone also with Fanny Elssler) seems highly improbable. Nevertheless, when in 1832 rumours circulated in Vienna of the birth of a child, a son, fathered by the Duke of Reichstadt with a lady of the court, the only such child born there that seemed to fit the description was Maximilian.

Melanie's family, her father Samuel, mother Anna (who was deeply upset by the turn of events), sister Julie and brother Lucjan could be relied upon to be discreet. Living in Vienna, their relatives and properties exposed to the wrath and power of the Habsburgs and the Romanovs, the child to be brought up in the hands of the Vatican, themselves devout Roman Catholics, they would not risk bringing disaster down on their heads or those of their dearest. That they complied with the solutions outlined to them is demonstrated by the fact Melanie's parents and sister lived out much of their lives in Vienna, close to the court. Graf Samuel Kostrowicki, the father, was involved in Polish cultural matters, becoming President of the Polish PEN Club[xliv]. He (in 1863) and later Julia and Anna Kostrowicka were ultimately buried in a Kostrowicki family plot in Hietzing Cemetery[xlv] (purchased by Samuel), close to Schonbrunn Palace, maintained to this day by public funds. We will, however, meet Melanie's father, Samuel, again later, as he features in another twist to this tale.

We know about the state of the affair between Gentz and Fanny during this period and of the comings and goings from Vienna of Fanny and her sister, Therese.

Early in 1832 more chaff was thrown into the rumour mill for a short time by the appearance in various newssheets of the suggestion of a possible marriage between Franz and the daughter of Archduke Charles. Unfounded, but nevertheless no one could suspect that the prince was already married.

That the Vatican would assist in this matter touching so delicately on the Emperor's family was obvious. Francis had, until 1806, been the last Holy Roman Emperor, promoter and defender of Christianity, and the Roman Church. He and his relatives ruled over much of Italy and the Papal States were his neighbours. Marie-Louise's mother had been the late Maria Theresa of Naples and Sicily (an Italian Bourbon). Church and State had long worked closely together, including in such sensitive matters; indeed, there had been speculation that Franz would, as a small boy, be handed over the Church for his upbringing, care and protection, but Francis had chosen to keep him in sight, at court. To have done otherwise would have antagonised the Bonapartists and potentially and unacceptably exposed the boy to kidnap or rescue, depending upon perspective. Marie Louise had probably also interceded on her son's behalf.

Franz's own son was now destined for the alternative upbringing to which he himself might have been exposed, but in his son's case, in secrecy, his true identity masked. The Vatican was expert in maintaining secrets - and it had no interest in a revival of the Bonapartes, especially fomenting unrest in Italy, where its hold on temporal control in the Papal States was challenged.

What of Prokesch and Franz himself? For much of 1831 Anton von Prokesch was in Italy, sent there by Metternich, who had appointed him Chief of Staff of the Austrian Army of Italy (there is some suggestion that Metternich wanted him gone from court, where he was becoming too close to Franz). He said goodbye to the prince on 31 March, before departing for Bologna. Prokesch was to be active in the campaign that Franz had dearly wished to participate in, alongside his friend and mentor in military matters. He was therefore far away when the lonely Franz and Melanie were becoming closer.

Prokesch had been a constant figure by Franz's side; it would be reasonable to assume that he might have noticed developments sooner than Dietrichstein or anyone else in the Prince's circle. Franz, however, must have been fully aware of Prokesch's loyalty to the Emperor, his proximity and dependency on Metternich and that he could not rely upon his friend not to disclose his liaison. Much that he missed his friend, his absence was in this important respect timely - Franz did not have to deceive his friend nor put him into an impossible conflict of interests by confiding with Prokesch about his affair and asking him not to give them away - an impossibility for Prokesch who would have been cashiered once discovered.

Prokesch was ordered to return to Vienna in early October 1831, to find himself drawn into the disaster recovery process. He resided in Hietzing.

Prokesch, who made no allusion to Melanie (other than perhaps the earlier reference to an interruption by the arrival of a lady of the Court to visit Franz in his apartment at Schonbrunn, sometime before Prokesch's departure, bound for Italy), would later write that the Prince was chaste throughout his short life.

Prokesch wrote that "I thought the duke looked good enough, though a little thin, and my impression was that he was being fatigued with too much care. What he needed was movement, material activity, to stifle the fire that devoured his soul. He seemed decidedly calmer. His desires had remained the same, but his hopes had diminished. during the long interval in which we had remained distant from each other, he had not perceived on the political horizon any sign which presaged that in France his wish was seriously desired; in Poland the insurrection was no more than an ordinary sedition on the eve of being repressed; in Italy secret societies alone were still agitated, and this country offered no arena worthy of the name. This name, which he regarded as a sacred inheritance, he saw to profane in many places by the Revolution. I myself did not have any further information, except that I knew that the members of the Bonaparte family, with no purpose other than to stir up trouble, took part in the impotent riots that took place in Italy, and that the party which, in France, was trying to overthrow [Louis-Philippe], was the republican faction and not the Napoleonic party. I had to suppose...that if the last of these parties existed more or less widespread in the country, it was there in a state of complete impotence. I was not unaware that openings had been made in Vienna, or that they had been rejected."

Francis and Metternich would not countenance a throne for Napoleon's son and heir.

In the late Autumn of 1832, the prince's health began to deteriorate. He developed a persistent cough and loss of weight and his appetite was poor - all noticeable in this very tall and thin young man. Count Dietrichstein instructed the renowned Dr. Johann Malfatti[xlvi] to examine Franz. Malfatti lived conveniently nearby on Küniglberg, a hill in Hietzing.

On 16 January 1832 the Duke visited his regiment, of which he was a Lieutenant-Colonel, for the final time as it would transpire.

Prokesch left again to return to Italy.

Louis Marchand, seeking to fulfil his late master's instructions and to deliver to Franz those precious items of his father's left to be given into his possession, applied to Metternich, the gatekeeper, for permission to see Franz. He was refused, on 'medical grounds' - Malfatti said that this was to avoid provoking too much emotional strain on a young man made fragile by his illness. No doubt it was also to prevent their communication, for whom better to relay his father's words for him, to tell him of his father's devotions and ambitions for him and to instil in him a confirmed sense of his own inheritance and destiny? We can also assume that Metternich was on guard to prevent communication between the prince and his family and supporters. Nor would he wish Marchand to assess the condition and circumstances of the Duke of Reichstadt and report these matters to the outside world, Bonapartists in particular. Worse than that, if Franz were to disclose that he would be a father, even that he was married and to a Pole, with deep roots in Russia! The consequences of these disclosures were unquantifiable. It could not be permitted.

Franz was more than ever a prisoner; and he knew it. These actions in locking him away from even meeting his father's valet and companion on St Helena and receiving his father's personal bequests, last gifts, to him, treasured items, mementos of his father's life and extraordinary career, must have been devastating.

The prince went into a decline over the sad, lonely days, weeks and short months that followed. On 4 February 1832 Franz wrote to his mother: "forgive me today for a trembling script, a short letter, but I am still very weak. I have been in bed for six days, and I am recovering for a week. The fever, vehement enough in truth, has completely stopped, but the chills, which harass me more than all the fatigues which I remember, return regularly each evening. However, I believe they will end one day. I am armed with a lot of patience, and I am looking for glory to suffer patiently."

He recovered for a time sufficiently as to hope that he might go to Naples, to visit Prokesch. He did not accept that he would never be permitted to go to Italy, in any capacity.

In April 1832 the Duke insisted on watching a horse race and was soaked by rain. He returned to his rooms with a fever, his coughing persistent, soon spitting up blood and complaining of a sharp pain on the right-hand side of his chest, day and night.

Princess Melanie von Metternich recorded in her diary that 'the Emperor told Clement that he had met doctors in consultation to decide on the condition of the Duke of Reichstadt and that all had declared that the situation of the patient seemed desperate to them. He is already spitting out pieces of lung and has only a few months to live."

Marie Louise arrived at Schonbrunn on 24 June, much distressed at the reports she had received of Franz's condition. Seeing him for herself she burst into tears.

On 21 July Dr. Malfatti advised that the end was near. Franz passed away in the middle of the following afternoon. It was reported that in his last words Franz called for his mother. Baron Karl von Moll[xlvii], who was present, reported the event to Count Dietrichstein, far away in Munich for the delivery of his daughter.

Who was with Franz at the end? Not his mother, no member of his family, no relative, not his friend Prokesch, not Dietrichstein. His mother and the Archduke Francis had attended upon his last rites, earlier. It is Moll on whom we rely to relate the Duke's passing. Although Franz had called for his mother, those present had not informed her, deciding to spare her this ordeal.

When an autopsy was conducted by Dr. Malfatti[xlviii], Dr. Semlitsch (the Court Surgeon) and Doctors Hieber and Rinna (doctors to the Court) and Zungerl (house doctor to those at Schonbrunn Palace) they concluded that lung cancer was the physical cause of death.

The news of the tragic death of the young and romantic Duke of Reichstadt was covered by news sheets and gazettes everywhere, provoking an emotional outpouring. Marie-Louise was distraught. In Rome a young, bereaved mother was also distraught and bereft, for her loss and her son's loss, their son's loss.

On his desk was a letter intercepted and delivered to Metternich. It said, "If the presence of a nephew of your father, if the sins of a friend who bears the same name as you, could relieve your suffering a little, it would be the height of my wishes that I could be useful in something to one who is the object of all my affection." Its scribe was the future Napoleon III. If evidence were needed of the continuing devotion of Franz's father's family, this was it.

Napoléon François Charles Joseph Bonaparte, variously Prince Imperial, King of Rome, Emperor of France, Duke of Reichstadt and heir to Napoleon I, was stifled. Stifled in the manner of an exotic plant or creature, forced by his circumstances to live in a space increasingly too small as he grew and developed into a young man, a man from whom all dreams, hope and opportunity were removed, denied by those who found his very existence threatened their place in the world, were he to escape their shackles. In this he was the unhappy and undeserving victim of his father's legacy - a curse on his own line.

Just as he was, for all practical purposes, smothered in life, so was his story controlled in death. Emperor Francis (and after his death in March 1835, his successors Ferdinand I - who abdicated in 1848 - and Franz Joseph I) and Metternich and their lieutenants, Dietrichstein and Prokesch, controlled the story with the power of the pen, later publishing careful memoirs and reminiscences of the Duke.

No one who was not a member of the Habsburg family or one of its dependents had been allowed sufficient access to the Duke in life nor to his writings in death to provide us with a picture of the prince that was not edited by the Habsburgs or on their behalf.

The Emperor and Metternich had, in effect, possession of the Duke's papers and personal effects, able to keep or destroy whatever they wished. In this context we should remember that Jan Kostrowicki has told us, as related to him by his father, her nephew Marcin Kostrowicki, that Melanie was (in the late 1880's) in possession of those items of the Duke of Reichstadt's property, papers and effects that she gave to him to take back to the Kostrowicki family home at Koscieniew, expressing "her desire to remove from her eyes what she associated with the world that reminded her not only of the joyful past, but also of ill-fated experience". Surely, these items could not have reached Melanie, or continued in her possession, living peaceably in Vienna and Rome, without the knowledge and sanction of the Imperial Court, most probably both reflecting and respecting the wishes of the Duke and trusting that she and her family would abide by the accommodation that had been made? An arrangement that appears to have held until 1916, when the World was at war on a scale never seen before, empires clashing and beginning to fall by the wayside, the international political and social order questioned, recast fundamentally and permanently and these once important matters were reduced to curiosities.

PART III - THE WARD

Melanie a frightened teenager, gave birth to their ill-fated boy far away in Rome. We may hope that her mother, Anna, could be with her, perhaps her father Samuel and sister Julie, too. These must have been difficult times for all of them.

When months later the news of Franz's illness and then death came it must have been devastating. Whatever hopes Melanie and they might have had for the future were ended.

The boy could not be removed from the Vatican, though she would be permitted to visit him. She herself would become a canoness, committed to living a life of piety. Her story could not be told to another suitor, even if she were to contemplate one, then so far from her mind. So early in life her path was determined - not for her a future as a wife and mother, living openly in society. She would live out her life quietly in the shadows, as would her child. Anything else would spell danger for the boy, her parents, sister and brother and for herself - and was forbidden. As with the father, now the baby was a hostage too.

We should not imagine that Melanie or her son (Marcin Kostrowicki passed away in 1905 without disclosing it to his young sons - we will call him Albert, until his true name is revealed; though we are told he used the surname Kostrowicki) were treated badly in terms of their daily needs. The Catholic Church has a long history of providing excellent tuition and education. We can expect that young Albert Kostrowicki was given such an upbringing.

Albert's 82-year-old grandmother, Letizia Bonaparte, was of course another resident of Rome, but this elderly lady would die four years later, and we do not know if there was contact between Melanie, her family and Madame Mère. It seems likely that rumours of a child of

Franz being born of a lady of the Austrian Court would have reached members of the Bonaparte family, and therefore maybe Madame Mère. Nevertheless, this child, even if legitimate, was too young to be a political player - and Franz himself had not been able to take up the mantle of heir to Napoleon.

Marie-Louise, the child's other paternal grandmother, Duchess of Parma, lived on until 1847, when he was 16 years old.

With the Duke of Reichstadt gone, the rising hope of the Bonapartists became the able nephew of Napoleon I, now 24 years old, Charles-Louis Napoléon Bonaparte, son of Napoleon's younger brother Louis and of Hortense de Beauharnais, the Emperor's stepdaughter, daughter of Josephine.

In Britain, France and Russia, the next two decades would witness simmering social tensions and change. The 1832 Reform Act saw the enfranchisement extended beyond landowners to include any man paying taxes of £10 or more each year (over £1,000 today). The British model, and that of the USA, were watched closely in Continental Europe, with fear and suspicion by the autocrats and with some envy by the liberals. In 1830 Charles X issued the Four Ordinances of St Cloud - abolishing freedom of the press, reducing the electorate by three quarters and dissolving the lower house of the French Parliament. The resulting uproar, the Three Glorious Days of 26 - 29 July 1830, brought about Charles' abdication and the installation of another

Bourbon, from the Orleans branch, Louis Philippe, giving rise to the so-called July Monarchy.

Louis Philippe was a very wealthy and successful businessman, among the richest men in France. His policies were more liberal and supported by the petite bourgeoisie and bankers, railroad developers, owners of coal and iron ore mines, forests and landowners. Opposition to his regime came mainly from the ultra-royalists (who regarded him haughtily as an upstart) and from industrialists and working classes, unlikely bedfellows all. Enfranchisement favoured the landed classes, to such an extent that by 1848 only approximately one per cent. of the population could vote, alienating many people who were not necessarily natural allies.

The King became viewed increasingly as detached from the concerns of broad sections of the people. Pointing to the British model, encouraged by the free press, a mood of republicanism took root. A financial crisis (in 1846), failed harvests and rising unemployment, inflation impacted bread prices and, together with corrupt government practices, became the fuel of revolution. Fundraising banquets replaced illegal political gatherings until even these were outlawed.

On 22 February 1848 the citizens of Paris rose, flooded the city's streets and demanded reform and the removal of Louis Philippe's chief minister, Francois Guizot. The citizenry erected barricades and fought with the municipal guards. Guizot resigned the following day, but the angry crowds were unappeased. In a melee before the

Ministry of Foreign Affairs soldiers fired on the pressing crowd, resulting in 52 deaths. The consequential anger turned on the King. With the crowds descending on his palace Louis-Philippe abdicated in favour of a small boy, his nine year-old grandson and, disguised, fled to England.

A Second Republic was declared, but that year would continue to witness upheaval and frenetic political debate and activity, workers riots, xenophobia, elections, radical calls for an international crusade for democracy, even calling for the restitution of an independent reunited Poland (where an uprising had started on 20 March - the Wielkopolska Uprising). The middle classes, fearful of a workers' revolt and all that could follow, pressed successfully for the Army to restore order, ultimately achieved by some 120,000 troops overcoming the barricades that had blockaded Paris. It was a victory, but it had driven a lasting wedge between the working classes and the bourgeoisie.

Elections held in December of that year resulted in Louis-Napoleon Bonaparte, Franz's cousin, being voted in overwhelmingly as President (he secured more votes than all of the other candidates together). Once again, a Bonaparte would lead France out of revolution, offering stability in very uncertain times. Louis-Napoleon garnered support as the man who could stand above the political fray, under the mantle of the glory days (as they were now remembered) when his late uncle bestrode Europe.

Louis-Napoleon set about re-establishing order. The economy grew, witnessing significant development in industrialisation and development of railway communications. In December 1851, rather than face elections, Louis-Philippe lead a coup that saw him enthroned as Emperor Napoleon III - the Second Republic was at an end and the Bonapartes were restored.

These momentous events were monitored and influential.

In Russia, after the untimely death from typhus of Alexander I in 1825 (aged 47) he was succeeded by his brother Nicholas I, an autocrat and soldier, distrustful of the nobility (many of whom nursed grievances against Tsarist rule, impacting upon their privileges) and of political reform. It was a vast, mainly underdeveloped and backward country, with a middle class forming only slowly. Although, as elsewhere in Europe there was developing industrialisation, economic expansion and pressure for increasing rights, these factors were developing more gradually and painfully in Russia and its domains, now a far-flung empire, covering vast territories, multiple peoples, cultures and faiths. In 1832 a secret police force was established (the 'Third Section'), overseeing a large network of spies and informers.

Having had experience of crushing and subjugating the Poles in 1830, Nicholas I responded resolutely to the call for aid that came from Franz Joseph I of Austria in 1849. An uprising in Hungary, determined to throw off the Austrian and Habsburg yoke, was winning ground, measured in victories over Franz Joseph's forces.

Nicholas sent a powerful force of 280,000 men (200,000 regulars and 80,000 auxiliaries), that, together with Austrian forces, crushed the hopes of the Hungarians (and of many others contemplating action). Hungary would remain, resentfully, under Habsburg rule until the aftermath of WWI.

The succession of the more liberal minded Alexander II in 1855 brought with it some reforms (in government, the military, in education and in the legal system and notably the emancipation of serfs in 1894). His assassination in 1881 - a bomb thrown under his carriage having caused extensive and horrible injuries, he bled to death, witnessed by members of his family - brought swift reaction. Alexander III, his son, cracked down on dissidents, strengthened the security police and addressed the situation of the peasants and workers, extending land ownership rights and worker protections (limitation of working hours, proscribing child labour, etc.), and encouraged industrialisation.

Amidst the backdrop of these swirling events the career of Fanny Elssler had continued to flourish. Fanny's appearances with the Ballet du Théâtre de l'Académie Royale de Musique (today the Paris Opera Ballet) were triumphant, especially her performances of the Spanish *Cachucha* (from *Le Diable boiteux* by Coralli and Gide, 1836), her signature piece. The popularity in these nationalistic times of such dances saw her performing a *Cracovienne* and an Italian *tarantella*. She was an international star, much in demand. In 1840 Fanny and Therese sailed to New York, the first prima ballerina to visit the USA. There she was seen regularly dining in the company of John van Buren, the son of the President, before returning with Therese to Europe in 1842, arriving in Liverpool on 28 July. Only recently arrived back in Europe, she soon crossed paths with Count Samuel Kostrowicki, Melanie's father.

By 1841 Samuel was professing his love for Fanny. A limited edition of 100 copies were published in Brussels under the title *Lettres à une artiste,* of extracts from correspondence, in which the author (unnamed, but likely to have been Samuel) disclosed that he had met Fanny shortly after the death of Gentz (this was consistent with Fanny's role in assisting Prokesch, Dietrichstein - and therefore Metternich - and Melanie's family in providing a plausible cover story). Samuel would have considered himself and his family in her debt - she had sacrificed her reputation to protect them from the storm that would have come. They were already united by this secret. Early in 1843 he asked her to retire from the ballet and to marry him.

In January 1843, Fanny made several entries in her diary revealing that Samuel was pressing her for an answer and that she was agonising over how to respond.

6 January 1843 - (Proverb: When all else fails, faith, hope and love remain.) I slept peacefully, thanks to Thee, O Giver of all good things. I had a quiet day. I could experience so much if I complied with the wishes of one person. Is it my own will, or am I still blinded by the glory of the world? I wish I could renounce this worldly glory. Yes, I believe I could, and am not afraid to admit it. In the evening I danced the *Cracovienne*; I was merry and so was the public. K. seemed calmer. At the end of this day I can truly say, "My God, I have faith, I love, and I have hope. Thanks be to Thee."

7 January 1843 - I have just received a letter from Reich. I expected more of him. Everyone seems to deceive me. Proven friends are the only ones one should call friends, but it is difficult to find them. I have such a one at my feet. Why do I not accept him? Oh, Fanny, Fanny, take care, such things do not happen twice in a lifetime.

8 January 1843 - Today brought me only joy, no pain. After Church I met some friends. In the afternoon I saw K and talked about the future. How carefully he plans everything for me, like a father for his child. In the evening I was at Liszt's concert. I find him not natural, and much too calculating. This detracts greatly from his art. I did not enjoy it. I saw many people at the concert, and many people saw me. An empty evening.

12 January 1843 - I was uneasy the whole day. K wrote to me that I should not go to Strelitz. I replied that I must. Then I went to work, and saw K beside himself at my decision. In the evening I was alone with Minna and talked of all that had happened. She felt insulted that I had not confided in her. K had foreseen that it would turn out like this. I was wrong not to have spoken of it immediately. But who is right in this affair? I have proofs that K means well towards me. Can I doubt it? No. Then why this weakness, this doubt? Life no longer has any value for me. Everyone says he means well towards me, but nobody ever thinks of me, but only of him. Only God knows my heart, and only He can protect me. I trust in Him.

That day Fanny and her brother Johann would learn the sad news of their father's death. They left Berlin to attend a requiem in Vienna, held in St Stephen's Cathedral. Fanny returned to Berlin for one more performance, on 3 February, before departing for London, where she resided at 13 Regent Street, performing at Her Majesty's Theatre. Her father's death and the distressing state of her relationship with Samuel were troubling her. Triumphant receptions of her performances at Her Majesty's Theatre and at Covent Garden did much to relieve her.

In her diary Fanny recorded:

11 March - First appearance in London. I was saving myself for the evening, and had such a violent headache that I lay down after dinner for two hours, after which I felt better. I saw nobody, but went quietly to the Opera to await my fate. Perrot sprained his foot. I was received with applause that left nothing to be desired. Victory was mine.

13 March - I was at Covent Garden early for rehearsal. In the evening I danced in *Bayadère*. What a difference from Berlin, I was often led to think. It was unbelievably bad here. I had an extraordinary reception and danced well. The Queen was present.

In July 1843 we learn that Fanny, who has been in Brussels for a five-week long tour, was invited to dinner by the Austrian Ambassador, Count Dietrichstein, renewing their acquaintance we must assume. It seems likely that Dietrichstein will have been aware of her liaison with Samuel Kostrowicki, a combination that is unlikely to have recommended itself to him or his masters in Vienna. Did he warn her off a marriage with Samuel? Maybe, but it also seems likely that Fanny, long the object of attentions from powerful men wishing to possess her, sometimes obliged to accede because of life's realities for a young woman in her position, enjoyed the self-determination and financial independence that she had won for herself and was not, ultimately, willing to subject herself to control by any man, however well-meaning and deep in her affections. Perhaps her doubts were confirmed by a warning from Dietrichstein, a warning concerning her own and also Samuel's well-being. Once again, we must remember the broader political and environmental context. These remained troubled times.

More years of performances in the capitals of Europe followed. Fanny was one of the greatest performing celebrities of her day, in demand by audiences everywhere, until she herself decided to call a halt and retire as she turned 41 years of age, performing for the last time, with 12 appearances at the Kärntnertortheater in Vienna, ending on 21 June 1851. The whole of Viennese society had wanted to see her, including Emperor Francis Joseph.

Fanny, wealthy and independent, settled for the time being in Hamburg.

Across the years in which her son Albert was growing up, the still young and beautiful Melanie lived in the shadows, dividing her time between Vienna and Rome, seeing her boy whenever she could, but unable to remove him from Rome. Her father, Samuel, provided for them, financed by his properties in Lithuania.[xlix]

Her brother, Lucjan Kostrowicki, met his own misfortune. As Jan Kostrowicki would later write[l] Lucjan, while enrolled as a cadet at the French military academy at St. Cyr, would have the unhappy fate of crossing the path of Tsar Nicholas I, who then visited Paris. The Tsar's obsession with military matters and his love of parades was well known and the French arranged for him to inspect the academy (L'École spéciale militaire de Saint-Cyr, founded by Napoleon I in 1802). The cadets were paraded before him and one of the Tsar's French hosts boasted to him of the fact that one of their best students was a Pole!

Having only recently crushed rebellion in Poland, subsequently stripping noble status from some 40,000 persons, Nicholas bristled and was swift to scent a dissenter. He considered himself the prime defender of ruling legitimism and enemy of revolution in Europe - he was proud of his nickname as the "gendarme of Europe". In 1830 had he not offered troops (including, unhappily, Poles, as we have seen) to suppress the rebellion in Belgium against Dutch rule?

He detested nobles who, to his mind, betrayed their rightful hereditary ruler in supporting liberalism, a cancer taking root and spreading in Europe. When the duc d'Orleans took the French throne as Louis-Philippe in 1830, the self-styled 'Citizen King' (a concept itself anathema to a Romanov[li]), displacing Charles X and his line, Nicholas was horrified. He judged his friend (as he had become in 1815, when he had first visited Paris) to have taken the side of revolution and liberalism. His foreign policy swiftly became anti-French, allied with Austria and Prussia (Nicholas saw eye to eye with Francis and Metternich - they faced the same problems).

Nicholas saw France, and Paris in particular, as a hotbed of liberals and revolutionaries. After all, had not the contagion started here?

After the collapse of the November 1831 Uprising some 5,000 Poles had fled to France, mainly Paris. Among these were not only many displaced aristocrats and political leaders, but also intellectuals and important cultural figures such as Mickiewicz and Chopin. The Poles considered that France was morally in their debt, due to their support for Napoleon and their recent resistance to autocratic rule - to Nicholas.

So here at St. Cyr Nicholas was faced with a Polish noble boy from a family that had long taken part in fomenting resistance to his and his forebears' legitimate rule! On learning the identity of this student, Nicholas called for him to be presented. Standing smartly at attention before the Tsar of All the Russias, Lucjan Kostrowicki found himself denounced as a traitor! Nicholas demanded he be released from the academy and repatriated, with which the French authorities complied - after all, they neither wanted another cause for argument with Nicholas nor, we may assume, the story of his sister and the deceased Duke of Reichstadt to emerge[lii]. Once back at home, at Papiernia, Lucjan was placed under a form of house arrest, required to report to the police authorities at all times and forbidden to leave the country and, expressly, to visit his family in Vienna (forever!). He was only permitted written correspondence with his family and this was censored (and no doubt reported on and filed by the Third Section).

The impact of these family disasters so upset their mother, Anna, that she left her daughters and husband in Vienna and returned to her family, the Zaleski's, in Volhynia.[liii] These were truly dark times for the family.

Fanny, meanwhile, maintained her home in Hamburg, where she brought up her daughter Therese (her sister's namesake) until she was 21, in 1855. In that year she returned to live in Vienna, where she moved into an apartment (at 14 Kärntner Straße, near to the Stephansplatz, in the city's centre). Here Fanny's lively dinners and receptions were attended by a mixture of old friends, of leading cultural lights and senior servants of the Empire. She was much loved by the city that had long since treated her as one of its own. She retained her beauty and her style of dress barely adjusted over time. This quirk was part of her charm; others grew old, but not Fanny.

Of course, in Vienna she was in close proximity to Samuel Kostrowicki and his daughters. Fanny and Samuel remained close loving friends until his death in

1863, aged 75 (Fanny was still only 53). Years earlier, soon after Fanny turned down his proposal of marriage, Samuel had purchased two neighbouring plots at the Hietzing Cemetery[liv]. One he kept for himself and his family, the other he offered to Fanny, in the hope that even if they could not be together in this life, they would be side by side in the hereafter, eternally.

Melanie, Julia and Lucjan each received substantial inheritances, according to Jan Kostrowicki. He wrote that "great-grandfather [Samuel] and great-grandmother were apparently very wealthy people and they had serious capital abroad. After their death, their foreign property was given to their daughters Julia and Melanie, their brother (my grandfather), it seemed inherited the property in Wilenszczyzna[lv] ([the estates of] Kowale, Papiernia and Koscieniew)." [lvi] After his difficulties in Paris and his return to Lithuania he settled at Papiernia, the main family home, where he married (Jozefa Sieklucka), giving up any hopes of moving to Vienna to build a career there. Jan also wrote that his grandfather Lucjan sold Kowale and Papiernia, that is, 2/3 of his property, and donated the sale proceeds to his sisters, Melanie and Julia. After Julia's death, all of this was inherited by Melanie. As Jan wrote, "here again, some mysterious factors had to play a decisive role in my grandfather's actions". It would seem that substantial funds were needed in Vienna (and Rome); although living comfortably by the standards of the day, there is no suggestion that these sisters were profligate - indeed one was a canoness, living a life of comfortable secluded piety.

As Jan would write to Anatol Stern in 1958, if you compare these circumstances with Melanie's son's birth, and then "with the efforts to get the Vatican to care for him, it seems logical to assume that this money was used to obtain and provide this care". In passing over to his sisters more than half of his inheritance, and so disadvantaging his own wife and children, Lucjan must have felt a significant compulsion.

In the context of a continent experiencing pressures for change, met by defensive autocratic and conservative reactions, a young man grew up in Rome under the aegis of the Vatican. When, in 1852 his uncle was crowned as Napoleon III, Franz and Melanie's son, Albert Kostrowicki (by which names we shall call him, as will be explained) became 21 years old. We know so little of how he spent his days.

Rome in his day was very different to the cosmopolitan city of today, political and legislative capital of a united Italian republic, encapsulating the entire Italian peninsula, teeming with pilgrims, visiting dignitaries, cardinals, archbishops, bishops, abbots, abbesses, priests, monks, nuns and others of the Roman Catholic faithful and thousands upon thousands of tourists. At the start of the 19th Century Rome stood at the centre of the Papal States, the Pope not just a spiritual leader and Christ's Vicar on Earth, the inheritor of the mantle of St Peter, but also very much a temporal ruler of a large domain.

Napoleon I had conquered the Papal States and they were annexed into his Empire, part of France. Declaring his son and heir King of Rome had been a calculated slap down to the Pope (and to the dethroned Holy Roman Emperor, permitted to remain as Emperor of a reduced Austria and King of Hungary), directing him to focus on matters of faith, not state. Most of the Papal States were returned to the Pope by the Congress of Vienna. The Vatican had reason to be grateful to Francis and to Metternich.

Austria controlled large swathes of Northern Italy and Italian nationalists, saw their opportunity to tap into the wider mood of rebellion against foreign totalitarian regimes. In the Papal States liberal views brought demands for independence from the Church, which was resented by many, even the faithful, for exercising too much influence over their lives. In 1848 revolutions broke out on the mainland and in Sicily. King Charles-Albert of Piedmont-Sardinia was the leader, seeking to unite Italy and drive out the Austrians. After losing to the Austrians at the Battle of Custoza in July a truce was signed - Austria remained in control.

A Roman Republic was declared in 1849, of which the famous Giuseppe Garibaldi was a leader. Again, this action failed. Austria and the Papacy shared a common interest in the status quo, although the next two decades would see continued strife and the retreat of the Papal States, with the Pope essentially clinging on to rule in Rome.

For a time, Pius received aid and troops from Napoleon III (ironically, one might observe), however the commencement of the Franco-Prussian War in July 1870, culminating in the defeat of France and Napoleon's abdication, ended this aid. On 20 September 1870 a three hour long artillery cannonade preceded the Italian Army infiltrating the city, which was occupied the following day. After a plebiscite in which the vast majority of Rome's citizens (over 130,000 voters) voted in favour, Rome was annexed to the newly founded Kingdom of Italy and became Italy's capital on 1 July 1871.

Albert Kostrowicki was now 39 years old. His mother, Melanie 58, Aunt Julia 59 and Uncle Lucjan 56. Fanny Elssler, their family friend, resident in Vienna, was an elderly but spritely 61 year-old. It would be another decade before Marcin Kostrowicki, hopeful of an inheritance, would be summoned to Vienna to meet his mysterious great-aunt, resident in the 'Kostrowicki Palace'.

In 1872, once it was safe to assume that the age of Bonapartism was well and truly over, Anton von Prokesch chose to publish, in Paris, his book entitled 'My relations with the Duke of Reichstadt' (*Mein Verhältniß zum Herzog von Reichstadt*). In 1871 Emperor Franz Jozef had appointed him Ambassador to The Sublime Porte[lvii] and, in gratitude for 60 years of distinguished service, a hereditary count. Truly he was a servant of the Habsburgs. He would live on until 1876.

Maurice Dietrichstein retired in 1845, but lived on to the age of 89, passing away in 1864[lviii]. It was not until 1927 that Jean de Bourgoing would publish a collection of papers in book form entitled "Dietrichstein - Papiers Intimes et Journal du Duc de Reichstadt", comprised of letters, journal entries and other papers in the possession of the Dietrichstein family that belonged to or concerned the Duke. Dietrichstein, faithful servant of the Emperor, remained discreet to the end.

Clemens Metternich, whose long and distinguished career placed him as Chancellor, in de facto control of the Austrian Empire, one of the key players in international events for more than three decades, was obliged to resign in 1848 over uprisings in Hungary and elsewhere in Habsburg domains - there was cheering in Vienna when his departure was announced - this confirmed conservative and believer in legitimism had outstayed his welcome.

After years of exile, spent mainly in England (in Brighton), Metternich returned to Vienna in September 1851, with the permission of Emperor Franz Jozef. Many senior figures who would play their parts in the years to come were interested to meet him. He passed away in Vienna in 1859, aged 86.

PART IV - THE POET

I Vienna August 1880 – the Kostrowicki Palace

A letter from Rome had been delivered. It was from her son. As she sat by the window in her now outmoded Viennese salon gazing into the street, occasionally sipping at her morning cylinder of coffee, she was lost in reverie. Her surroundings reflected her life, vestiges of her White Ruthenian roots and the style of a lost era, that sparked by a Corsican who through his remarkable genius and military prowess had shaken Europe over half a century earlier but was not forgotten. Especially today.

Melanie's thoughts drifted far back across the years. Years of careful silence. In this house she had grown up. Those were happy, noisy, colourful days, of new discoveries and joy at home. She remembered her dearest papa, Samuel Kostrowicki and mama Anna, her sister Julia and brother Lucjan, of whom she had seen so little once he had left for France so many years ago, still a boy, and the impressive if austere elegance of the Imperial Court at the Hofburg and, in Summer, at magnificent Schonbrunn, in those days before everything changed. The elegance of it all, the formality, the wonderful lilting music, theatre, skating and later precious invitations to balls and soirees which began to arrive after she was presented at Court by her proud parents to the Emperor and Empress. She was young, clever, well-educated and beautiful with life's promise before her, and so many dreams.

She had soon found to her shy heady delight that she was attractive to men, but perhaps (which she did not yet understand), as the daughter of an émigré, a political exile, a little too exotic and not what aristocratic Austrian parents, concerned to advance their sons, would prefer. The young Melanie was all the more desirable for this, her reverie assured. What young woman would not have been excited by those times? What old woman would not be warmed by such occasional sweet memories? To have been beautiful and loved passionately and romantically, secretly, by a powerful force of nature once in her life is not offered to many women.

Most of all she thought, happily and then painfully about the glittering sensitive young man whom she had come to know, dared to love, had won and so swiftly lost. Of what was and what might have been, perhaps. Memories burnished over time, as she sat surrounded by mementos, his few possessions that had come to her.

A movement of flight caught her attention, broke the mood and brought her back. The years had made a realist of her very early. Of course, it was never possible, she remembered now, understood as a mature woman, just as she had come to recognize this unbending reality most painfully many years ago. It would never have been allowed.

The now tired elderly lady looked down at the letter in her hand and softly, inadvertently, remarked aloud "and so it begins again, poor boy". In this uncommon way did she greet the news, the mixed blessing, that she had a grandson - her own son was now nearly 50 years old and she had not entertained thoughts of his line continuing, or what that could entail. Some ten years earlier, after Sedan, the reins had gradually slackened, but nevertheless they were not free, they would never be free.

II The Chancelleries

Unbeknown to the author or its intended recipient, though neither would have been surprised, indeed it was to be expected, she was not the only reader of this letter or alone in knowledge of its delicate news. Letters which passed between monitored persons through the Imperial Austro-Hungarian Postal Service were easily read, copied and re-sealed by the Secret Police. In any event her son had always been watched, reported on - information reaching the authorities and even the Emperor, if need be, faster than the mail would reach her.

The birth of a child to Angelika de Kostrowitzky[lix] (or Olga, which she went by) had come and this sensitive fact could no longer be ignored, due to the child's paternity.

The expected arrival was known about, of course, and plans had had to be made, a handful of very important people informed.

The Imperial Chancellery of the Austro-Hungarian Empire quietly informed the Emperor. This news was also relayed very discreetly through the most sensitive channels to the Heads of State and government of the major European Powers. All were assured that the matter was under control, Paris in particular. The existence of the secret was itself incendiary, maybe even now.

Vienna and the Vatican would continue to manage the situation. There was calm, the problem was now nearly fifty years old and had not come to light, the World had moved on, but not entirely. There was civil unrest to be managed, movements to be controlled, monitored and even stamped upon and empires were under threat from within and without.

In Vienna there was no doubt on the part of the Dyrektor of the Evidenzbureau[lx] that things needed taking in hand - the genie to be kept firmly in the bottle. In his regular private audience in the Emperor's study, where this hard-working man took a detailed and personal interest in the goings on across his vast empire and within his large and sometimes troublesome family, Emperor Franz Joseph had made it clear to him with few words. There must be no trouble. The Emperor had a long memory and an unforgiving nature in such matters. The Dyrektor knew his place, he was there to serve, to be effective and useful, not to fail.

III Rome – the Vatican

They had met to discuss a dilemma. The now elderly, Antonio Saverio De Luca, Vice-Chancellor of The Holy Roman Church (and Prefect of the Pontifical Congregation for Studies, Cardinal-Priest of San Lorenzo in Damaso and Cardinal-Bishop of Palestrina) was tired. On days like this he regretted the complexity of his offices that usually and for many years had driven and sustained him, even though he was now well into his seventies. Before him sat a man, now of middle age, of still remarkable visage, a man whom he had known for decades, a man brought up since birth in the shadows of the Vatican City and under the care of the Roman Church. Kindly care, but within firm limitations and supervision. That these factors had not prevented the events which brought them together again this morning had at first, months ago, come as a shock, now the challenges were more tangible and present.

Thinking back to their first conversation on this matter some five or six months ago, the Cardinal remembered that among the jumble of thoughts he had first entertained was surprise that his visitor, now in his late forties, should after all of these years produce a child and, remarkably, that the mother, in her early twenties[lxi], many years his junior, should be his cousin (of sorts), albeit so distantly related as not to be more than curious (this was not unknown among noble, or for that matter even royal families)[lxii][lxiii].

It was the very fact that there had appeared to those monitoring Albert to be nothing unusual in what had become his increasingly lengthy and regular visits to call upon his Kostrowicki cousins that had thrown his guardians off the scent. They had not guessed at the relationship developing between this mature man and his much younger pretty cousin. Any other female interest would have been reported on, with either party warned off. It had happened before. They were all caught out this time, but how could they have known?! The history of these families was impenetrable to most.

His musing over, his mind turned to the present. Now if this newly minted father were willing or even enthusiastic about denying paternity, and the mother not so stubborn, matters could be handled quite simply and traditionally. The child could be placed in an orphanage or found adoptive parents. That would be much the best outcome and would suit the Holy Father and those other very important persons who were looking to him to resolve this unfortunate and unwanted matter.

Strange, Antonio thought, that of all the pressing and complex matters of Church, State and Theology that sit upon my table, far away from my younger, simpler days in Sicily and as a priest in Monreale, I am drawn back into a matter of this kind, a pastoral, human, delicate and political matter. His visitor looked to him as his friend, in many respects his father, in place of the man he had never known, whose legacy, such as it was, he had been denied.

His visitor coughed politely, and the Cardinal turned his gaze, which had for a few glazed moments been trained out of the window of his large office in the Palazzo della Cancelleria and focused on him. "I suppose I must start by congratulating you. That would be usual. As you very well know, however, little that involves you is usual. Certainly not this. This should not have happened. I know that you know that. As your friend I understand the loneliness that your restrictions have placed upon you. I am a priest and chose the life I have led. You had no such choices to make."

His anxious visitor replied "but surely we can lead together the discreet life here in Rome which I have always lived and complied with? I have proved that I can be trusted. Together we can bring up our son as I was brought up, living here quietly for so many years. Our secret remains safe, for the safety of my child even more than my own. You of all people should understand that. When he is an adult, he can live a normal life, without attention, nearly a century will have passed, and the World will have forgotten. Please do this thing for me. I have asked for little, but this I ask for, I insist, I, I demand!", his emotion coming to the surface, pleading.

The Cardinal replied deliberately in his quiet measured tones that habitually never varied, "you are in no position to demand and I hope I need not remind you of the dangers for you, your child, his mother and those close to you. Threats can only make things worse, much worse even. Remember, I am your friend in this as in all things. Come again to see me in a few days - I will send for you. I must think and consult. Talk to no one; all depends on discretion. I will give you a final answer then."

IV Rome - the apartment

Torn by his mixed emotions - love for Angelika, for his new son Wilhelm and by his concerns and frail nascent hopes - Albert returned slowly and thoughtfully to the apartment shared by Angelika and her father, and now his new problematic grandchild.

Michael Apolinary Kostrowicki, Angelika's father, a soldier by profession, was a Papal Chamberlain, receiving a small stipend[lxiv], and devoutly Catholic. Michael, his wife, Julia Floriani, and young Angelika had emigrated to Rome in the 1860's, after the collapse of the 1863 Uprising, in which Michael Apolinary (then an officer in the Tsarist Army) and his brothers Jozef and Adam, with other relatives, had participated. Michael had escaped, but his brothers were marched off to Siberia in chains. The family's property was confiscated.[lxv]

In Rome they were grateful to find cousins. Albert became a regular visitor to their home, where he could hear stories of his maternal Ruthenian roots. Several Kostrowickis had served in his grandfather's armies. The secret of his birth was known by some within the family. This household had been a home to him, a place of refuge, for him and his mother, Melanie, during her visits to Rome. 'Family first' was the saying.

This home was now a place of complex emotions; very little heartfelt joy had greeted the new arrival, or earlier the revelation of this prospect. A pall hung over the place. These were damaged people living damaged lives. They were like criminals awaiting their sentencing. Powerless to intervene.

Practicality was the order of the day. Into this environment was born the great grandson of Napoleon Bonaparte and Marie Louise Habsburg. What was to be done?

V Rome – the Vatican

Colonel Karl Freiherr von Ripp paced uncomfortably and
irritably before Antonio De Luca. Although he thought
there were better uses for his time, he had impatiently but
nevertheless personally come by train from Vienna to
meet alone with the Cardinal. The Dyrektor of the
Evidenzbureau had no illusions as to the weak security
both of the telegraph and postal communications systems
between Rome and Vienna – after all, his agency
monitored them. They collected intelligence from various
sources and put these into daily reports to the Chief of
Staff and weekly reports to the Emperor. He also knew
interesting gossip material when he saw it! This
discussion was best had in person and best reported on in
person.

In the preceding minutes the Cardinal had related the
news, including the wishes of his ward.

"Your Eminence, this is a problem that we believed had
been managed and, in a decade or two, perhaps sooner,
would naturally and tidily end."

"Indeed Colonel, we are all responding to this unhappy
change of circumstance. You have no doubt been
apprised of the full situation by your predecessor,
Colonel von Leddihn, including of the existence of, shall

we call them certain longstanding sureties?"

Annoyed that the Prince of the Church seated in front of him should have casually questioned his access to sensitive matters touching on the Imperial Family, the Freiherr bristled, but let it pass.

"What does the Church suggest, your Eminence?"

"The Church, indeed, the Holy See, has been a sanctuary and a home, overseeing this situation these many years. The child became a man, and he caused no upset, no harm. Political foundations have not been challenged or shaken, despite the storms that blew abroad or even here in Rome. His mother and her family have sacrificed much over the years to support him. He has asked for little. Now he asks for his son. A son that at this stage in his life he did not expect - but greets with understandable joy."

"Yes, yes, but come to the point please your Eminence", the Colonel urged rudely. He wanted to get to his reserved cabin on the evening overnight train and back to Vienna.

The Vice-Chancellor of The Holy Roman Church, Prefect of the Pontifical Congregation for Studies, Cardinal-Priest of San Lorenzo in Damaso and Cardinal-Bishop of Palestrina was not to be rushed, certainly not by a jumped up policeman, for in his eyes that was what this colonel truly was.

"Indeed, Colonel. Please do sit down," he urged. Colonel von Ripp looked closely into those orbs of dark

Sicilian stone and sensed for the first time the inner strength of the man he was dealing with. Between the owner of those imperious eyes which bore into him weekly as he reported in a private study in the Hofburg or, more inconveniently, at Schonbrunn, and those of the Prince of the Church now contemplating him, the Colonel was coming to feel his options were limited, an uncomfortably deflating sensation for one usually handled with care, even fear, and not at all what he had expected as he travelled here and even when he had arrived. Of course, he had not met Antonio De Luca before. De Luca's time as Apostolic Nuncio, or ambassador, to the Imperial Austrian Court had preceded his own elevation into court or diplomatic affairs. The young man from Sicily, who had won friends in Vienna, had come much further, he respected that. Von Ripp slowed and sat down where indicated, looking at the Cardinal. He would listen.

"Certainly, the initial news that there would be another generation was an unwelcome surprise. That was months ago, and we have had time to anticipate Signor Kostrowicki's state of mind and likely paternal affections and wishes. He is a lonely unfulfilled man of promise but with no outlet for its application. What else should we expect? He is not heartless, far from it, something of a romantic, which I believe is endemic in his mother's family and probably why we are where we are and he is where he is, for that matter. It does appear that history is repeating itself, if you will pardon the use of the expression here [the Colonel's face sought to be disappointingly impervious]. He is also in love and with a lively young woman many years his junior who is willing to make a life with him. He imagines himself on the verge of a new life. Something of The Count of Monte Cristo perhaps." This was too much for the Colonel.

"Your Eminence, I really must insist...." He began, to be cut off. "Quite so, Colonel. You have to admit, however, that in all of this there is an extraordinary story, a love story against a background of power and loss, one fit for the theatre or even opera. Even Cardinals are allowed such occasional pleasures."

Having caused the Colonel's mind to begin to race and heat, the Cardinal moved on. "So, let us be serious. Where we succeeded before we can succeed again", and with that the two debated and eventually agreed upon a course of action, one that had worked before.

Before taking his leave the Dyrektor of the Evidenzbureau spoke. "Can you assure me that the Kostrowicki's, all those involved, will abide by this? It doesn't seem to me that Albert is in a frame of mind to listen, as for the child's mother....".

De Luca replied: "He will argue but he will come to agree. She will resist, with even greater passion at first, but she will agree more readily than him, because I can offer them something that they will truly prize" and, looking into the quizzical blue eyes of the Austrian policeman before him he added one word.

When later the evening train to Vienna pulled out of

Rome, the Dyrektor of the Evidenzbureau sipped at a glass of chilled delicate Gavi di Gavi, sighed, examined the menu on the white and silver bedecked table before him and enjoyed the moving views of the City of Seven Hills, satisfied that his journey had been worthwhile and that he could now again face the Emperor. He dined alone, secure in the knowledge that he had taken his own precautions. After all, from what he had learned through studying the chapters of this ongoing story, the women involved were not to be underestimated.

VI Vienna

At her bureau, by the window, in the mixed rays of the setting late Summer sunshine, warmed by glow of the gas lights only recently lit by her housekeeper, Melanie Kostrowicka sat writing, a short letter. It contained an invitation that would have unsettled von Ripp had he been watching over her shoulder. Melanie had reached conclusions that afternoon. Over the course of much of the night before – she regularly suffered from insomnia – and during the day she had been alternately travelling back in her mind and running through broken images of those events which had come to shape her life, that of her son and now would define the path of the grandson she had believed would never come. The cycle would continue.

As she wrote she felt the unexpected beginnings of

optimism. It brought the hint of a smile to the once beautiful face of this now old lady who had had to be strong from so early, for so many years, strong for her son, strong for the father he had never known and with whom she had shared only a short, exciting, heady and frightening time, once she had entered the 'gilded cage'. Through such powerful emotions, lives are shaped, and some are drawn to the flame where most others draw back. It was in her blood and he had recognized it in her and drawn her in, willingly. Strength she only later learned she possessed. She had loved him from the first. He was a beautiful, clever, witty, talented caged bird. Not to be petted or trained, but a bird of prey, an eaglet eager to soar - chained by circumstance. A man who could nevertheless change her life and did. A man who could have shaken and shaped wider events, but who was crushed by the mantle of his inheritance and expired. Too, too early. A tear fell. Rare these days; she was nonplussed.

VII Rome

Angelika was unhappy. Angry and plain difficult. Kostrowicki women were not be messed with, a genetic trait. And she was still feeling tired, sore and unwell from the birth, the result of which was announcing himself less endearingly and with more regular noise and demands than she had anticipated, despite prescient voices of experience.

He had returned to her the day before in low spirits. Hoping for understanding, she had dis-abused him of the notion. He had eventually spent a miserable night alone in his own rooms.

That Angelika was fiery, intelligent and strong minded was part of her appeal. He had watched her growing up. She was wonderful when in a silken mood, could even be gay and brilliant, but that was small comfort when the mercury dropped, clouds came over and the thunder and lightning swiftly followed, or worse, froideur, which she did very well.

Becoming a father had its exciting and alluring side, but it was dawning on him rapidly that the theory and practice of these conditions were not aligned and that his experience to date was based upon the solitary life of a bachelor, the only self-determination he had really known. Other than, of course, the heady affair into which he had found himself steadily, and then suddenly and deliciously drawn once his cousin had manifestly grown up. He loved her of course and the boy, the wonderful boy, even more, if that were possible, he reminded himself. He would have to fight - finally he had a cause! Something truly worthwhile. Thank God. It must be meant. Surely, they would agree.

VIII St Petersburg

Alexander II Aleksandrovich Romanov, Tsar, Autocrat of

All The Russias had at least this in common with his ally Emperor Franz Jozef, he kept a close eye on problems and smaller problems which could become bigger ones, even threats. There was an endless stream of problems, he thought wearily. Despite all the ministers, courtiers, aides-de-camp, generals, secretaries, other officials, bureaucrats and hangers-on at his command, eager to be seen to help and to advance themselves, he knew that he must keep a firm grip on affairs himself. How else would things get done?

He was helped in this regard by the Third Section - his eyes and ears, they extended tentacles across his vast empire, with many paid informers and others eager for rewards, large or small. The Third Section was feared, he was sure this was necessary. He had, so far, survived several assassination attempts, the most recent only months ago. How else could he protect his people, his huge domain, his family and his inheritance, God-given as it was. The misguided had to be dealt with, it was the only way. It was not a matter of a lack of finer feelings, quite the opposite, but he could be ruthless when necessary.

It was in this frame of mind, and with this inner certainty, that he sat, surrounded by family photographs, reading the letter which had come for him by hand under the seal of Franz Joseph.

After the usual pleasantries came a paragraph which caused him to put down the coffee cup he held in his other hand, sipping at it absentmindedly until now.

Franz Jozef had written: "There is news from Rome concerning the matter relating to the bee that once buzzed around both our houses. There is another bee in the hive. The grandson has begotten a son of his own. By one of your subjects and, by remarkable coincidence, another young woman of the same family that gave rise to the problem in the first place - Angelika Kostrowicki[lxvi]. She is the 22 year-old daughter of an émigré subject of yours, Michael Apolinary Kostrowicki, who lives in Rome also. A soldier and Papal Chamberlain. We are informed that he and his brothers were rebels in 1863 and he was a deserter from your Majesty's Army. It was reported long ago that the two had met because of the obvious coincidence of being in this small city. The matter is being managed."

Yes, it would certainly have to be managed, thought Alexander to himself. It was long ago, but from a boy he had been made well aware of how nearly the Romanov throne had been to being toppled by Napoleon and of the terrible destruction and loss to the Motherland which had been wreaked in 1812, when the vast Grande Armee had crossed into the Empire, with Moscow itself shamefully abandoned to the enemy - then burned by its defenders. That his namesake and forebear and his generals had turned this series of bloody defeats into final victory, could not disguise how close they had been to disaster. It was through the inner strength of Russia and its people that, with God's will and anger at this insult, we sacrificed, suffered, fought, prevailed and inflicted a terrible just retribution.

He sent for Count Mikhail Loris-Melikov, the very capable Head of the Third Section and his Minister of the Interior.

IX Paris

The Third Republic established after the loss at Sedan had somehow survived the period of turmoil, self-doubt and examination that had followed ignominious military defeat at the hands of Prussian military might, wiping away what had remained of French military pride. Disagreement over selection had prevented the enthronement of a monarch, however constitutionally constrained and so some ten years later, despite wide political and economic divisions amid the weight of reparations to Prussia, a true French republic was beginning to take root. A country that did not see itself as needing a paternal dynastic leader and figurehead. In this it represented an existential threat to the established hereditary monarchies of Europe. One compounded by the role Paris had long played as an incubator of free thinkers and liberals. Only in the USA could a similar political experiment be found on such scale. To Autocrats such as the rulers of Austria, Russia and Prussia, to Britain under Queen Victoria and to lesser monarchs, these were dangerous precedents.

Only a very few were aware of the existence of Albert Kostrowicki. The communications from the Vatican, from Vienna and from their own agents in Rome revealing the birth of another generation, was unwelcome news - it reminded them of an old problem, so far contained.

X Berlin

Prince Otto von Bismarck, now the elder statesman of Europe, had served his Kaiser, Wilhelm I, to great effect. Together they had united the German states, kingdoms and lesser principalities, under Prussia and created the German Empire, the predominant military and economic power in Central Europe. Resented by Austria and France (both smarting from military defeats and losses) and a wary Russia, Bismarck saw it as his task to prevent cooperation between these powers and neighbours against Germany.

He too received news of this birth, news that he shared with the Kaiser, together with the assurances that the matter would be contained.

XI Vienna

The following evening at precisely 9 pm the doorbell rang. Her neighbours would have been surprised to see that Melanie open the heavy front door herself (her servants having been dismissed for the evening). Her maid, Agniezka, had not thought to question the motives for the gift of a pair of tickets to the operetta, or the encouraged absence. Her employer had long been kind; she was more of a companion, carer and even friend than a housekeeper. Another noble daughter of the East whose family had fallen on hard times, also punished for standing up against the foreign invader. Her loyalties were firmly with Melanie.

There was only the low glow of an oil lamp in the hall, barely lighting the interior or the face of her visitor, unremarkably dressed in a well-cut black woollen overcoat and hat, having unobtrusively descended from the curtained black cab (a fiacre), typical of the street cabbies for hire in Vienna (though closer examination by an expert in horseflesh of the pair of dark potent animals that drew it would risk belying this picture), with its stocky driver seated patiently upon it. He knew what his master expected of him, absolute discretion and unwavering vigilance, ready (and armed) when needed, anticipating danger, exciting no unwanted attention. An Empire might depend on it, an Emperor certainly did. He was proud of his job, as only a Guardsman can be. He loved his master, whom he had long watched over, as he was doing now, unobtrusively vigilant, noticing everything.

It was sometimes difficult to remember to slouch, too stiff a posture would be remarkable, he must remember. Some habits were ingrained. Hardest of all had been learning, when in sight or earshot of strangers, to treat his charge with the apparent respectful indifference cabbies habitually show their passing trade. Also deflecting those other cabbies who showed too much interest. He only ever carried a very few passengers - his master, his mistress and those whom they occasionally instructed he carry. How else could an emperor and empress get about in private? Safety relying on anonymity.

With the sounds and any prying eyes of the street shut out, Melanie curtseyed as best she might these days. A sight that certainly would have gained curious attention as would the mustachioed face of her visitor, an image readily recognizable by the millions over whom he ruled. Her Imperial caller removed his overcoat and hat, placed them on a hall chair with his cane and greeted her with the words: "I am here Madame." "Thank you for coming, Your Majesty. We are alone. Please come through." With that she indicated politely the door to her salon and without saying more they went into the heavily curtained room and he, having motioned her to do so, they came to sit by the fire, facing one another. He did not accept the refreshment offered. He had no intention of staying longer than strictly necessary. This was not a social call, but business, awkward business at that.

The Emperor considered himself experienced at gauging those he met. It was a vital attribute. Briefed on events in Rome he believed he knew the subject matter to come. What else could have motivated her to write that she needed to speak to him in person on a matter touching on "L'Aiglon" (the Eaglet), a term he had not heard for many years, knowing he was hardly likely to refuse, much that he might prefer to. He had sent back a brief handwritten note by the same messenger, also a Polish woman, who at his bidding was ushered to him and then waited as he had asked.

That evening he had used his preferred most private means of getting about Vienna (indistinguishable from the average bourgeois, he assumed). It was sometimes necessary and occasionally a discreet means to pleasure, even a little adventure. Von Ripp and his predecessors must surely have its registration number and receive reports from his driver, but he paid the driver very well, more than enough so that not all of his excursions would be reported. Even an emperor must have some secrets from his own agencies. He waited, and regarded this elderly, but still handsome woman, who had been beautiful to the point of turning the head of a king who never ruled. Franz Joseph (himself born not long before Albert Kostrowicki) realized that he was curious to meet her. That thought made him feel better for coming.

Melanie began "Your Majesty I have disturbed you because I feel I must. I have heard news from my son. News that ..." "you have a grandson, Madame", her august guest completed the sentence. Melanie's eyes narrowed, "I have a grandson, Your Majesty", she agreed. There was a pause, while Melanie took in the obvious conclusion that, as she should have anticipated, her mail was intercepted or, just as likely, the Emperor's information network still extended its interest to the affairs of her family, or perhaps both applied, as he had chosen to remind her. They were in a web and its threads lead back to the autocrat now in her salon.

"I have asked to see Your Majesty so that I may, for my son and my new grandson request, beg if that will help, as my son deeply desires, that they, with the child's mother, be allowed to live together in Rome as did I and my son those many years ago."

"Madame, I have been made aware of the arrival. You will have to pardon me for not greeting this information with joy."

"Your Majesty know that if anything untoward happens to this baby boy his great-grandmother's instructions will be followed. His legacy and his loss will be made public in the broadest manner. He is to be protected as has my son been protected."

"You are very clear Madame. Impertinent, but very clear. We are in 1880, not 1820. Remember that. The World has moved on."

"It has moved on, but some memories are long. Your Majesty would not have come to see this old woman if my words could have no meaning for you."

He made no promise, nor did he object. Melanie was wise not to press him harder. She knew he would not be pushed by her to express a commitment, that like all men of great power and responsibilities, he could be very dangerous and should not be provoked, unless no other option existed. She could also read the faces of men. Without further meaningful communication he departed much as he had come.

Melanie went back into her salon and seated herself in her habitual chair. She was satisfied; he would not allow harm to come to her new grandson. Franz's mother had seen to that long ago, but she had not needed to remind him, she now knew. Warmed by this thought she mused and then slept until, an hour or so later, an excited Agnieszka returned with news of the evening's merry dramatic entertainment, oblivious of the visitor she had missed. Melanie instructed her to make hot chocolate for both of them and to sit down and tell her all about her evening.

XII St Petersburg

Count Mikhail Loris-Melikov, Head of the Third Section and Minister of the Interior, stood as he addressed his sovereign, Tsar Aleksander II, the man to whose life, family and Empire his own destiny was attached. "Your Majesty, her father, Michael Apolinary Kostrowicki of the crest Prawdzic, is the brother of two of the Kostrowicki's banished to Siberia for treasonous participation in the 1863 rebellion, their property confiscated."

"You also asked about Melanie Kostrowicki. She would be about 67 years old, the daughter of Count Samuel Kostrowicki, crest Bajbuza. This branch of the Kostrowicki family comes from Papiernia and Koscieniew, near Lida. He was a captain in the army of

Bonaparte that invaded our Motherland. He emigrated and settled in Vienna, where he was received at the Court and was active in emigre and opposition circles. It is an old Ruthenian family with deep roots in Belarus and Lithuania and before, under the name Obakunovich, in Veliky Novgorod, until it was shown the error of its ways by Ivan Vasilievich[lxvii]. Those who were either already there or who fled became office holders and courtiers of the Lithuanian Grand Dukes and Polish Kings and landowners in Belarus and Lithuania. Three hundred years ago, after The Time of Troubles[lxviii] this family took in the descendants of that Oscik whose mother was a Mstislavska and who supported Fyodor Ivanovich's candidacy to be King of Poland and Grand Duke in Vilnius. They were cousins of Prince Fyodor Ivanovich Mstislavski, whom Your Majesty will remember was leader of the Council of Seven Boyars, of which your great uncle Ivan Nikitich was a member, before the enthronement of your Blessed great great grandfather Mikhail Fyodorovich". He waited; there was a nod and he continued. "The descendants of these Osciks and this Mstislavska are that branch of the Kostrowicki family who lived near Minsk, whose property, Navasiolki[lxix], in the district of Dzierżyńsk, near Kojdanów, Your Majesty confiscated in 1864 and members of which were sent to Siberia, for conspiracy and treason against Your Majesty in the 1863 rebellion." Aleksander looked stern.

"This family has no reason to love Your Majesty. What, however, has caused Your Majesty's particular interest now, may I ask?", with which question he stopped and looked closely at Aleksander Nikolayevich, hoping to have his curiosity satisfied. The Kostrowicki's (whether Obakunovich's or Oscik/Mstislavskis) were perhaps interesting, but no more so than many other reluctant subjects from Moscow's more recently acquired Western domains, noble families of boyar origins whose privileges had been restricted, removed or squeezed. This was to be expected. A byproduct of the extension of the Romanov view of a greater Russia, a new Rome, the successor to Byzantium, Constantinople, the Roman Empire of the East, until its fall, in 1453, the centre of the Orthodox Church, a mantle now inherited by Moscow.

Having received his master's request for information he had asked his deputies in Vilnius and Minsk for background information and details and suspicions of current activities. There appeared to be nothing which would warrant the Tsar's own attention, nor, in particular (which irked and worried him) would have given rise to his master hearing about it before him, or otherwise than through him. Something might be very wrong, and he felt exposed. They must have missed something. If so, his deputies had better watch out! They would feel his anger. Networks of spies and secret policemen required a goodly dose of fear, as well as the prospect of reward. Zeal was not enough or reliable as a driving force.

Aleksander, who had listened to him impassively as he had delivered his report, moved on to the next topic. Now that was interesting, thought Loris-Melikov. I really must look further into this. It did not occur to him to expect an explanation or to be annoyed; autocrats are different to other men. He himself expected his own subordinates to be respectful and dutiful.

XIII Rome

It was days later that Albert was summoned to his follow up meeting with Cardinal De Luca. Days in which they had fretted.

The judgement was what he had hoped for. They could be together, in Rome, but only in Rome.

On 31 August 1880 the Registrar of the City of Rome was 'informed' of the birth, five days earlier, of a male child whose mother wanted to remain anonymous and whose father was 'unknown' (entered as 'N.N.'). The child's name was given as Guillaume-Albert Dulcigni. On 29 September 1880 the same child, now said to have been born on 25 August at 5 a.m., was baptised with the names of Guillelmus Apollinaris Albertus de Kostrowitzky, son of Angelica de Kostrowitzky (sic). The father was still not identified. A month later, on 2 November, Madame de Kostrowitzky officially recognised her son. She would always call him Wilhelm.

Angelika and Wilhelm continued to live in Rome until 1887, when they moved to Monaco. We do not know for how much of this time Albert was with them. Another son was born in 1882, named Alberto Zevini, father 'N.N.', not known and mother not named (hence 'Zevini', the name provided by the registrar, as was custom in such cases). In 1888 Angelika 'recognised' Alberto, who was re-registered as Alberto de Kostrowitzky (later, in France, he dropped the 'o').

We should note an important event. In South Africa, in 1879, a brave young man, a soldier brought up and educated in England had died, his body pierced many times, by the hands of the Zulu enemies of Britain. Queen Victoria was deeply saddened, she had been very fond of Napoléon Eugène Louis Jean Joseph Bonaparte, Prince Imperial, the son and heir of Napoleon III, who had moved to England with his family when his father was dethroned in 1870. When his father had died in 1873 hopeful Bonapartists had declared him Napoleon IV, but of course this had not transpired. It was widely recognised as the end of any hope for the House of Bonaparte to rule in France again.

Napoleon III (1808–1873), his wife Empress Eugénie (1826–1920) and their son the Prince Imperial (1856–1879) were exiled from France in 1870. They came to live in Chislehurst, in England. Napoleon III died in 1873 and was buried at St Mary's in Chislehurst.

After the tragic death of her son, Napoleon IV, or Prince Imperial, Eugénie built a lasting monument to her family. She founded the Benedictine Abbey of St. Michael in Chislehurst in 1881, there erecting a mausoleum, the Imperial Crypt, for her late husband and son (based upon on the altar of St Louis, where her husband had wished to be interred). Empress Eugénie was later interred together with her husband and son. They lie in granite sarcophagi (as arranged by Queen Victoria).

In Vienna, on 27 November 1884, Fanny Elssler, who had been ailing in recent years, passed away, aged 74. Her body was interred at Hietzinger Friedhof Cemetery[lxx], with a splendid gravestone, in that grave bought many years earlier by her late friend and would-be-husband, Graf Samuel Kostrowicki. They would finally be side by side.

We do not know when Albert Kostrowicki, Melanie's son, passed away. That Angelika moved with her sons from Rome to Monaco in 1887 would be consistent with him being gone by then.

You will remember that Jan Kostrowicki in his letter of 28 November 1958 to Anatol Stern, wrote "Now to tell [about] my father and the events of the story [above].... A dozen or so years before the day when my father related this to me and my older brother, he visited his aunt..., Melanie Kostrowicka, already an old woman, living in Vienna in her own home on one of the main streets, the name of which I do not now remember." He also informed Stern that his father, Marcin, had related this story to him and his brother in 1903 or 1904. On this basis we may assume that Marcin visited Vienna in about 1888, in effect soon after Angelika and her sons had left Rome. That Melanie would also then be tidying her affairs, finally, passing Franz's relicts to her family at Koscieniew rather than to her son in Rome is consistent with Albert being gone. To pass these items, themselves a burden and clear tell-tales, to Angelika for her sons, would have been both dangerous and impractical. She could see no better solution - and it was impractical for her brother's family to come and continue in Vienna. This was closure.

Melanie, born in 1813, was now an elderly lady too and would pass away in 1889 (the year in which Jan Kostrowicki was born). She was buried at Hietzing in the same plot as Fanny Elssler, next to that of her family[lxxi] Marcin Kostrowicki, Jan's father, son of Melanie's brother Lucjan (who had died in 1867), owner of what remained of the family's property in Belarus/Lithuania, living at Koscieniew, learned that he would not receive the 'Kostrowicki Palace' in Vienna, visited by him, nor indeed its contents or any other property from his Viennese relatives, save for those curiosities, boxes, papers, portraits, paintings, maps and other items, some bearing references to the erstwhile King of Rome or Duke of Reichstadt, that his Aunt Melanie had sent back home with him, now kept at Koscieniew.

The Church had not forgotten them, nor various secular authorities, in Vienna and elsewhere. The Benedictine Order was close to the heart of the matter, of which we shall learn more.

An old respected noble family, servants of the Vatican and of King Ferdinand II of the Two Sicilies, closely related and allied to the Habsburgs (his paternal grandmother was Maria Carolina of Austria, his second wife Maria Theresa of Austria) and therefore to Franz, supplied a cover story for Angelika and her two now 'fatherless' sons as they moved to Monaco. It was a scandalous one - a difficult service for such a conservative family - but therefore all the more plausible.

232

Francesco Costantino Camillo Flugi d'Aspermont[lxxii] was already the black sheep of the family, a colourful adventurer - a little more colour would not make much difference, especially in a good cause supported by his family, the Church and the authorities (in fact these features probably amused him).

It was put about that Angelika had been Francesco's mistress in Rome and that, it could be inferred, her sons were by him - an aristocrat who lived for a time in Rome, with close links to the Church, whose brother, Dom Romarino Flugi (born Niccolo Flugi d'Aspermont), was General (Abbott) of the Benedictine Order - an order with strong historical affiliations with the Habsburgs and one that had become associated with the Bonapartes, as we have seen. From 1885 Francesco was gone from Rome - and disappeared, conveniently.

Angelika would, for a time, receive money from Dom Romarino[lxxiii]. Dom Romarino also arranged the education of Wilhelm and Albert by Marian Fathers in Monaco. Wilhelm excelled, remaining in Monaco until he moved to Nice early in 1897 to study for his baccalaureat. He lived in France for most of his life.

Angelika lived on, close to her sons. She would outlive Wilhelm (Apollinaire), but only just. Many colourful stories would continue to be attributed to her.

So much has been written about Guillaume Apollinaire, regarded as one of the leading French language poets of the 20th Century, defender of Cubism, forefather of Surrealism, friend to many now famous artists, writers and others. Others are much better qualified to write of him and on his contributions to his times. That he struggled with his identity and with how to respond to it is known. In his own way, he told us much, but he will have known more. It was only in 1916, during WWI, that he revealed his identity in 'Le Poète assassiné' - by then revolution was in the air. Wounded in that year, he never fully recovered and passed away on 9 November 1918, one of so many victims of the flu pandemic who had survived the carnage of the Great War. Wilhelm was interred in the Père Lachaise Cemetery, in Paris.

As Apollinaire died, so did the age of empires - Austria, Germany, Russia, all swept away, their dynasties no longer relevant. We now cannot know what more he might have felt free to reveal in subsequent years. A relatively young man, aged 38, he left his widow of one year, Jacqueline Kolb, but no children.

What happened to the precious items (proofs) kept at Koscieniew, those brought back from Vienna by Marcin Kostrowicki after his visit to his Aunt Melanie? In his letter of 28 November 1958[lxxiv] to Anatol Stern, Jan Kostrowicki explained that, his father having died in 1905, he and his brother Stanisław learned no more from him. The boys were sent away to school. Jan wrote that there were numerous documents, including letters in trunks that his father had brought back from Vienna to Koscieniew. Access to them was difficult, because only a few years after their father's death, he and his brother were sent off to school, and their stepmother and her relations remained at Koscieniew.

It was not until 1914, when the German army occupied Poland, and their stepmother had left for the Lublin region to go to her parents, that he and his brother remained and, even though they now had access to Great Aunt Melanie's memorabilia, there was no time to read the documents and letters. Instead, the brothers packed these mementos, including all of the portraits, pictures, prints, engravings and drawings, into strong sealed chests so that at any time they would be easier to hide or move.

In 1914, the Tsarist Russian Army chose Koscieniew as their staff headquarters. Jan and his wife were allowed to stay in the manor house, living in one room. His brother Stanisław was managing the estate (of approximately 1,000 ha.) of their uncle, Wincenty Sieklucki, at Strzelica[lxxv] - Uncle had left the house and gone to join their stepmother (he was married to her sister, Felicja Nowakowska).

The Russians told him to remove anything of value. All valuables, carefully and securely packaged, were moved to Strzelica, which lay on the sidelines of communication roads, among swampy lakes and forests. They hoped their possessions would be safe there. News from the front and from areas under German occupation soon had them worrying. The retreating Russians were destroying everything, leaving nothing behind them. The Germans were plundering anything of value and repatriating what they took to Germany.

The Russian forces were falling back to the River Niemen, where they intended to hold a new line and halt the German advance - Strzelica would be overrun.

Responding to these rumours, Stanisław decided to take all of the portraits to Sieniezyce[lxxvi], a property belonging to another of their relatives (Stanisław Jundziłł[lxxvii]), behind the intended Russian lines. He also, alone, took all of the remaining chests of items and buried them in the Strzelin forest.

Jan found that, although he had fulfilled his military service obligation and should not have been required to do so, he was ordered by the Chief of Staff of the Russian Army Corps operating there to prepare to leave, with the staff. Despite protests and holding the relevant discharge papers he had to comply.

The result was that at the end of the Summer of 1915 Jan and his wife, each driving a cart, were obliged to leave Koscieniew in the middle of night, taking only some personal items and food. They were not trusted by the Russians and their carts were parked later in the midst of a large staff camp. It was not until the staff departed for Minsk that they were able to leave.

Stanisław Kostrowicki had remained at Strzelica. He suffered under the German occupation and died in 1918. The German forces were not held at the Niemen and soon seized Sieniezyce, from where they stripped everything of value, including the portraits brought from Koscieniew for safety, sending these back to Germany to a (so far) unknown destination or fate.

Jan wrote to Stern that "When, after the end of the war, I returned to Koscieniew, I did not find my brother of course, and the people in Strzelica[lxxviii], although they knew about my brother's removal of the chest (with files and other things), they could not point out where all of this was hidden. So all traces that can cast light on Apollinaire's interest [for us] have disappeared for now."

It is therefore possible that, whether through investigative research or quirks of fate, some of the missing items - including those that were once the precious mementos of Melanie Kostrowicka and Franz, Duke of Reichstadt - may in time be found, whether in Germany, in Belarus or elsewhere.

It is easier to find something that you believe exists. Of course, the Church itself, keeps records.

----

[i] Alexandre Florian Joseph, Count Colonna-Walewski (born 4 May 1810; died 27 September 1868).

[ii] Lucien Bonaparte, fell out with Napoleon, his brother, and tried to escape to America, was captured by the British and well treated in Britain, where he was seen as anti-Napoleon, being allowed to live comfortably with his family at Ludlow and later in Worcestershire, until he returned to France in 1814.

[iii] He wrote in French (the diplomatic language of the age)
"Altesse royale, en butte aux factions qui divisent mon pays et à l'inimitié des plus grandes puissances de l'Europe, j'ai consommé une carrière politique, et je viens, comme Thémistocle, m'asseoir au foyer du peuple Britannique. Je me mets sous la protection de ses lois que je réclame de votre altesse royale comme du plus puissant, du plus constant et du plus généreux de mes ennemis. Ile d'Aix, 13 juillet 1815. Napoléon".

[iv] Savary, one of the last to leave the Emperor on his abdication in April 1814, had been among the first to welcome his return from Elba. From Plymouth he and Lallemand were taken to Malta and imprisoned ("interned"). They escaped after two months. Savary made his way to Smyrna. In financial difficulties, he travelled. He later was permitted to return to France, settling later in Rome. After the July Revolution (1830) was rehabilitated and commanded a French army in Algeria.

Lallemand made his way back to England. In Liverpool, together with another French officer, he was smuggled on board an American merchant vessel, the Triton. They were then moved by small boat from ship to ship to avoid the British authorities, boarding and inspecting vessels and their rolls. They arrived in Boston in April 1817. Lallemand became president of the French Emigrant Association, which obtained a grant of four townships in Alabama for a vine and olive company. Rumours circulated that Lallemand would attempt to rescue Napoleon and put Joseph on a throne in South America. He returned to France after the July Revolution of 1830, serving as military governor of Corsica (1837-1838).

[v] Aside from two wives, more than 20 mistresses have been

recorded; he was often financially generous toward them.

[vi] A French officer who had met Schulmeister wrote: "I was curious to see this man, of whom I had heard a thousand marvellous tales. He inspired the Viennese with as much terror as an army corps. His physique is in keeping with his reputation. He has a bright eye, a piercing glance, his countenance is stern and resolute, his gestures are abrupt, and his voice is sonorous and strong. He is of middle height but very sturdy...of a full-blooded temperament. He has a perfect knowledge of Austrian affairs and his portraits of its leading personalities are masterly. On his brow there are deep scars, which prove that he has not run away from dangerous situations. He is generous too: he is bringing up two orphans whom he has adopted."

[vii] Schulmeister made various attempts at new business ventures, each of which failed. He eventually acquired a tobacco shop in Strasbourg, through a friend, where he lived out a quiet life, in full view of the watchful authorities. He died in 1853.

[viii] Gourgaud remained an ardent and loyal supporter of his patron. He remained an active member of the Bonapartist Party until 1830. Rehabilitated (Commander of the Artillery in Paris (1830), appointed Lieutenant General (1835), made a Peer of France (1841), he was among those who returned to St Helena in 1840 to accompany Napoleon's body on its return to France. He then sought to include de Montholon in this mission, but unsuccessfully – de Montholon was imprisoned at the time with Louis Napoleon (later Napoleon III)), Gourgaud attended the interment of Napoleon at Les Invalides (along with an estimated one million others who turned out on the streets of Paris for this momentous spectacle).

^{ix} Marchand kept a meticulous written record in the form of a diary. This was published for the first time in 1955. He also kept hairs from the head of the dead Emperor, shaved off his corpse a day after his death on St Helena. Scientific analysis indicated substantial doses of arsenic over a long and intermittent period. This has been disputed.

^x Louis-Joseph Marchand subsequently married Mathilde Brayer, daughter of Napoleonic General Michel Silvestre Brayer. He was confirmed as a count by Napoleon III in 1869 and admitted to the Order of the Legion d'Honneur.

^{xi} The French writer and poet Auguste Barthelemy sought to meet the Duke to present his own latest work. Count Maurice Dietrichstein was charged by the Duke's Grandfather, Emperor Francis, and by Metternich with overseeing the upbringing, security and affairs of the Duke; in effect he was his gaoler and keeper, responsible to the Emperor and his chief counsellor. Dietrichstein refused permission for Barthelemy to meet the Duke, describing the Duke's situation with these words. This prompted Barthelemy to compose the poem 'Le Fils de l'homme" and to coin the the concept of an Eaglet in the Golden Cage of Schonbrunn Palace.

^{xii} The Dietrichstein Family owes its wealth and position to its long service and devotion to the Habsburgs, to whom they are related. Siegmund von Dietrichstein (1484 – 1533) was elevated to the noble rank of Freiherr by Emperor Maximilian I and purchased Hollenburg Castle in 1514. Siegmund married the Emperor's illegitimate daughter Barbara von Rottal (1500 – 1550), and he was said to have been favoured by the Emperor as a son. Siegmund and Barbara's great-granddaughter, Regina von Dietrichstein (d.1630) was married (2nd voto) to Kryštof Adam Vencelík z Vrchovišt a na Třešťi (d.1626). Jeremy Moczarski's Great Grandmother, Maria

Waleria Wentzl (1854 – 1937), wife of Ludwik Antoni Moczarski vel Mocarski, was from the well-known Polish Wentzl Family, patrician Krakow merchants and bankers, descended from the Vencelík z Vrchovišt a na Třešťi Family, from Bohemia.

[xiii] Born in Hungary to a family of Saxon aristocratic origins, he was a Dominican friar and military chaplain. In 1817 he became the confessor of Marie Louise and worked to regularise the cohabitation between her and von Neipperg. He received various honours and became Bishop of Parma in 1843 but was unpopular with both the local clergy (he was intransigent) and the local population (he was seen as an Austrian stooge).

[xiv] In 1854 an additional $8 million was allocated to fulfilling the testamentary dispositions of Napoleon.

[xv] Barings had had a longstanding acquaintance with Napoleon. In 1802, Barings and Hope & Co. (as it then was) facilitated the Louisiana Purchase (the largest land purchase in history). This was done (with political support in London) even though Britain was at war with France, and the sale helped to finance the French war effort. After a $3 million down payment in gold, the remainder of the purchase was made in United States bonds, which Napoleon sold to Barings through its partner Hope & Co. of Amsterdam. Alexander Baring, working for Hope & Co., first made the arrangements in Paris and then sailed to the United States to collect the bonds and then back to deliver them to the French Treasury.

[xvi] In 1853 Petrucci revealed this secret and testified that Revard was Napoleon I. It was safe to do so - in 1852 Napoleon's nephew, Louis-Napoleon, had ascended to the

French throne as Napoleon III.

[xvii] In 1872, there were published in Paris Anton von Prokesch-Osten's memoirs of his time with the Prince, entitled 'My relations with the Duke of Reichstadt' (translated from the original german into french as 'Mes Relations avec le duc de Reichstadt', edited and re-published by Jean de Bourgoing in 1925). This was two years after the decisive German victory at The Battle of Sedan, that resulted in the fall of the Second French Empire, the surrender, capture, and abdication of Napoleon III and the end of Bonapartism. It was published with official sanction, by the then elderly career diplomat, soldier and author, heavily rewarded by the Austro-Hungarian Crown, to whom he had remained a grateful and loyal servant throughout. It painted a kind but insipid picture of the prince, loved by his Austrian family and loving of his grandfather, Francis, willing to be a king, but only if the pathway were clear, with popular and official support and with the approval of his grandfather. A picture calculated to deflate any remaining Bonapartist talismanic reverence for this previously romantic figure. It largely succeeded. These impressions were reinforced by the publication of the "Intimate Papers and Journal of the Duke of Reichstadt" kept by Count Dietrichstein - itself translated into french, then edited and published by J. de Bourgoing in 1927. Censorship is an old concept. In the words of Dietrichstein, Prokesch was an "assiduous [agent] of Metternich and Gentz" who supported his advancement. Gentz would later write "what Prokesch got on ten different occasions is fabulous".

[xviii] Prince Eugene of Savoy (1663 – 1736) a general and statesman of the Holy Roman Empire and the Archduchy of Austria and one of the most successful military commanders in

modern European history.

xix The Polish–Russian War / November Uprising (1830–31), was an armed uprising in the centre of partitioned Poland, the heart of Europe, against the Russian Empire. It was started in Warsaw on 29 November 1830, when the young cadet officers attending the military academy of the Army of Congress (the proud rump of that army that once fought for Napoleon) rose in revolt. They were soon joined by large segments of Lithuania, Belarus and western parts of the Ukraine, all parts of the former Polish-Lithuanian Commonwealth (Rzeczpospolita). Despite some smaller successes, the uprising was eventually crushed by the much larger, better equipped and organised Russian Army of Tsar Nicholas I, who decreed that henceforth Poland was an integral part of Russia. Further repression followed.

xx The Rzeczpospolita was the Crown of the Kingdom of Poland and the Grand Duchy of Lithuania, after 1791 the Commonwealth of Poland, the confederation of Poland and Lithuania, ruled by a common monarch, who was both the King of Poland and the Grand Duke of Lithuania. It was among the largest and most populous countries of 16th Century and 17th Century Europe.

xxi At the invitation of Emperor Francis, the Bourbons moved to Prague in late 1832/33. After Francis died in March 1835, the Bourbons left Prague Castle, moving initially to Teplitz. Kirchberg Castle was eventually purchased for them.

xxii The Mayerling Affair (involving the mysterious death of Crown Prince Rudolf and his young lover Baroness Marie Vetsera in 1889), would in time shed light on what steps touching on the House of Habsburg were on occasion deemed necessary.

xxiii In 1850 Frederic Chopin published love letters, 'from the Duke of Reichstadt to his cousin'.

xxiv The Mexico adventure did not go well for him, he was later deposed and executed by firing squad.

xxv By Count Anton von Prokesch-Osten.

xxvi After Gentz's death Fanny was soon consoled in the arms of Anton Stuhlmuller, dancing by her side in Vienna and then Berlin, where Fanny, Therese and Anton went to appear in the Autumn. In Berlin they had a brief passionate affair, resulting in a daughter (born in Edinburgh on 26 October and cared for, for a time by Mrs Grote, with whom she stayed when the sisters visited London to perform, arriving in April 1833). In London Fanny was introduced to Count Alfred d'Orsay, and soon there were rumours of another affair; Fanny attracted such rumours.

xxvii Dubrovnik, Croatia.

xxviii From medieval times communities of secular canonesses were formed in which unmarried daughters and widows of the nobility could lead pious lives of devotion in relative comfort, with servants available, remaining free to marry, as some did. Some remained in their own homes. It was a form of retreat, without taking irrevocable vows. Such communities continue today.

xxix see p. 166, "Napoleon II" by Jean Tulard (pubd. by Fayard, 1992 ISBN 978-2-213-02966-5).

xxx Addressed to the surrealist poet and author Anatol Stern and shared by him on pp. 218 - 229 of his book "Dom Apollinaire'a" (House of Apollinaire), published in Krakow in 1973. This is an extract from that longer letter.

xxxi Marcin Kostrowicki h. Bajbuza (1855 - 1905).

xxxii Prince Nikolai Vasilyevich Repnin (1734 – 1801) was an Imperial Russian statesman and general who played a key role in the dissolution of the Polish-Lithuanian Commonwealth (Rzeczpospolita). In 1763 Empress Catherine (the Great) sent him to Poland as Minister Plenipotentiary, where he was the de facto governor. This privilege or letter was probably dated from that time. The original in the possession of this branch of the Kostrowicki family was lost in WWI and the consequent destruction and upheavals affecting Kosceniew, the family's estate situated near Lida. It was the practice of the Crown Chancellery to keep copies and records of such documents and this original may yet be found to have survived in one such collection still known today, e.g., the Moscow State Archives. Many of these items have not yet been catalogued or published.

xxxiii Count (in Latin) (the nearest British equivalent is an earl).

xxxiv A typical look of Polish and Lithuanian magnates and nobility in the 16th Century.

xxxv Manor house home of that branch of the Kostrowicki family, West of Vilnius.

xxxvi Also visited by your narrator's grandfather, Samuel Andrzej Lew-Ostik-Kostrowicki, his brothers (Daniel and Andrzej) and sisters (Maryla, Barbara and Krystyna).

xxxvii In 1812 Count Samuel Kostrowicki was a lieutenant in the

Horse Artillery of the Lithuanian Army, formed to fight for the freedom of Lithuania and which became part of the Grande Armee of Napoleon I that marched to Moscow. In January 1813 his unit was folded into the forces of the Grand Duchy of Warsaw, under Marshal Prince Jozef Poniatowski, in which Samuel was appointed a Captain of the Honour Guard of Prince Poniatowski and a Chevalier of the Legion d'Honneur. He would later be granted entry to France, listed as a 'Prussian Count'. A photograph of the undress uniform, epaulette and waistcoat of Lieutenant Samuel Kostrowicki, as an officer of the Horse Artillery Regiment of the Duchy of Warsaw (1810 - 1814) may be seen on p. 179 of 'Napoleon i Polacy' (Napoleon and the Poles) by Dom Wydawniczy Bellona, Warsaw and the Muzeum Wojska Polskiego w Warszawie (Polish Army Museum), ISBN 83-11-10121-3.

xxxviii Volynskaya region, which is situated in the north-west of Ukraine, borders on Poland and Belarus. Since the earliest times the region was a part of Kievan Rus. Later it was included into the Galitsko-Volynskoe principality ruled by the Rurikovich dynasty, then it became a part of Lithuania, Poland, and subsequently the Russian Empire.

xxxix Believed to be St. Cyr.

xl Melanie Kostrowicka (1813 - 1889) turned 18 in 1831; she was three years younger than Fanny Elssler.

xli The only such person at the Austrian Court was Franz, Duke of Reichstadt.

xlii Marcin Kostrowicki, the father of Jan, the author of this letter, died in 1905, the year after the conversation to which Jan refers took place. His widow, Princess Maria Massalska

(1863 - 1915) survived him by 10 years. His sons Stanisław (1888 - 1918) and Jan (1889 - 1967) were 17 and 16 and their sister, Zofia (1886 - 1943) 15 when their father died. The opportunity for Marcin to reveal more was lost with him. Only Jan survived WWI and WWII and into the years of the Soviet Union and Communism to disclose what he wrote carefully, for posterity. Jan was the father of two sons, Prof. Jerzy Samuel Kostrowicki (1918 - 2002), geographer, and Prof. Andrzej Samuel Kostrowicki (1921 - 2007), biogeographer. Jerzy (married to Irena Halina Czapska) had one daughter, Ania Kostrowicka.

[xliii] As your narrator can attest, the Kostrowicki ladies tend to be strong willed, forthright and independent, used to getting their way! These characteristics were typical of noblewomen from Eastern Poland/Lithuania/Belarus (known as Kresy, in the time of the Second Polish Republic, in the interwar period, 1919 - 1939).

[xliv] Essentially, a literary society, for authors and poets.

[xlv] Ehrengräber Friedhof Hietzing, Gr.06, Nr. 13. Here may be found the graves and tombs of many distinguished persons, soldiers, thespians and artists - such as Alban Berg, Franz Grillparzer, Otto Wagner, Gustav Klimt, Franz Conrad von Hötzendorf, Engelbert Dollfuß, Rudolf Prack, Heinz Conrads and many others (including, as we shall see, Fanny Elssler) - it is a beautiful place in a lovely setting.

[xlvi] During the Congress of Vienna he enjoyed an excellent reputation and became the personal physician of Archduke Karl and Archduchess Maria Beatrice d'Este of Modena. On 31 December 1821 he married Polish countess Helena Ostrowska (1794–1826). The mother-in-law of Dr. Ambrozy

Samuel Kostrowicki (the narrator's maternal great grandfather) was Aleksandra Ostrowska (d.1919), wife of Albert Wojciech Boguszewski.

[xlvii] A statesman and naturalist.

[xlviii] On 10 April 1837 Malfatti was awarded the title of Count of Monteregio for his contributions to medical science. Malfatti had founded the society of general practitioners in Vienna in 1802. He was buried in an honoured grave in the Heitzinger cemetery, and the *Malfattisteig* in Hietzing is named for him.

[xlix] His landholdings included some 17,000 hectares.

[l] Letter to Anatol Stern from Jan Kostrowicki dated 28 November 1958 - see pp. 218 - 229, "Dom Apollinaire'a", by Anatol Stern.

[li] A boyar family that obtained the Muscovite throne in 1613, ending the 15-year long Time of Troubles - a period of famine, civil war, invasion, opportunists and contenders for the throne that had followed upon the death of the last Rurikid Dynasty Tsar in 1598.

[lii] It would be reasonable to assume that the French intelligence service knew of Lucjan's Viennese family connections; perhaps also that he was the uncle of a well-connected child in Rome; related to the Bonapartes and to the Austrian Imperial Family. Lucjan was effectively placed under a form of 'house arrest' on his enforced return home, however this was unpleasant but lenient treatment by the standards of the time. It was control, surveillance, not punishment.

[liii] She would return to Vienna some years later and died there.

liv Gr.06, Nr. 13 (Kostrowicki); Gr.06, Nr.12A (Elssler) - Friedhof Hietzing

lv The Vilnius region of Lithuania.

lvi Samuel Kostrowicki owned: Papiernia (about 23 km SW of Lida, Belarus) comprised of farms and forests of c. 3,000 ha; Wiewiórka c. 6,000 ha, Kowale c. 3,000 ha and Koscieniew c. 3,750 ha, about 17,000 ha in all.

lvii Istanbul, the Ottoman Empire.

lviii He lies buried in close proximity to Fanny Elssler and to Samuel Kostrowicki and his family members in the Hietzing Cemetery. His grave reference is Gr. 06, Nr. 15.

lix The name is spelt Kostrowicki (Polish), Кастравіцкі (Russian), Kastravicki, Kostrovitski, Kostrowitzky (phonetically) and other variants.

lx Austrian military intelligence, which oversaw the *Kundschaftsbüro*, tasked with monitoring foreign states.

lxi Angelika de Kostrowitzky 1858 - 1919, c. 26 years younger than [Albert] Kostrowicki. NB the narrator's mother, Jolanta Lew-Ostik Kostrowicka (1933 - 2009) was 16 years younger than his father, Stefan Ziemowit Moczarski vel Mocarski (1917 - 1993), who was 43 years old when the narrator was born; your narrator was 44 when his youngest child was born. Older fathers and younger mothers were not uncommon in this family or more generally.

lxii The Kostrowicki Family is an old Ruthenian (White Russian) noble (boyar) family with several branches holding different crests. The branch of Angelika Kostrowitzky (sic) came from Kostrowicze near Słonim, south east of Grodno in Belarus and had the crest Prawdzic (descended from Hrybun - Bakunowicz - see *Le Flaneur des Deux Rives*, Bulletin d'Etudes Apollinariennes, No.1 Mars 1954, p.12 - *Les ancêtres maternels d'Apollinaire* by Maria Kostrowicka-Dabrowa). The branch of Melanie Kostrowicka (and her son) came from Koscieniew, near Lida, west of Minsk and used the crest Bajbuza. The Kostrowicki family is descended from the Obakunovich or Avvakunovich (Avvakun meaning 'lover of God') Family of Wielki Novgorod, boyars (including posadniks, centurions and the Tribune (hertzog, or dux bellorum) Oleksander Obakunovich), referred to in The Chronicle of Novgorod. The name Kostrowicki was derived from their earlier crest of Kostrowiec (the Cross). Members of the Obakunovich Family came to Mstislav Province of Lithuania in the 15th Century - Ivan served as Podskarbi (Silver Treasurer) to Prince Yurij Lukgvenovich Mstislavsky (aka Jurij Semionovich (Lengvenaitis)) (Prince of Veliky Novgorod (1432 - 1440) and Duke of Mstislav (1431 - 1442, 1443*, 1445 - 1460)). There were strong links between the Obakunovich/Kostrowicki family, Mstislav and that branch of the Lithuanian Royal House (descended from Giedymin) that was the princely/ducal house of Mstislav and provided princes to Wielki Novgorod (forebears of the Mstislavski princes). Wasil Kostrowicki was the ancestor of Melanie Kostrowicka, via his son Jan-Rafał.

* See 'Gediagináičiai, Enciklopedinis Žinynas, pubd. Vilnius 2005, ISBN 5-420-01558-7, p.71, where it is stated (in Lithuanian) in this section on Jurgis Lengvenaitis (Prince/Duke Yuri Lengvenovich) that "1443 jam buvo dovanota, atgavo tėvonija Mstislavlio kunigaikštystę. Po konflikto su didžiuoju kunigaikščiu Kazimieru 1445 vėl teko

bėgti, bet 1446 kunigaikštystę atgavo." (English: "In 1443 the Duchy of Mstislavl was granted to him and so he regained his father's land. Due to conflict with the Grand Duke Kazimierz he had to flee again in 1445, but he regained the Duchy in 1446."

The first known person to use the name Kostrowicki (a Polonised use of the family's crest) was, appropriately, Protas Kostrowicki. Mstislav Boyarin* Yakov Fedorovich Obakunovich "Levtik"**, accompanied by his son Protas Kostrowicki podstarosta (under-sheriff) of Mstislav and King's Courtier, on 8 March 1561 appeared before King Zygmunt II August (King of Poland and Grand Duke of Lithuania) and received from him a Privilege*** confirming Yakov as the holder of the village of Steckovo (alias Kostrowicze) in Mstislav Province, first granted by Kniaz Yurij Lukgvenovich Mstislavsky in 1443 to his Treasurer (Podskarbi) Ivan, Yakov's grandfather, which Privilege was also later confirmed to Ivan by Kniaz Ivan Yurievich Mstislavsky. Protas' brother, Bohdan z Kostrowic Kostrowicki, was the father of Wasil Kostrowicki (married to Regina Zambrzycka), above. Yakov Obakunovich also had a third son, Małofiej. [*A 'Boyarin', or Boyar, was a member of the highest rank of the feudal Kievan, Moscovian and Wielki Novgorodian (Ruthenian) aristocracies, second only to the ruling princes from the 10th century to the 17th century.**Levtik was a diminutive of Levontik, itself a diminutive of Leontii - lion-like - a nickname, said to have been given for bravery by Helena Ivanovna of Moscow (19 May 1476 – 20 January 1513) daughter of Ivan III the Great, Grand Prince of Moscow, and an uncrowned Grand Duchess of Lithuania and Queen of Poland, wife of Aleksander Jagiellonczyk. *** recorded in the 41st book (pages 217 – 218v) of the Metrika of the Grand Duchy of Lithuania – the original is in The Russian State Historical Archive or RGIA (*Rossiiskii Gosudarstvennyi Istoricheskii Arkhiv)*]

[lxiii] Your narrator's mother, Jolanta Lew-Ostik Kostrowicka came from a branch of the Kostrowicki family that used the crest Wąż, a serpent, similar to but not the same crest as Bajbuza. This latter branch was in fact descended (via Jan Ościk) from the grandson of that Hrehory Hrehorowicz Ościk (or Ostik) famously executed in 1580 in Vilnius, son of Jurgis Grigorievich Astikas (died 1546), Court Marshal of Lithuania, and his wife Princess Marina Mikhailovna Mstislavska (died 1563), descended from Giedymin, Grand Duke of Lithuania, via both his sons Algirdas and Jaunutis (themselves Grand Dukes of Lithuania). Ościk's grandson was effectively 'adopted' into the Kostrowicki family, by Wasil Kostrowicki (Secretary to King John II Casimir Vasa, King of Poland and Grand Duke of Lithuania (1648 - 1668)), with the use of the crest Wąż. This family lived at Nowosiołki, near Minsk from the 17th Century until Karol (Lew-Ostik) Kostrowicki was dispossessed and sent to Siberia after participating in the 1863 Uprising. The Lithuanian Astikai (variants: Ostik, Ościk, Oścyk, Oścykowicz) Family is descended from Kristinas Astikas (Krystyn Ościk z Kiernowa) (1363 - 1442/4) (n.b. Kiernowa, or Kernave, is an ancient capital of Lithuania and a UNESCO World Heritage Site), Castellan of Vilnius (from 1419) and progenitor of the Astikai and Radvilai (Radziwiłł) families, through two of his sons, Stanislovas / Stanko Astikas and Radvila Astikas. According to the Lew-Ostik Kostrowicki and Radziwiłł families and some historians, the Ostiks are descended from Narimantas (a.k.a. Sirputis/Sirpuc) (crest: Hipocentaurus), Duke of Kernave c.1280, brother of Grand Duke Traidenis, via his son Lizdeiko, a well known pagan high priest (c.1320). There was a poetic strain in this family and

among its relatives - for example the Belarusian poet, playwright, linguist, sculptor, national and cultural activist known as Karus Kahaniec ('The Lamp') was Kazimierz Rafał (Lew-Ostik) Kostrowicki (1868 - 1918), son of Karol (above) and brother of Dr. Ambrozy Samuel Kostrowicki (1870 - 1937), the narrator's great grandfather, who in 1917 was Chairman of the Congress of Belarusian National Organizations in Minsk, created by the Belarusian National Committee.

[lxiv] Possibly he had been or still was a Colonel in the Papal Guard - perhaps either the Palatine Guard (infantry) or the Noble Guard (cavalry), as distinct from the Swiss Guard.

[lxv] The estate of Doroszkowice, pow. dziśnieński (Dzisna County), Lithuania.

[lxvi] Angelika de Kostrowitzky. Kostrowicki in Polish is equivalent to 'de Kostrowic' (or Kostrowiec) in French.

[lxvii] Ivan III, who conquered Veliky Novgorod (Lord Novgorod the Great) in 1478, ending the Novgorod Republic, founded in 1136 and annexing it into Muscovy, forming Russia.

[lxviii] A period between the death of the last Russian Tsar of the Rurik Dynasty, Feodor Ivanovich, in 1598, and the introduction of the Romanov Dynasty in 1613, with the enthronement of Mikhail I. During the Polish–Russian War (1605–18), Russia was occupied by the Polish–Lithuanian Commonwealth, and experienced civil uprisings, usurpers and impostors.

[lxix] Meaning "New settlement". Nowosiółki Małe (Little Nowosiółki) was confiscated; neighbouring Nowosiółki Wielkie (Large Nowosiółki), with its 1820s neoclassical

palace, was sold by Kazimierz (Lew-Ostik) Kostrowicki in 1860. Karol (Lew-Ostik) Kostrowicki, Kazimierz's brother, the narrator's great-great-grandfather, was marched to Siberia in chains for participation in the 1863 Uprising, released in 1874, he died soon after.

^{lxx} Gr. 6, Nr. 12A.

^{lxxi} Gruppe VI, Nr. 12-a, Einfache Gruft SL. Charakter: Gräfliche Familie Kostrowicka. 1. Fanny Elssler, Wien. 29.XI.1884; 2. Katharine Prinster, 11.IX.1888; 3. Melania Gräfin Kostrowicka, 12.VIII – 1889 (Armutshalber gratis); 4. Elssler Wilhelm, Flugkapitän, 1936.

^{lxxii} None of whose given names coincided with those of Wilhelm (Apollinaire) or his younger brother Albert.

^{lxxiii} Was this connected with the fact that Melanie Kostrowicka did not leave her Vienna property (and perhaps any Roman assets) to her nephew Marcin, as had been hoped for by her relatives (per Jan Kostrowicki's letter), but rather to the Church, of which she was a secular Canoness? Had she in fact made an arrangement with the Church to provide for the welfare and education of her grandsons, Wilhelm Albert Apolinary Kostrowicki (Apollinaire, as he was to become known as by the rest of the World) and his younger brother Albert (a name that reappears consistently) and for their mother? The names Albert and Wilhelm become strong candidates for those of the son of Franz and Melanie - names that Franz's mother, Marie-Louise, had given to her daughter (Albertina Maria, Countess of Montenuovo, later Countess of Fontanalleto) and to her son (Wilhelm Albert, Prince of Montenuovo) by Adam Albert von Neipperg, Franz's half-sister and half-brother, both born illegitimate and later

legitimated. Wilhelm Albert named one of his daughters Albertyna Leopoldyna Wilhelmina (married name Wielopolska). Such families chose and repeated given names for good reasons, often to clarify lines within families or to celebrate or remember an ancestor or relative. Was the son of Franz, Duke of Reichstadt and Melanie Kostrowicka in fact Albert Wilhelm [Samuel] Kostrowicki (or in fact Bonaparte)? Franz's mother, still mourning the loss of her husband, von Neipperg a couple of years earlier, grandmother to Franz's son, was a necessary ally and guardian for this child. The name Napoleon surely could not have been given.

[lxxiv] pp. 224 - 226, 'Dom Apollinaire'a', by Anatol Stern.

[lxxv] c. 100 km south of Vilnius. When the Sieklucki family returned to Strzelica ('The Shooter'), theirs for c. 300 years, they found the remains of buildings and ruins - valuables, family portraits, old documents, and the library were destroyed. Outside the manor house, a dozen farm buildings were also destroyed. The Germans had only weak control of the area and lawlessness was rife, with gangs of armed stragglers and bandits operating.

[lxxvi] In the Nowogródek (Navahrudak) region, in North-Eastern Belarus.

[lxxvii] Zofia Jundziłowna h. Łabędź was the wife of Jan Hrehorowicz Ościk (in Lithuanian, Jonas Astikas) (d.1611), whose son by him (Jerzy Janowicz Ościk – see pp. 310 & 439, 'Herbarz Rycerstwa W.X. Litewskiego' by Wojciech Wijuk Kojałowicz (published in Krakow in 1897)) assumed the name Kostrowicki (the progenitor of the Lew-Ostik Kostrowicki line) - he was the great...great grandfather of your narrator. Zofia married again (her third husband) after Jan's death.

Also written by Jeremy Moczarski:

A Man of Power and a Goblin on a Fork

The complex origins of a Man of Power and a Goblin on a Fork forged against the background of WWII and the Cold War, their lives in Nigeria, Gambia, Ethiopia (the Danakil Desert), Afghanistan, Yemen, Lesotho and Iran and the gifts bestowed on their children. The intertwined stories of historical families of Belarus (White Rus'ia), Bohemia, Lithuania, Poland, Russia (Muscovy) and Wielki Novgorod (Lord Novgorod the Great). Published by Amazon Kindle Publishing, March 2019, ISBN-10: 1797659219; ISBN-13: 978-1797659213.

Poetry in the blood

One of the most respected poets, dramatists and authors of the 20th Century, Guillaume Apollinaire (friend of Pablo Picasso, Georges Braque, Henri Rousseau and Marcel Duchamp) and Karuś Kahaniec, the poet, author, sculptor, artist and Belarusian social and political activist Kazimierz Rafał Kostrowicki were cousins. This anthology of poems, mainly by other Kostrowicki / Kastravicki family members and close relatives, speaks from the past, evoking powerful images of the turbulent times - the heavy yoke of Imperial Russia, WWI, the Russian Civil War and Revolution, the 1920 Bolshevik Russo-Polish War, WWII and the Cold War - in which they lived, fought, endured, loved and lost so many and so much that was dear to them. It reveals that poetry was a commonly shared medium of expression in this family, rooted in the history of Belarus, Lithuania, Poland and Russia. Published by Amazon Kindle Publishing, November 2019, ISBN 9781703104271.

Spring blossoms, Summer fruits

A forbidden relationship unbalances the lives of a student, a
musically talented Eurasian heiress, and of those closest to her,
with profound ramifications involving China, Russia and the
USA. Love, jealousy, politics and wealth collide. A novel,
published by Amazon Kindle Publishing, February 2021,
ISBN - 13:979-8711501565; ASIN: B08XPG3RZY.

Printed in Great Britain
by Amazon